MW00849771

COLD
ETERNITY

ALSO BY
S. A. BARNES

Dead Silence
Ghost Station

S.A. BARNES

COLD ETERNITY

NIGHTFIRE

TOR PUBLISHING GROUP

NEW YORK

This is a work of fiction. All of the characters, organizations, and events portrayed in this novel are either products of the author's imagination or are used fictitiously.

COLD ETERNITY

Copyright © 2025 by S.A. Barnes

All rights reserved.

A Nightfire Book
Published by Tom Doherty Associates / Tor Publishing Group
120 Broadway
New York, NY 10271

www.torpublishinggroup.com

Nightfire™ is a trademark of Macmillan Publishing Group, LLC.

The Library of Congress Cataloging-in-Publication Data
is available upon request.

ISBN 978-1-250-88495-4 (hardcover)
ISBN 978-1-250-88496-1 (ebook)

Our books may be purchased in bulk for promotional, educational, or business use. Please contact your local bookseller or the Macmillan Corporate and Premium Sales Department at 1-800-221-7945, extension 5442, or by email at MacmillanSpecialMarkets@macmillan.com.

First Edition: 2025

Printed in the United States of America

0 9 8 7 6 5 4 3 2 1

To everyone who dared to peek behind the curtain at ShowBiz Pizza or Chuck E. Cheese. You are my people.

COLD

ETERNITY

1

Seven Fathoms, the establishment in question, is on station level twenty-three.

I've never been down that far, and when the lift doors open to reveal my destination, I hesitate. Theoretically, the narrow oval concourse on this level holds a variety of commercial and trade operations—places for residents on nearby levels to eat, drink, buy new boots, or trade for whatever you might need that someone else is willing to give up.

But a lot of the businesses appear shut down, closed up with heavy security gates . . . which have been trashed and bent inward anyway. People are gathered loosely in groups, talking loudly between fits of coughing, or sit crouched near the floor, their heads bent toward one another and their hands outstretched toward the warm air pumping out through the vents.

It's darker here, too, lights pulsing erratically overhead in twitchy blue-white strobes, on the edge of breakdown. The air is worse, thicker somehow, like I can feel particulates lodging themselves in my lungs.

In my five weeks here, I've never ventured more than a few station levels from my very shitty hostel room on SL-9. Theoretically EnExx17 station security is present, keeping the peace everywhere. But they don't seem to be here right now, not that I can see, anyway.

Today, though, I don't have any choice.

The lift gives a warning ping, about to close its doors, but I've spotted the pub on the far side of the concourse, almost directly opposite me. Seven Fathoms is one of the few doorways still lit and seemingly operational. Raucous laughter spills out toward me.

Ignoring the nerves coiling and twisting in my gut, I step out of the lift and tug at the ragged edges of my sweater hood to shadow my features as much as possible. In doing so, though, my fingers collide with the swollen and tender flesh around my left eye. Sizzling lines of pain explode outward.

I grit my teeth, but after a moment, the sharpness fades, the injury resuming its regular dull ache.

All the more reason to get on with it, Halley.

I stride toward the pub, trying to find the fine line between moving with confident purpose and, well, running. The second I move, I can feel eyes on me, attention stripping away my illusion of invisibility.

I don't belong down here, and they know it.

These people need help. Better conditions, a small voice in my head insists. *If you—*

No longer your problem, no longer within your power to play hero, remember? A louder, mocking voice cuts off the other.

Right as I near the pub, a man stumbles out, almost colliding with me at the entrance. His eyes are glazed, his coveralls still covered in white dust from his shift at the desalination plant. A briner.

Swaying in place, he stares at me, and I flinch and duck my head automatically, but there's no shout of recognition, no slurred proposition.

After a moment, he stumbles off to the right, staring up at something no one else can see.

I grimace. That's not alcohol. Daze, if I had to guess. At levels that might have him forgetting he needs to breathe, if he doesn't topple over a safety railing or down a set of stairs first.

Nothing you can do about it, keep going.

I duck into the pub, tension building in my shoulders. My contact better be here. I *need* them to be here.

It's even dimmer inside the pub—for atmosphere, for privacy, maybe. More likely to save credits on power. It takes a moment for my eyes to adjust. The dingy floor has given up any ghost of its one-time shiny metal surface. A thin coating of salt crunches beneath my feet with every step. Practicality for absorbing spills? Or a side effect of so much brine, all the time? I don't know.

On the other side of the darkened room, closer to the bar, a half dozen or so surface workers gather around a larger table, their ruddy faces bent over their ale mugs.

In one of the privacy booths ahead of me, the curtains are only partially drawn, so I have a view of a slick-looking woman, dressed better than anyone in a six-level range and her hair pulled so tight into an elaborate braid that it barely moves as she argues with someone on the holocomm in front of her. A man, another briner in silt-covered coveralls, lies stiffly in the booth next to her, eyes wide and fixed on the ceiling.

Daze. I *knew* it. Dealer and another buyer.

People will always find a way to step on others, to create a seedy underbelly to any location, even on a remote space station, where it's better to keep your head down and your eyes to yourself.

Before the dealer notices me, I make myself look away. I don't need any more trouble.

I turn cautiously in a circle, checking the pub's other occupants. Very few of them sit alone at a table, and those who are alone don't appear to be waiting for someone.

My heart plummets. The posting—on a hidden branch of the EnExx17 internal net—*had* seemed to be too good to be true.

*Caretaker/security monitor wanted for dry-docked ship. No experience necessary. Low wages, but room and board included. **Must** be comfortable with isolated working environment and limited outside contact.*

Room and board without prying eyes or hands around sounded perfect. Maybe too perfect. But my weary brain sought—and found—rationalization. It was probably some wealthy owner, one with more vessels than good sense, who didn't want his baby sitting empty for months at a time out here, no one but the quartermaster half paying attention to it. I wasn't thrilled about the low wages part—I couldn't live like this forever, and credits were the only thing that would eventually get me out, even if it was just to return home.

In my former life, the idea of responding to a post on a black-market employment board—one I'd only learned of by overhearing the other hostel residents discussing it—would have sounded as bizarre as shimmying naked on the floor of New Parliament. And equally as likely.

But that was the old me. The new me needs to eat. And find a safe place to sleep.

I draw in a breath, ignoring a protest from my ribs, to calm myself.

I'm probably too early, that's all. I wanted to arrive before my contact. To be *sure*. Of what, exactly, I don't know, as I have zero identifying information on who I'm meeting, other than the initial K.

I head for the nearest empty table with a view of the door.

"Oi," the bartender calls as soon as I pull out a chair. "No drink, no table." She points to something behind me. Her arm is tattooed with rivets and metal joints drawn on the skin with startlingly realistic detail, and I try not gawk at the artistry of it.

I turn to see what she's indicating.

NO DRINK, NO TABLE. The words are scrawled on the wall in

flickering and partly burned-out digital letters. Everything out here on EnExx17 runs on a shoestring.

Touching my hood to make sure it's still in place, I head to the bar, keeping distance from the patrons who are hunched over it on their stools.

"Tea, please."

The bartender arches an eyebrow but says nothing.

A moment later she has one of my last loose credits, and I have a thick and lumpily printed mug with a "station-conserved" tea sachet—gray and slightly fraying around the edges where it's been less than delicately restitched after new tea leaves were inserted—bobbing around in my beverage like an elderly dumpling.

Once, I would have pushed the mug away, disgusted.

Today, I hold it tight, circling my hands around its heat, and inhale deeply as if the scent alone will help fill the growling hole in my belly.

I return to sit at my table, keeping an eye on the entrance. Willing K, whoever he or she is, to come.

I'm so busy watching the door, I nearly miss the bartender approaching my table. Her shiny metal prosthetic legs flash with the movement even in the dim light, catching my eye as she smoothly clicks toward my table. The tattoos on her arms match her legs.

I look up and automatically put my hand over the top of my cup—I can't afford a refill.

Her gaze moves over my face, her mouth tightening at the sight of bruises. "You the one expecting a call?" she asks.

"Oh." I sit up straighter, removing my hand from my cup. "No, I'm supposed to meet—"

"Then this is for you." Her mouth pursed in distaste, the bartender holds up a holocomm, the round disc pulsing with a green light, indicating a waiting party.

Before I can respond, she slaps the holocomm down on the center of my table and clicks away, back behind the bar.

I stare at it for a moment, attempting to work out what's happening. If this call is for me, maybe K is canceling?

No. No, no, no! Desperation makes an ugly crease in the calm I've been clinging to. I need this meeting to work out.

I reach out and tap the center button. The green light goes solid, and a wavy projected silhouette appears above the holocomm, a head and shoulders, facing away from me. The connection is terrible, loose and staticky, so it's hard to see much more than that. Machinery rumbles in the background on the other end. "Hello?" I say.

The figure turns to face me, the holocomm image blurring with the movement and then reconstituting itself. It's a man, his rumpled dark hair shot through with strands of silver, and eyes so pale they nearly seem see-through. The dark circles under his eyes, however, are plainly visible, as is the scraggly scruff on his chin from several days—or weeks—of not shaving. He's at least a decade older than I am, late thirties or even early forties. "Finally!" he shouts over the background noise on his end. "You're the one who responded to my posting?"

I sense heads turning in my direction. Wincing, I tug the holocomm closer and fumble to turn down the sound on the side. I would have taken a privacy booth if I'd known he was going to call in. "Yes," I say, my voice hushed. "But I thought we said we were going to meet—"

"Listen, I can't get away right now, so this is the next best thing." He rakes a hand through his already messy hair. "I need someone right away. I'm in the middle of a massive system overhaul, and I can't be bothered with this shit. I'm trying to meet their deadline, but I can't be in two places at once. And the fucking board rules are ridiculous—"

"What shit, exactly?" I interrupt.

He pauses, looking surprised. "What I said in the posting. You walk around, keep an eye on things. Document any new repairs required. Alert me if anyone arrives. Punch a button for the micromanaging board of directors so they know someone's awake and paying attention. That's it. A 'bot could do it if they weren't so paranoid." With a scoffing noise, he shakes his head. "I've never seen such fucking neoluds."

The latter clearly sounds like the greater sin of the two, in his mind.

"I need someone reliable," he says, turning to look at something behind him, off camera. Metal clanks against metal, and he swears softly. "Someone who's not going to panic and fuck off in the middle of rounds like the last one." His voice is muffled, but the disdain comes through loud and clear. "Stowed away on a transport during a resupply."

Panic? Why would someone panic?

I open my mouth to ask that question, but he keeps talking, facing forward again. "What's your name again . . . uh, I have it here somewhere." He scowls at the something below the sight line of the holocomm camera.

I clear my throat. "Halley. Halley Zwick."

"That's it!" He grins. "As in Fireman Flick and Spaceman Zwick?"

This is the problem with relying on low-end criminal help; you get low-end results. Like someone thinking it's funny to give you a false last name—to go with your equally false first name—based on a famous children's cartoon character. Perhaps I should be grateful that I'm not Halley Mouse or Halley McDonald, though the latter, at least, could be a real name.

"The very same," I say tightly.

His smile fades a bit, an avaricious look of curiosity sliding to the forefront.

"I noticed you didn't include UNOC creds," he says, his tone light. "*Halley*, was it?"

I stiffen, resisting the urge to retreat into the shadows behind me. I can't tell if he recognizes me. Even with the damage to my face and the steps I've taken to alter my appearance—chopping off my hair, buying a cheap color enhancer to turn it an awkward auburn, and contact lenses without the comm hookup for their pale violet shade alone—it's not impossible. Especially after that fucking press conference the other day. My mother in a soft and shapeless pale blue sweater that I'd never seen before—that she would have died before wearing—her hair loose around her shoulders, my father with his shirt rumpled and tie loose at his neck. *"Come home, Katerina, please."*

They were the very image of worried parents. If you didn't know them. But I do.

I make myself stay still, my face the practiced impassive mask I'd learned long before coming here. "Yes, it's Halley," I confirm. And nothing else. "K" was welcome to interpret silence however he liked—as if someone going by a single initial has room to criticize—but I wasn't going to help by filling in the gaps.

"Uh-huh. Looks like someone did a number on you, eh?" He eyes me speculatively, waving his hand around to indicate his own face, and I brace myself for more questions.

But then he seems to come to a decision, shaking his head. "Listen, it's an easy gig. You do your rounds, you pay attention, you press a button for the board of directors. You don't mess with the residents or their shit, but keep an ear out for any of the pre-alerts, because the system is slow sometimes and every minute counts when you're talking about—"

"Wait, wait. Residents?" I lean forward, heart sinking. "Your posting said the ship was empty." Actually, it said dry-docked, and I *assumed* that meant empty, but still.

He grimaces. "It is. Technically."

Technically? Not good enough. "Mr. K, or whatever your name is," I begin.

"Karl," he interjects.

"Fine. Karl. The ship either has passengers or it doesn't," I say.

"It's both. Sort of," he hedges.

"Okay," I make myself say, reaching for the holocomm. "I think this is where we should part ways—"

"'Residents' is the term the board prefers," he says quickly. "But it's not what you're thinking—not *who*."

"Board? You keep talking about the board." Corporate-owned ships might have a board of directors somewhere in the mix, but never this hands-on. There would be whole departments, maybe even divisions, responsible for their fleet.

Hesitation visibly shows on his face. "It's the *Elysian Fields*," he admits after a moment, with chagrin.

I rock back in my chair in surprise, before I can hide it. "You're kidding. That's still around?"

Irritation flashes across his face. "Why does everyone say that? It's not going anywhere."

I raise my eyebrows.

He makes an exasperated sound. "Except on its preprogrammed course, yes, yes, okay."

So, not dry-docked at all, then. But not a normal ship, either. I could see why he maybe hadn't wanted to try to explain that in the limited space of an illicit job posting.

"But I remember reading that it closed, what, thirteen, fourteen years ago," I say. My class trip there, when I was twelve, must have been one of the last groups through.

"We closed to tourists, yes, but the Winfeld Trust ensures we're still up and running." He glances over his shoulder with distaste. "Barely, at any rate."

The *Elysian Fields* is a relic. Over 150 years old, probably, at this point. I don't remember the exact date it started. It was back in the early days of system colonization. Colonies were established and growing rapidly on Mars and the moon, along with the ill-fated attempt on Venus. Not to mention the first batch of residential space stations. More people were living in space or off-Earth than ever before.

And dying there, too. From accidents, like Venusian II, but also from normal causes, too—old age and disease.

Which raised the never before considered issue of what to do with the deceased. For large-scale contamination events, like the Ferris Outpost tragedy, protocol was the same then as it is now: the deceased, habs, and equipment are destroyed, burned to ash. But for individuals back then, it was more complicated. Cremation polluted the hard-won breathable air. Burial within the colony domes took up incredibly valuable land that could be used for crops or building. Ejecting bodies from the stations created minefields of tiny human missiles in orbit around them, making it difficult—and extremely horrific at times— for ships to navigate . . . without collision.

In this narrative space, Zale Winfeld, the wealthy trillionaire and tech genius, became the hero. Winfeld had one of those late-in-life conversion experiences, only instead of finding God, he seemed to think God had found him. He'd received a vision, he said. God had chosen him to spread the word of the new world that was to be. He "donated" a former hospital ship, converting it to the latest in cryogenics. According to Winfeld, death was only temporary, until technology caught up and allowed everyone to live forever. Defeating death—that was to be his big legacy. Available for a price, of course.

In an irony of ironies, Winfeld himself didn't get a chance to use his own innovation. He vanished not long after a shuttle crash took the lives of his three children (and his fourth wife). His company desperately tried to suggest he'd simply retired from public life, but persistent rumors were that he'd committed suicide, out of range of *Elysian Fields*, unwilling to be "saved" without his family at his side.

Eventually, the better part of a century later, the ship was turned into a public memorial and an educational experience (aka revenue generator).

A history lesson, a field trip for the kiddos, with a side of morbid gawking. Not all that unusual, I suppose, considering a few centuries ago people used to picnic in graveyards on Earth, and stare at the mummified dead inside glass cases at museums.

Still weird, though.

I remember looking through the frosted side of a cryotank

at an aged pop star, someone who had been dead before my grandmother had even been born, her light brown cheeks still so perfectly preserved that I could see traces of makeup and the delicate fuzz on her hardened, frozen skin. Glass display cases around her "room" housed sequined tour outfits, guitars, and replica wedding rings from her famous marriage to a vid actor that lasted less than a week. Holos of her much younger self gyrated around us, as the boys in my class unsuccessfully attempted to peer through the tank privacy shield protecting her naked corpse. Or near-corpse, if she was frozen in time.

And the "show," featuring AI versions of Winfeld's deceased adult children welcoming you to the ship and expounding upon the benefits of joining *Elysian Fields*, was especially eerie.

Even now it sends an uneasy prickle over my skin.

Most of the "dead ships," Winfeld imitators, went out of business a long time ago, especially once biocremation became accepted as a practical solution. But apparently *Elysian Fields* is still out there.

"I can't manage their stupid security requirements and finish this upgrade in time. But the board won't hire anyone to help me, so I'd be bringing you on . . . unofficially," Karl says.

Illegally, is what Karl means. *Elysian Fields* is an Earth ship, of the former United States, so Earth law applies. That means UNOC credentials are required, and Earth citizenship is vastly preferred. Yet another way the legacy governments try to stem the tide of progress, by implementing stiff fines and even short stints in prison for employers who don't follow the rules.

The Winfeld Trust would never take that chance, but Karl apparently will.

"I will, of course, have to tell them you submitted fraudulent credentials if we're caught," he continues easily.

There it is.

Creating fraudulent UNOC credentials is an automatic sentence to a decade of labor on one of the asteroid mining camps, which is why I hadn't gone that route. So far, nothing I'd done had broken the rules, just . . . bent them at a severe angle. I still want my life back. Someday.

"Of course," I say dryly.

"But I'm sure we would both prefer that not be the case," he finishes.

It would be his word against mine, if that were ever an issue. He might find himself surprised at who was willing to fight for me, if only to have me back within their control. Still, Karl wouldn't want that trouble, and neither do I.

And the primary benefit of this arrangement remains: I would be hidden away where no one, including my former employer's vast network of contacts, would expect to find me—or even consider looking, really. I wouldn't have to try to sleep with my back against the door, knowing that even that measure wouldn't be enough. Instinctively, I trace the lower edge of the swollen skin around my eye.

Metal screeches loudly in the background on Karl's end of the connection.

"I have to go. If you think you can manage it without letting this place get into your head like the last guy, you've got the job. Seven hundred fifty credits. I'm expecting a water resupply shipment from EnExx17 in, uh, twelve hours. If you want—"

"Seven hundred fifty credits an hour? That's barely minimum wage by UNOC standards."

He makes an exasperated noise. "Seven hundred fifty credits a *day*."

I gape at him. At 750 credits a day, it'll take six, almost seven months to save up enough for transport back to anywhere civilized. Way longer that I anticipated being on the dark side of nowhere. And that's if I don't spend any.

"Housing and food are included in this gig," Karl reminds me. "As for UNOC standards, you can go ahead and report me." He grins.

"Twelve hundred," I say quickly.

Another loud crash echoes on Karl's end.

"One thousand credits. Final offer. If you want it, be on the transport ship in twelve hours. Terminal B, Gate Thirty-Four."

His image vanishes, the connection cut, before I even have a chance to respond.

I sit back in my chair, staring at the space where his holographic image was. His offer is insulting, not to mention illegal, but if I say no, he'll have plenty of other takers. By the time I sent my information in, the number of responses, ticking upward in the corner of the posting, was already in the hundreds.

I'd been surprised when I got a pingback to meet for an interview at the Seven Fathoms. Surprised and relieved. If "relief" can adequately convey the warmth of muscles relaxing for the first time in months and dizzying rush of a true, deep breath.

It was one of those moments when you don't realize how worried you actually were until you can finally see your way out from under whatever it is that's sitting on your chest like a six-hundred-ton baroque cruiser.

But . . . an isolated ship of the dead, by myself, except for one guy who has already admitted to the potential criminality of his character by posting this job to begin with.

I shudder. It's not ideal.

But creepy as it is, the *Elysian Fields* is at least somewhat familiar. And the job sounds easy enough.

Plus, I'm not sure I have an alternative.

Two nights ago, I woke to hands yanking roughly at me, rolling me off my thin mattress. A bash to the side of my face stunned me, and when I hit the ground, a fist in my hair at the back of my head held me down. A harsh voice, telling me, "Stay quiet if you know what's good for you."

Numbness washed over me, even as a little voice in my head kept protesting that this couldn't be happening, even though I'd been half expecting it. *But I was so careful!*

The fear, so sharp and bright, a knife's edge glinting in the

darkness, felt unreal. Not the hazy featureless terror of a nightmare, but the pure disbelief. Life colliding at speed with my false
sense of security.

When the numbness finally wore off, only a few seconds later,
I lashed out, flailing, kicking and bucking. I would not be taken
quietly. And if they were going to kill me, I would not make it
easy for them.

That "fight" earned me a likely orbital socket fracture—
the auto-doc holo could only give it a 75 percent accurate di-
agnosis without more personal information that I refused to
give—a concussion, and several cracked ribs.

But they didn't drag me out of the room, didn't slip a blade
between the ribs that now pained me.

They took my hard credits, though. Without my UNOC credentials, I have to rely on a physical credit chip to hold most of
my money. Once they found that—poorly hidden in the toe of
my boot, I realize now—they left.

A robbery, plain and simple and ugly. Reassuring in its mun-
daneness if nothing else.

Or that's what they wanted it to look like.

I try to ignore the little voice in the back of my head.

It's not as if my credit chip was a big secret—the pinkish
scar on the back of my hand where my UNOC implant used to
be is a dead giveaway that I have to use some other means of
payment. It makes me an obvious target for random criminals
who are paying attention.

The problem is, I can't be sure.

*You saw the mark on his wrist. How many people have that
exact tattoo?*

Except I don't *know* what I saw. It *might* have been the angled line of a shield, the tail end of a familiar Latin phrase,
peeking out from under a sleeve as one of the intruders held
me down. Or not.

The brain is notoriously unreliable in stressful situations,
and it was only a glimpse. I might have . . . filled in the gaps

with my worst-case scenario, letting my worries get the best of me.

With something that looks like "Mors mihi lucrum"? *Really?*

The memory—the cold metal floor pressed into my face, the acrid scent of sweat above me from the man whose rough hand tangled in my hair—fills me with a bright bolt of pure, crystalline fear.

If it was them . . .

I shake my head, refusing to follow the thought any further. It doesn't matter. What does matter is that I'm not as invisible as I thought I was. And if random criminals can find me so easily, what about the professionals who might be looking?

I can't take that chance.

I stand up and grab the holocomm. Life is full of hard choices, but this isn't one of them. I have nothing to fear from the dead, and one possibly shady man is nothing compared to a station full of them.

Pulling my sweater cloak tighter around me, I head toward the bar. The bartender is occupied with another customer, a man hunched over the bar, his face turned away from me. He's dressed all in black, unusual out here, and his shirt and pants are pristine. Not even so much as a smear of salt on them.

Like, say, a UNOC Investigation and Enforcement agent's uniform with all the shiny bits and bobs, ceremonial braids and division patches, removed to help him blend in.

Shit. I slide the holocomm onto the scraped and battered bar surface and turn to head for the door. Quickly.

"Hey," the bartender calls after me.

I freeze, heart skittering in my chest like a small frightened animal. "Yeah?" I make myself say, without turning around. Never turn around.

"That guy? He's 'interviewed' people from here before," she says with distaste. "Never seen any of them come back."

Because they panic and take off in the middle of the night,

apparently, if what Karl says is true. Or at least the most recent one did.

I nod, acknowledging the warning. "Thanks," I say, and then keep walking, expecting a shout of recognition from the possible IEA agent—or, worse, a hard hand gripping my shoulder. But I make it to the corridor without interference. For now.

In truth, if this *Elysian Fields* thing works out, or even if it doesn't, I won't be coming back here, either.

2

Terminal B, the transport deck, is a patchwork of chaotic sounds and colors. Failing lightbars overhead flicker a sickly yellow or pulse a dull gray-blue. Dozens of voices speak over one another, in as many languages, competing with transport captains shouting for any last-minute passengers. Food vendors demand attention for their hot and (theoretically) fresh wares. All this is punctuated by monotone departure and arrival announcements on the overhead, creating a din that feels as if it should be solid to the touch in the air around me.

I keep my head down, watching as discreetly as I can for UNOC IEA agents. I haven't seen that one from the bar again. But now that I'm here, so close to escaping, it feels inevitable that dozens of them are lurking in the shadows, waiting to surround me.

I press the loose edge of my sweater cloak against my nose as a barricade to the smell. It reeks up here, despite the higher level. Beneath the bacon-flavored soy dogs rotating on a spit, the sweet-salty scent of teriyaki noodles from the stand farther down, and the hot-oil aroma of paddle cakes behind me, a strong odor of rotten eggs and old fish lingers. My throat works in a precursor to gagging, and I press the woven fabric tighter, as if that will help filter clean air through to me. But there's no escaping that smell, not here. That's the brine.

Huge barrels of it are being carted this way and that to various transport ships, some for local stops, most to transfers to larger depots that will take the brine to farther-flung locations. Earth, even.

Water, too, rolls by, on thundering carts filled with equally large barrels, but transparent, the better to advertise the quality of the product. All of the barrels are branded with the EnExx17 designation, as are the well-armed station security guards accompanying each cartload.

Not that anyone out here cares. Clean water—or a lack of it—is not an issue on this station. It's the reason most of the workers took the job. Comes with the wages, part of the benefits package. Though in that way, I suppose it costs dearly enough.

Exhausted-looking briners talk in small groups, awaiting transfer to a different EnExx station. Some of them have their families with them, children, too. Dressed well enough, in clothes from the exchange, but too quiet, too skinny. The ashen quality of their skin speaks to too much time on the lower levels without any access to the limited sunshine or even the sun lights in the simulated outdoor areas that are supposedly for everyone. Knobbly joints, visible through their thin layers, say they're not getting enough of their nutrition from actual food, relying instead on VitaPlex. Supplies aren't reaching them, or the higher-level executives aren't sharing. And no one in the local gov is paying attention.

Or they've been paid to direct their attention elsewhere.

One of the children, a boy of about eight or so, points to the paddle cake vendor behind me. His father reaches down and takes his hand, lowering it, before shaking his head and speaking quietly to him.

I can't hear the words, but I get the gist.

My eyes burn, and I have to look away, stuffing my hands into my pockets. In the bag strapped tightly to my side, I have only a few clothes and toiletry items—nothing of any value.

If I had the credits, I would buy that kid his paddle cake. His sisters, too. Not that that would come close to assuaging my responsibility. But I don't have it. Once I reclaimed my advance from the hostile hostel for the nights I wouldn't be staying—the manager tried to keep it, claiming some kind of deposit until I pointed to my banged-up face and reminded her that I had no problem advertising what kind of establishment she ran, which, of course, I couldn't actually do, but she didn't know that—I had just enough for a ticket out of here.

In my pocket, I close my hand over the battered token, a physical chip of blue plastic with the transport's designation crudely carved into its surface. Because I had no UNOC credentials to hold my ticket. Another reminder of my current status in life—a nonentity.

And that was the best choice I had, my only choice.

If you'd sucked it up and stayed, played along like a member of the team . . .

Guilt pulses through me, and I turn away from the little family, focusing on something, anything, as a distraction. A battered departure screen, jagged white lines running through the transport designations and times, hangs crookedly on the wall opposite.

It's mostly impossible to read, but that doesn't matter. It's a safe place to fix my eyes for the moment.

Until it starts flashing images of people with the designation "MISSING."

Grigory Eachairn

Julia Jordan

Caspian Ahmad

Shikoba Ludwig

Johannes Salvi

Trinity Boothe Hopkins

Astra Sandberg

Giannina Ngo

And with every picture, a repeated refrain: *"Please report any sightings! Hard credit reward! We want our [child/daughter/son/parent] to come home!"*

Families desperately searching for their lost loved ones who've disappeared from EnExx17—they must be desperate if they're relying on this method to reach people.

Some of them are probably runaways. A handful of the disappearances might even be human trafficking, given the volume of transports out of EnExx17. But based on my station experience, I'm betting a good percentage of them are folks who descended into the lower station levels in a Daze haze and never resurfaced. Eventually, they'll be presumed dead, then found sometimes many months or years later, as a funky smell or bones in a passageway thought to be closed off.

I can't seem to look away. As I watch the faces flicker overhead, part of my brain automatically conjures possible programs and initiatives that might be implemented to address this issue, from the introduction of an on-station rehab facility (UNOC-funded, of course) to tighter restrictions on cargo haulers that might be tempted to include humans among their wares.

Until, of course, my own face appears. Right there, on the board above me.

My lungs lock up, and I can't move. The noise of the terminal drops away, leaving only a high-pitched buzz in my ears. *Who . . . How did they . . .*

It takes a moment for my stuttering brain to begin to process information again. But eventually, more details seep in. The name next to the face: Sarai. The last known location: here on EnExx17, somewhere on SL-19. Her brother's contact information.

My breath rushes out of me in a quiet *whoosh*. It's *not* me. I don't even have a brother.

This girl, Sarai, bears just enough of a superficial resemblance to me in my old life—blond hair, blue eyes, though she's several years younger—that my paranoid, sleep-deprived brain filled in the gaps.

Also, Halley, *your face wouldn't be on that board for panicked families.*

It would be on the holocomms of every passing security guard and IEA agent on the whole fucking station.

Jesu, I need to get out of here.

["Hey, *gerla,* are you getting on or what?"] A man's voice behind me shouts in Russian, the sharpness of the demand cutting through the noise around me and inside my head.

I turn around. The first mate I bought my ticket from, a broad, balding man with an impressive beard, is gesturing at me with wide exasperated movements that translate in any language. The small cluster of waiting passengers, including that little family, is gone, presumably already boarded.

Without thinking, I call back, ["I'm coming. Don't rush the horses."]

His brows rise.

I ignore his expression of surprise and duck my head to hurry toward him, my worn boots clacking hard across the gritty floor and onto the loading bridge.

["Okay, strange woman,"] he mutters.

The inside of the transport is like every other independent transport ship I've been on, which is to say, like the one I came here on—a former cargo hold retrofitted as a passenger area because ferrying people became a more profitable endeavor and lower licensing fees made it possible. About thirty mismatched seats of varying colors and ages are intermittently and randomly bolted to the metal floor in haphazard "rows." Several unevenly placed windows carved into the sidewalls offer a little additional light, along with something that might be generously considered a view. Everyone else is already settling in, talking in low murmurs as they rustle and shift their bags into place, restraints clicking.

I head for the only open seat, crammed against that sidewall—the first to be sucked out in the event of a hull breach. Probably not quite legal. A man, a midlevel EnExx manager, based on his too-clean beige jumpsuit and the designation on his shoulder, is already in the seat next to it, blocking my path, his eyes closed and his hands folded in his lap.

I know this trick. He wants this "row" to himself. It doesn't work, though, when there's only one available seat left.

"Excuse me," I say, keeping my voice low but firm. "I need to get through."

He doesn't so much as twitch.

"Sir?" I try again.

Again, nothing.

My temper flicks to life. I want out of here. And this guy is determined to make things difficult. His workers probably hate him. A self-important asshole who thinks that because he runs some tiny square inch of the world, he's better than everyone else. Particularly an annoying woman in worn-out clothes from the station exchange who thinks she has the right to take space he's already mentally claimed as his.

Fine.

"Sir, I don't think you should be touching yourself like that here!" Not too loud, don't want to cause an actual stir. Just make him think I might.

Midlevel Asshole bolts upright, eyes bulging open, hands flying away from his lap, like his thighs are electrified. "I'm not!" he blusters immediately.

I smile politely. "My mistake."

He glares at me and then wrestles to free himself from his restraint with a huff.

It used to work better, when I was in a crisp suit, official insignia on my lapel, and UNOC credentials prominently displayed on the back of my hand instead of the still healing scar from their removal—a signal to some that they have permission to offer abuse and mistreatment without fear of consequences.

But it still worked.

With grim satisfaction, I back up to give him room to stand and step out of the way. That's when, through one of those odd hushes that sometimes falls over a crowd, I hear a woman's voice behind me, clear, smooth, and professional.

"*. . . entering week six of the hearing. The prime minister of the United Nation of Colonies has continually denied the allegations, calling them 'ludicrous' and 'a conspiracy' to muddy his good name.*"

I freeze, my brain shouting contradictory orders at me: *Duck down! Pretend everything is fine!*

I manage to twist around to see where the woman's voice is coming from.

An old vid screen is welded—and then apparently duct-taped for good measure, the silver tape framing the edges—to the bulkhead wall at the front end of the "passenger compartment." One of the perks of choosing this transport, apparently. At the moment, it's playing a fragmented, jumpy picture of SNN and one of their political reporters, Lanna Charles. No holo, but this is bad enough.

My heart immediately trips with anxiety.

Are they going to show a clip, archival footage with my face in the background? Worse, what if they run that press conference again?

"Are you sitting down or what?" Midlevel Asshole demands, at a far higher volume than I used.

I swivel automatically to face him, his flushed cheeks. Other passengers are staring. At him. At me.

Sit down. Halley Zwick *has no reason to care about this story. Go!* The exasperated voice in my head, so familiar, immediately spurs me into action.

I turn my back on the screen, pretending it doesn't exist, and squeeze past manager man. I unclip my bag and force myself to settle into my seat. Next to me, the midlevel manager drops back into his seat with a loud, disgruntled exhale, before pulling a holocomm from his pocket and flicking through his messages. By fate or poor luck, though, I have a clear view of the vid screen between the headrests of the seats in front of me. And I can't make myself look away.

"... *representative from the Ministry of Justice has indicated that the possibility of criminal charges for Bierhals's alleged role in inciting a riot has not been ruled out at this time,"* Lanna continues. *"He is alleged to have planted operatives of his own in the crowd, as false supporters of his rival to encourage the lawlessness that resulted in twenty-seven injured and three dead. One thing we know for certain is that the violence on Nova Lennox likely changed the outcome of the most recent election. With that violation of terms, UNOC removed the station's capacity to vote as a probationary member of the body. But anonymous sources have indicated that Nova Lennox would have cost Prime Minister Bierhals his election, giving the win to Rober Ayis."*

On screen, Ayis appears, red-faced and gesticulating wildly. I can't hear his speech, but I don't need to. It will be about the evils of UNOC and Earth's legacy governments and how each station needs to put itself first. One Station is his program for self-sufficiency.

Then, it cuts to Prime Minister Mather Bierhals, young, handsome, flashing a modest grin—*Not so many teeth, goddammit, Math!*—and holding a hand up to a crowd in a benevolent wave. He stops briefly to shake hands, bending down to speak to the children directly, Mather's go-to move for winning attention from the press and the public. Kids greet him with bundles of wheat grown in the dome fields, and teens hold up holos of their art projects, sponsored by Mather's new Art Is Universal program.

The contrast is striking. And beneath layers of despondency and exhaustion, pride swells in me. Just a little.

The camera catches Mather chatting with one girl in particular, his face intent on her words, nodding as she speaks. That is his gift, making people feel heard. Behind him, his team follows, discreetly taking notes on everyone he speaks with, making sure to mark a need for additional communication or perhaps even a personal note.

An odd distant ache starts up in my chest. Watching him, watching *them*, is like seeing someone you used to know, an ex-boyfriend, a friend you no longer have contact with, from across a busy shuttle station. You are no longer part of their life.

I tear my gaze away from him to study the background of the video. This looks like a clip from a visit to the Columbia Hills colony, based on faux Greek architectural elements in the printed housing behind him. It was a big deal at the time, moving away from the practical but sterile hab style that has dominated dome living for so many years. One of Bierhals's innovations, back when he was in Parliament, to make a house feel more like a home. Studies showed improved mental and physical health as a result.

Theoretically. I don't know. I don't know anything anymore.

"Much of this will depend on the results of the New Parliament's ongoing committee investigation into the allegations, including finding witnesses to testify," Lanna says, *"which has been difficult, given the high turnover in the new Bierhals administration. Some have even suggested that it's a conspiracy to keep former staffers from speaking out."*

Feeling the heat of an invisible spotlight that only I'm aware of, I sink down farther in my seat, now grateful to have the innermost, instant-death position. It feels more protected, less visible.

"There's really no story here, Lanna. Turnover early in a new administration is completely normal." This new voice from the news freezes me in place. It sounds like the one in my head.

Niina.

Except the real Niina sounds more wryly amused than the

version in my head. And her true voice has the tiniest tinge of irritation that makes you want to rush to soothe, appease. To win her approval.

Or maybe that's just me.

In the gap between the seats, I catch a glimpse of Niina on the screen. As always, her confidence projects outward, from the precise cut of her black hair—perfectly even at her chin—to the ruthless arch of her eyebrows. She looks as if she's never been stressed or worried about anything in her life. She's someone who knows her value, who knows the power she holds and doesn't bother to hide it.

She is who I wanted to be, once. And she made me believe it was possible. Another, stronger pang of longing clutches hard at my heart, before I ruthlessly push it down.

Niina had her own reasons for doing what she did and none of them had to do with me.

Though I can't see him on screen, Harrison Butler, my replacement, is surely lingering nearby. Ready to jump in with facts, contact information, or Niina's current nicotine fixation. He's a high-cheekboned, camera-ready Harvard grad who favors tidy eight-button suits and doing what he's told. That will serve him well.

"*We're transitioning from campaigning to active governing, and some people aren't cut out for that. So we've had to make some adjustments.*" Niina's gaze seems to bore straight into me.

My face flushes hot with a confusing blend of humiliation and fury, and I have to look away, studying the lumpy seam of metal around the window until I can wrangle myself back under control.

"*That was Bierhals's chief of staff, Niina Vincenzik,*" Lanna says. "*She indicated that every member of the campaign staff has been encouraged to testify as called upon. With the appropriate subpoenas. But as some have pointed out, it's hard to subpoena people you can't find.*"

I brace myself for a clip from the press conference. My parents "pleading" with me to return.

But the anchor moves on to another story, thankfully, this one about a grain disease destroying huge swathes of crops in the New Boston dome, triggering worries about a lunar famine.

A to-do list forms in my mind before I can stop it: contact the New Boston governor to ascertain food stores, hound our media contacts into drawing more attention to the impending crisis because people can't care about what they don't know about, and pound on doors (metaphorically speaking) until I can get someone in the UNOC liaisons office to pester those cheap bastards back on Earth in the RusAmerSino Alliance for aid. The residents in New Boston pay taxes like everyone else and they—

No.

Not your job anymore. Not your place.

The despondency I've been battling for the last six weeks rises up and drags me under.

It doesn't matter. *None* of it matters. It's all bullshit. Fake power politics and manipulation. The world is a game, one in which you can't win unless you cheat.

And, for better or worse, I'm out of the game.

I turn sideways, away from the screen and toward the sidewall all the better to be sucked out into space, if the opportunity arises—and drape the ragged side of my sweater cloak over my face to pretend to sleep.

Surprisingly, exhaustion is a relatively effective cure for my brand of fear-based insomnia. Or maybe it's being on the move again, the engines thrumming beneath my feet in a reassuring hum that speaks to escape. Again.

I hadn't realized how much tension I was holding, in my gut, in my shoulders, until the knots in both relax as soon as the transport clears the EnExx17 dock. No unexpected ATC holds or delays, no interruptions from an official IEA vessel demanding to board and search.

They always tell you when you're lost to stop moving so searchers can find you. I'm hoping the opposite holds true as well.

I wake abruptly, with a stiff neck, sore knees from the tight space, and the vague knowledge that I've just missed some kind of announcement overhead. The vid screen is, thank God, dark now.

A quick look around the compartment shows that I've managed to sleep through several stops, including that of the manager next to me. His seat is empty, restraints dropped to the floor, as if they're somebody else's problem.

Asshole. I lean over and pick the ends up, piling the straps in the seat for the next passenger.

Gasps from the other side of the compartment draw my attention. A handful of people are whispering and leaning toward a window.

Oh, fuck.

My hands go numb. Are we getting stopped? Now? Out here?

But when I make myself stand, to the stares of the remaining passengers near me, and angle my body to peer outside the window, all I see is the sheer cliff wall of metal, growing closer as the transport edges into alignment.

We're pulling up to a ship. A big one. The cargo hold doors are exposed, the connecting bridge already juddering forward toward us.

"See, right there," a briner whispers to his colleagues, as he points upward out the window. "I told you."

I give up any appearance of discretion and move closer to the window for a better look, excusing myself past the remaining passengers.

The briner looks up at me when I arrive next to his seat, but he doesn't seem surprised. He points again.

ELYSIAN FIELDS is painted along the side of the ship, in enormous sweeping letters, each one probably larger than this entire transport.

Oh. The ship is bigger than I remembered. But then again, I'd arrived last time on public education transport, holding several hundred students. And we had been welcomed into a public entrance rather than the (enormous) cargo hold.

The transport glides to meet the extending bridge, but the connection is more of a controlled crash, with a big jolt rattling the vessel around us, forcing me to grab an empty seat to stay on my feet.

"A supply drop for *Elysian Fields,*" the briner says a little louder, in response to the questioning looks around him. "The dead ship?"

My acknowledgment of curiosity seems to act as permission for everyone else to sate theirs; restraints click open left and right as passengers move closer to the window for a better look.

Grateful for the distraction, I slip through them, retrieve my bag, and head toward the rear of the passenger compartment for the cargo hold door.

A blast of brisk air greets me as soon as the door retracts. It's much colder in here and reeks of ship mechanicals. Hot metal, dried-up grease, and unwashed bodies working round the clock. I suspect the crew may sleep in here, when they have the opportunity to sleep at all.

I wend my way through the stacked crates and barrels of cargo, toward the open door and bridgeway to the larger ship.

The first mate from before is directing crew members as they drag rumbling, squeaky-wheeled carts full of supplies from the transport across the bridge.

The *Elysian Fields*'s extendable bridge feels solid enough beneath my feet as I take my first step onto its patterned metal floor; I've heard enough horror stories about older ships to be cautious. The seal behind me isn't hissing with a leak, and the much heavier carts don't seem to be making the bridge itself wobble.

I reach the threshold on the other side without any incident. The *Elysian Fields* cargo hold is several levels tall and echoingly wide. I expect a clinical, antiseptic smell inside, but it's mostly . . . old. That scent of decaying paper, glue, and materials that seems to inhabit any building over a hundred years old. Apparently that applies to ships as well.

On one wall, the towering metal launch framework for emergency escape shuttles stands empty. The shuttles themselves were probably removed when the museum was shut down. Less to maintain.

On the other three sides, mostly bare shelves line the walls to a dizzying height. A reminder that before this was a tourist stop, it used to be an active hospital ship, serving multiple colonies and thousands of people. One section holds boxes upon boxes marked DREXELL'S SNACK MIX-TRAVAGANZA, stacked well above my head. Left over maybe from the food court days? I'm not sure.

Other crates on the lower levels of shelving are marked with scrawled names and numbers, making me wonder if they belong to the "residents." A dozen or so empty cryotanks are shoved into the far corner, their attached tubes and wires stretching out in every direction, crawling across the floor like they're reaching out for connection.

I shiver in spite of myself. Extra tanks, left from when the ship was still taking new residents probably. Or maybe spare ones in case of a malfunction. But they look so dusty and discarded, it's hard to imagine them being of any use.

The supplies brought by my transport—dozens of crates marked with chemical compounds that I don't recognize, plastic tubing on a roll that's taller than I am, a few barrels of water, and a few small boxes of food—sit in the center of the cargo hold, an island in an ocean of empty space.

A blast of static makes me jump, and then Karl appears on the vid screen across the room.

"Thank you, gentlemen," he says, his voice tinny and thin from the speakers. "I'll take it from here." As the crew members depart with their now empty carts, Karl's attention turns to me, pale eyes laser-focused. "Halley. Good. The service lift is forward and to your left. Take it up to the main exhibition level, and I'll give you a tour."

I feel small suddenly, alone, here in this space with nothing but my tiny bag full of dirty clothes. Following Karl's directions with my gaze, I see a darkened corridor at the front of the cargo hold with what might be an elevator entrance on the left-hand side.

At the opening to the corridor, a large sign with a directional arrow points deeper within the ship: PREP ROOMS.

Of course. It makes sense that they would have received people here on the brink of death, cleaned them up, emptied them out, whatever was required to preserve someone back in those days.

I imagine pale limbs stretched out on shiny metal tables, hands flailing, blood running red and thick over the edges into a floor drain.

Knock it off. Nobody's been bleeding on this ship in better than a century.

I don't consider myself superstitious or even easily frightened. But something about being here with the idea of staying, rather than a short visit with a definitive end and accompanied by other people, feels . . . creepier than I imagined. And that's without considering what possibly waits upstairs, in the auditorium.

"[You sure about this?]" the first mate behind me asks, startling me into turning to face him.

He's at the threshold to the bridge, his presence keeping the cargo hold doors open and the bridge extended. His brow is furrowed almost into his former hairline. His skeptical expression takes in the dusty, oversize space, and me along with it. It's as if he's reading my mind.

Irritation flares within me. Not at him, at myself. No. I am absolutely not sure. But I am certain that I can't afford to be unnerved by imaginary dangers and childish fears when very real, adult ones await me elsewhere.

I wanted isolation, I wanted the freedom to stop hiding, a safe place to plan my next step. Well, now I've got it.

Plus, I have no money for a fare back. There are exchanges that could be made to guarantee passage, but I've already bartered away enough of my soul to get this far.

I nod. "[I'll be fine. Thank you.]"

Then I make myself walk away before I can change my mind.

3

The heavy cargo bay doors close as I reach the elevator, sending a powerful reverberation through the metal floor beneath my feet. An overwhelming silence follows.

I press the button for the elevator and wait, listening to the rough whir and click of machinery as it responds, and beyond that, the dull roar of the mighty engines powering *Elysian Fields*'s endless flight.

This corridor isn't as dim as it seemed from the brightly lit cargo area. But the lighting is certainly . . . feebler here, revealing a shadowy T-junction a dozen or so feet to my right.

I resist the urge to investigate. I'm not here to satisfy some kind of morbid sense of curiosity. This is a job. And safe space to wait while I figure out my next move.

But when the elevator lingers several floors below my current location, according to the digital readout above the doors—perhaps picking up Karl along the way—I take a quick peek. Dozens of closed doors line both sides of a long hallway, running perpendicular to the one in which I'm standing. Frosted glass windows for visibility and privacy, now darkened, are set in each door.

The prep rooms.

I shudder, a tiny chill skittering over my skin—superstitious bullshit; what could anything in those rooms do to me?—and return to stand before the elevator.

Seconds later, it chimes its arrival softly, as if aware that people in close proximity might be easily startled. The industrial doors peel back, revealing an oversize interior. The walls are padded with quilted moving blankets. But it is otherwise empty. No Karl.

I step inside, feeling small and out of place, as if I'm trespassing instead of simply following directions.

But as soon as the doors open on the third floor, revealing the main exhibition level, the rush of familiarity, the relief of it, overtakes any of my misgivings. After six weeks of hiding and wariness, always on guard, perpetually alert to my new environment, the sight of anything I actually *know* gives the sensation of being able to properly exhale for the first time in months.

The service elevator is on the far side of the welcome pavilion, tucked behind some fake trees in terra-cotta pots and a Doric column. But when I step out from behind the trees and column, I find myself where I once stood what feels like a lifetime ago.

The design mimics a villa courtyard. Delicate black and white tiles form an elaborate mosaic on the floor. A brass plate set among the tiles reads AD VITA AETERNAM. To Eternal Life. It's Zale Winfeld's motto, part of the message he supposedly received from a higher power. Strange symbols line the outer edge of the plate—more from Winfeld's "vision." I suspect they were more for effect than anything else—no one has ever been able to identify them.

Real-looking grape leaves and vines twine around every available vertical surface. Frescoes on the wall depict scenes from life several thousand years ago. Beautiful women with haunting eyes and piles of curls in elaborate styles, held in place by shining bands that still scream exorbitance, luxury. Men in poses of power, hoisting weapons over their shoulders or leaning casually against a table while a shopkeeper holds out wares in a desperate bid for approval. And as mythological characters, like Leda and Jupiter. The Hall of News stated that Zale Winfeld had paid a ridiculous amount of money to mimic a coastal villa uncovered in an archeological dig in Italy, in keeping with the *Elysian Fields* theme.

The fountain at the center features a girl in a simple shift holding a traditional amphora at a decided angle to pool its contents at her bare feet. But it's dry. Just as it was when I was here the first time. The water feature is another relic of the luxury that once existed here when it was a private endeavor.

An old gilded sign remains on the far wall, pointing to a Welcome Center that no longer exists, replaced by a gift shop. Tiny stuffed dolls, mimicking the inhabitants of the ship in terrible taste, remain in the dusty display windows.

On the opposite side of the shop, a food court, with metal rails to push trays along and a checkout stand with a UNOC credentials kiosk for payment, still gives off a faint scent of stale popcorn, adding a commercial crassness that clashes with the eternal elegance theme.

The whole thing, though, seems . . . dingier and older than I remember. No more soft lighting overhead, bringing to mind the warm candles and firelight of another life. It's the bleak white of an industrial workspace. The precise mosaic tiles beneath my feet are cracked and crumbling now. The enormous metal doors on the far side, the primary entrance, where hundreds if not thousands of school-age children entered once upon a time, are of course closed, but streaks of soot or grease from the aged machinery leak from the top, in a slow race to the bottom of the now dull surface.

"Hello?" I call, grimacing at the echo of my own voice as it bounces around the pavilion and then vanishes down the darkened corridor opposite me. "Karl?"

Straight ahead of me, through the welcome pavilion, should be the Hall of News and the bathrooms, if I remember correctly.

Everything is dark and silent in that direction, though.

I turn to look down the corridor at my back.

On this side, the emergency lighting at the baseboard level is on. Cheaper, maybe, than turning the lights on for real?

"Karl?" I call again before starting in that direction, uneasiness beginning to chafe. Is he playing a game of some sort?

Ahead on my right, the glass display beams a faint shadow of myself back at me. It's a life-size replica of part of a high-speed rail train car, re-creating the moment when Zale Winfeld was "blessed" with the idea for *Elysian Fields*. The details of the private car are difficult to see at the moment, but I remember that the table held a variety of gadgets and screens that our teacher, Mx. Hugo, explained would have been the communication devices of the late twenty-first century. The window showed rivulets of rain, real water, to represent the storm that had washed out the tracks and some of the surrounding community, stopping the train in place.

Normally a hologram of a distressed Zale would pace back and forth, hands stuffed in his pockets. Until he stops, staring out the window into the distance, at the new crossroads created by the rising floodwater across the tracks. And then a literal bolt of lightning strikes the train car. At which point, the narrator kicks in and describes Zale's epiphany.

This egocentric feature has actually been here from the beginning. Like a depiction of Moses receiving the Ten Commandments or Noah learning about the upcoming flood, this is Zale as spiritual leader. It's over the top, on the nose, and, I suspect, more marketing tool than accurate record of events.

The vid screen next to the display—old tech that offers the explanatory patter that a tour guide might have once provided—is dark as well.

I keep going. Farther down, I see the first doors to the "resident" displays, as well as the glint of the gold-worked sign for the Winfeld Auditorium.

A chill slithers down my spine and across my skin. The presentation was creepy enough when the lights were on and people were everywhere. Now, in the dim corridor, I can't help but imagine those blank-faced holos of Winfeld's children, still on stage, projecting brightly artificial smiles toward rows and rows of empty seats.

Mouth pursed, I deliberately look away from the auditorium signage and entrance. That's when I notice one of the resident doors, the second one down, about fifteen feet from me, standing about halfway open. A faint clicking noise, followed by a labored wheezing, seems to be coming from within.

A rush of cold fear leaves my fingers numb and tingling, before I regain control of myself. There's nothing here that can hurt me. Except possibly Karl, it seems. "Karl," I say firmly. "What are you doing?"

There's no response.

The clicking continues, followed by another round of wheezing. I try not to think about how it sounds like someone struggling to breathe.

It can't be. It's too even, too regular, I tell myself. Plus, no one here is breathing. Except for me. And Karl, wherever the fuck he is.

Still, I brace myself as I push forward toward the door, my bootheels clacking loudly against the tiles.

The slice of room revealed by the open door is darker than the partially lit corridor, but the clicking and wheezing is definitely coming from inside.

Son of a bitch. If this is a joke or a prank or some kind of scam . . .

Human trafficking. Ransom. Daze smuggling.

Or maybe he's just planning on turning you over to the authorities. Whoever is willing to pay the highest price. At this point, I don't even know which side that would be. But at least Ayis's people want me alive to testify. I'm not longer sure I can say the same about some of my former colleagues at the prime minister's office. And the Investigation and Enforcement Agency working on behalf of New Parliament? That depends, I suppose, on how far the corruption has spread.

I tighten my grip on my bag. I've had enough unwelcome surprises dumped on me simply by paying attention when everyone assumed I wasn't.

I shove the door open, and bright lights set in the ceiling trigger at the movement, telling me two things.

First, the room was unoccupied before I walked in. Second, the noises—clearly now bursts of static rather than the imagined wheezing—seem to be coming from the vid screen, set in the wall to the right of the door. A faint wavy horizontal line wobbles across the screen, back and forth, indicating that it's on and malfunctioning.

The resident and her accompanying cryo equipment are as still and serene as one would expect from someone in her condition. Though the holograms are off, the guitars on display and the glass case with several pink- and purple-sequined jumpsuits are immediately familiar. This is the room of Chessley Max, the former pop star I saw on my first trip.

Drawn irresistibly toward the tank, I edge closer until I'm looking down at her, her head resting on the traditional purple satin pillow. Her dark curls lie spread out in an arc on the satin. Her long eyelashes—more natural than the ones I remember from her holograms, which had pink and purple lights attached—rest peacefully against her cheeks, which still have the slight roundness of youth, perhaps artificially created through surgery or other means.

I frown. Weirdly, she somehow looks different, younger than my memory of her. Less of the ornate makeup meant to disguise age, fewer wrinkles near her eyes.

Probably my own misperception. When you're twelve, everyone over thirty looks ancient.

Because that is, after all, the benefit of cryogenics. Chessley is as perfectly preserved at fortysomething as on the day she . . . Almost died? Died temporarily? I'm not sure what the proper terminology is. From what I recall of her story, she overdosed and her team rushed her here, to Zale. So she's not dead, not exactly, but attempts to master cryo-awakening were abandoned decades ago. Best efforts usually result in a temporary revival that devolves into multiple organ failure within hours. Zale Winfeld sold these people—and his own family—a future he couldn't fulfill.

What else is new?

It's the small things that make Chessley so poignant, so *human*. There's a cluster of tiny curls cut short near her ear, the remnants of an ill-considered attempt at a new look, or maybe she twirled her hair when she was stressed. The now permanent colony of pimples on her chin. Tiny lines from a dimple when she smiles, carved around her mouth. All those years of projecting happiness out to thousands in a darkened arena, millions over holocam. Dark circles from exhaustion or her addiction are visible on the skin beneath her eyes.

Had she lived long enough, she likely would have corrected that. Along with the disastrous hair choices.

I grimace on her behalf. I'm sure this is not how she envisioned her future, preserved on her worst day for all eternity.

I mean, that would be like if I . . .

An image immediately bursts into view in my mind: me, staring down at myself in one of these tanks with my bruised face and badly dyed hair prominently displayed above the privacy shield. My hands, displaying the scar from the removal of my credentials and my bitten-to-the-quick nails, folded over my upper chest. Dead. Perhaps with a bloody hole on the side of my head.

Or a still red ring around my pale neck, fingerprint bruises plainly visible.

It's so vivid I can almost feel the cool satin beneath my head, feel the rush of icy fluids in my veins . . .

Jesu. My breath catches. I step back from Chessley's tank, shaking my head. Sleep deprivation and paranoia are eating away at me again. It's not like I'll ever be stuck in a tank here. No one is, anymore.

"Now that you've had time to snoop your fill . . ." Karl's voice booms behind me.

I jolt and then whip around to face him. Except he's not there. His face is on the vid screen near the entrance instead.

"I wasn't snooping," I say acidly, ignoring the heat rising in my face. "I was looking for *you*."

He arches a skeptical eyebrow.

I open my mouth to argue, but then I remember: the emergency lighting leading in this direction from the pavilion, the open door to this room, the sounds over the "malfunctioning" vid screen.

"Was this a test?" I demand.

Karl grins at me. "Can't be too careful. You won't believe how many journalists I've had to dissuade. And after my last experience, if you're easily unnerved, I don't want you here."

"A little late for that, don't you think?" I snap.

"Can always make a stop at the next available station," he says idly, but it feels like a threat. This ship doesn't stop unless there's a request for a visitor to board, supplies are needed, or, apparently, to boot a fired employee.

"Well, you caught me. I was curious. I fell for it," I say, crossing my arms over my chest, oddly defensive. Is he going to kick me off the ship for that?

"Nah. You didn't try to take anything or record her," he says. "You're good."

I glare at him, annoyed with both his "test" and the utterly childish but completely ingrained rush of relief I feel at being told I passed. I have always been an overachiever.

"I thought you were coming to give me a tour," I say.

Karl splutters out a laugh, gesturing to the engine room behind him, mostly quiet for once. "If I could leave this place for that, I wouldn't need you, would I?"

Apparently not?

"Now, come on. I'll show you SecOffice and where you'll be staying."

I head back out into the corridor. Each vid screen flickers to life a few moments before I reach it. He's obviously tapped into the screen system, or maybe it always had some kind of monitoring component. And his tour basically amounts to telling me what something is and reminding me not to touch it or take anything.

We pass by Winfeld's Inspiration (yes, it is really called that, and yes, it is nausea-inducing), head through the main pavilion again (the fountain girl, per Karl, is not a replica but an actual ancient Roman artifact that sounds, in my opinion, dubiously sourced), and down the opposite corridor.

The baseboard emergency lighting switches on as I approach. The Hall of News remains dark, as do the public bathrooms.

"You'll have facilities up in staff housing," Karl says. "No need to bother with these, except during rounds."

"And these rounds consist of . . . ?" I ask.

He blips off the last screen and it's a moment before he arrives at one farther down, near a door at the end of the corridor. Words are faintly burned into the screen over his face. DO NOT ENTER. EMPLOYEES ONLY. "Walk the floors through all the public areas, listening for alerts, watching for signs of anything unusual. That's it," he says, sounding impatient, as he jerks his head to the side, indicating I should approach the door next to him.

I ignore him, staying put. "Unusual like what?" I ask.

He makes a frustrated noise. "I don't know, a water leak? Lights that won't come on for a floor or section. A tank alert that doesn't trigger on the main board. This ship is old as shit, and I'm holding it together with soldering tape, refurbished microchips for God's sake, and sheer fucking determination." He pauses. "Speaking of which, your primary responsibilities will be this floor, which is the main exhibition level—ME in all our documentation—and subresidential levels one through five. We call those SB-1, SB-2, et cetera. I can check on the rest." He avoids my gaze, fidgeting with something out of sight.

This level holds all their high-interest exhibits. On the next couple of floors down, SB-1 and SB-2, apparently, you've got the politicians, including the second- or third-to-last vice president of the United States. I can never remember which. Then there are the CEOs and other corporate execs—lots of "titans of industry" in that section—along with heroes whose medical or technological advances won them a spot. More artists, musicians, and creators, acclaimed but less revered. After that, it's regular people. If you can term anyone who has enough money to buy into a sketchy promise of a rebirth as "regular."

There is one little girl whose family and community fundraised to be able to buy her place, according to the display inside her room. Viviane, I think. The reason I even remember her is because of how lifelike she looks. She has a perfect purple bow on her still perfect brown curls.

"Why not SB-6 through . . ." I pause, thinking, and realize I don't know the total number of floors in the ship. "The rest?"

Karl sighs, as though I've asked him to explain quantum mechanics in full. "The uppermost level on the ship is the bridge and . . . a special exhibit. Unfinished. Nothing for you to do up there. On the lower residential floors, the ventilation system needs updating, and I can't do all of them at once," he says, still not quite looking at me. "I've had to shut some of them down. It's dangerous down there. For the living, anyway."

I frown. "But I thought you were working on engine—"

"Just check out the SecOffice," he cuts me off. "There'll be plenty of time for questions, and all of this will make more sense when you see the boards."

Reluctantly, I push the handle on the security office door (how quaint) to open it. On the other side, it's probably ten degrees warmer, and it smells of stale air, aging dust, and—I sniff, wrinkling my nose—moldy sesame noodles.

The room is small, not much larger than my room at the hostel, with two chairs in cracked black simu-leather shoved in behind an L-shaped board full of buttons and controls. A forgotten gray biodegradable cup, tucked under one of the chairs with a spoon still inside, is likely the source of the odor.

Screens line every square inch of the walls, stacked and staggered above one another. A dozen or so of them are dark. Broken, maybe. The rest are showing resident rooms, empty corridors, the silent train replica, the dim auditorium with the black curtains still drawn back after the last "show." One of them even seems to be focused on what must be the bridge, based on the viewport full of stars in the background and the helm controls, including a very antique ship's wheel, at dead center.

A ship's wheel that looks to be moving on its own. Ghost captain.

I catch my breath and step back automatically, even as my brain kicks in. *Don't be ridiculous.*

"Yeah. I've jury-rigged it so I can run most everything from down here."

I jolt at the sound of Karl's voice and turn to see his face bobbing inside one of the formerly dark screens.

"And what I can't, you have to," he continues. "But mostly, your job is to press that button, every three hours."

Recovering from the start he gave me, I step forward for a better look. "Which—" But then I see it. It's the one marked with words carved into the plastic surround of the board— THIS ONE—with an arrow pointing for good measure. If carved words can portray a tone, these suggest that Karl barely refrained from adding the word "dummy" to the end.

"What does it do?"

He makes a sour face. "Not much. It's the board's way of keeping tabs on me out here. They say it's about safety and maintaining security protocols. But you know what would help with that? More staff. When we were up and running for real, we had thirty-two people on board. Living, breathing people," he adds with emphasis.

"So the button," I prompt, hoping to distract him from what seems like a well-worn diatribe.

He sighs. "You push the button, it's basically a check-in. The board knows everything is fine. We don't push the button, they send in the guards. Lots of rich ice cubes out here with plenty of less-rich relatives who'd like to reclaim their memorabilia and shit. But they can't because it's all willed to the *Elysian Fields* trust, and the board's not letting it go. But if someone can petition the courts that the board isn't keeping up their end of the bargain, endangering their legacy or opening it up for theft or whatever, then . . ."

"Are you talking about grave robbing?" I ask, incredulous.

"Not a grave if you're not technically dead, but same idea. Piracy, I suppose, would be more accurate. We've had a few attempts, but nothing too serious."

I pride myself on a fairly steady poker face, a necessity in my previous profession, but I can feel my mouth hanging open an inch or two at his casualness.

"Look, *Halley,* you'll be fine. No one's bothered with us in years. They hardly even remember we're out here." He sounds sullen, disappointed even, as if the thought of not battling criminals, scavengers stealing from the dead, is a massive bummer. "The board barely shows up to check on things themselves."

I am . . . less than convinced.

A realization occurs to me belatedly. "Wait a minute. If you're not allowed to hire anyone, and if I'm not supposed to even be on the ship, then how am I doing check-ins?"

"You don't actually talk with anyone. Any calls go directly to my holocomm," he says.

The rest of the implication clicks into place. "And they think you're the one pressing the button, obviously." So, essentially, I'm pretending to be Karl. Not quite signing his signature but close enough.

A twist of nausea floods my mouth with saliva. What is that

saying about those who ignore history? Not that this is an exact repeat of what happened with Bierhals, but it's enough of an echo to give me second thoughts.

And what are you going to do about it now? You're already here illegally. Stay safe, save up, and start over, that's still the plan. The only *plan.*

"You got it." Karl doesn't seem to notice my moment of inner turmoil. "If you have any trouble, you can get me by pushing the big blue button, right there." He jerks his chin to the opposite end of the L-shaped panel. "Now, let me show you where you'll be staying," he says.

The on-screen version of Karl leads me back into the corridor of the main exhibition level and then through another door to an echoey, shadowy metal staircase, which I'm to take up to the next floor. My steps clang loudly, reverberating through the narrow vertical space. Before I open the door to the next level, I peer cautiously over the railing, seeing the metal-grate stairs spiral downward into darkness. I shudder and retreat to safety.

When I open the door and step through, I'm in another corridor, though it looks nothing like the one a level below. More emergency lighting, but it's just a long string of closed doors at regular intervals. For the first time, I get a glimpse of the *Elysian Fields*'s former life as a hospital ship. These are old patient rooms, turned into staff rooms—first for Zale Winfeld's "this is totally not a cult" endeavor and then for the employees who managed the ship as a tourist stop—now turned into . . . nothing, I suppose.

"Wash-fac are about halfway down," Karl says. He's on the only vid screen in view, on the wall directly to my right. The words DAILY ANNOUNCEMENTS are burned into the screen across his forehead. "There's a galley too, but . . ." He pauses, frowning at me. "Where's your food?"

I raise my eyebrows. "I'm sorry?"

"The food from the transport," he says impatiently. "You didn't bring it up with you?"

And how would I have known to do that? I want to ask, but I tighten my grip on my temper. It's lack of sleep, that's all. I'm normally much better at handling difficult people. It used to be my job. "It's in the cargo hold," I say, keeping my voice even.

He shakes his head. "Fine. You'll have to come down and get it. And grab whatever snack mix you think you'll want."

I stare at him for a second, not sure I heard him correctly. "You're talking about the Drexell's? Those boxes?"

"The CEO is a grand-something nephew of Winfeld. He's on the board. That's his contribution. Unlimited snack mix." Karl shakes his head again. "Like that's going fix the engines or repair hull damage," he mutters.

Hull damage? Okay, yeah. *Elysian Fields* is a good *temporary* resting point. No one will find me, but also clearly not a place to linger.

"You can choose any of the rooms you want, but the one on the left there is probably the cleanest." Karl jerks his chin toward the door across the hall. It's open a crack. "It's the one most recently used."

By the last guy, who fled in the middle of the night, and I'm beginning to understand why. Karl seemed to think he was too easily spooked, but maybe he just didn't want to die of carbon monoxide poisoning or get sucked out of a window.

"All right." I start for the indicated door. Might as well check it out, see if it truly is the best of the available options.

"One more thing." Karl's voice stops me.

I glance back at him.

"I assume you have a personal holocomm?"

One I had not shared when I applied for his posting because I couldn't afford to get a new one if the job didn't work out. Anonymous comms, ones not connected to UNOC credentials, are hard to come by, even harder without spare credits at my disposal.

I nod reluctantly.

"Our connectivity is shit. We've got the emergency comm channel and all the alerts and reports for the button bullshit go through that. But if you want to reach out to someone on your own, you'll have to wait until we're close enough to a station or a ship to piggyback on their signal."

I stare at him. "You're kidding." The *Elysian Fields*'s long and meandering flight path around the solar system was based on long-outdated settlement numbers. It only cruises by the largest and oldest space stations and colonies. Twelve, maybe fifteen locations on each circuit—Earth, Bellaterra Station, Amster-York, the moon and the old lunar resupply stations, Mars, MarsAmz Stations 1 to 5, Venusian IV, Europa-7, New Kazan, Tian Station, a few others. I had to take a transport from EnExx17 to catch the ship on its way to Tian.

There might be other big ships out there that we could borrow a signal from as we passed, but anything military would be encrypted and the Traveler colonies, who permanently reside on their vessels, aren't always predictable.

I might be cut off for days at a time.

"You can send text pretty much any time you want, but that's about it. Sometimes you can download media packets, but again, text only." Karl pauses, cocking his head to one side with a sly expression. "In case you need to . . . keep an eye on anything."

I go very still. *He's guessing. He doesn't know. Does he?* I try to will the blood away from my cheeks and neck.

"I mean, someone must be missing you." He gives me a wolfish grin. "I don't think you got that shiner by chance."

What an asshole. "I did, actually," I say stiffly.

He cackles. "And that name, Zwick, is so clearly fa—"

"My name is Halley Zwick," I snap. "That's it. All you need to know."

The amusement fades from his expression, replaced by an ugly hardness that makes me instantly question my choice.

"Yeah, sure," he says. "You keep telling yourself that." He clicks his tongue in disgust. "You've got forty-seven minutes till button time."

Then his face vanishes, leaving me staring at the blackness of the screen and the darkness of the corridor beyond.

4

I take a peek in the room with the door open a crack, the one Karl indicated. It appears to be a standard, if small, setup, though still slightly larger than the one I had at the hostel.

A teardrop-shaped window on the far wall presents a curved cutout of deep black space sprinkled with stars. Our movement is so slow that the pinpricks of light hang motionless, frozen in their dark setting. A single bed with folded-down rails on the sides is the central attraction. A leftover from when the *Elysian Fields* was the *Clara Barton,* most likely. Lovely. An antique.

A set of three built-in drawers is cut into the wall to the right of the door. And that's about it.

The most interesting—or disturbing, depending on your perspective—detail is the bedding. Worn white sheets with a faint blue flower pattern and a woven green blanket with obvious holes in it are still on the mattress. Except they're tangled together and spiraling off the edge of the bed, as if someone got up in a hurry, tossing the covers aside in their rush to not be there anymore.

A single large work boot, tipped over on its side and resting on a small but oddly plush and expensive-looking patterned rug near the bed, speaks to the same idea. You have to be in a special kind of hurry to leave a shoe behind.

In other words, it's pretty much exactly as Karl led me to believe. No surprises here.

My attention is drawn toward the rest of the corridor. The series of closed doors on either side, facing one another in solemn lines. Sixteen on the right, fifteen on the left.

Something about them sends a little shiver down my skin. The blank faces of the doors staring out at each other reminds me of the tank occupants on the levels below. Hiding their secrets, their pasts, their lies behind frozen, impenetrable expressions.

Curiosity—along with troublesome attention to detail—remains my one truly persistent character flaw.

Jesus, kid, stop asking so many questions, Niina used to whisper to me, shaking her head. I wonder now if that was simply more for her convenience.

In this case, though, I find a whole lot of nothing. The other rooms, identical in layout to the first, are empty except for dust and musty smells. (Karl is likely right—seems like there might be a water leak somewhere.) Even the built-in drawers have been ripped out of most of them, indicating that renovation or salvage was at one point in consideration. One of the rooms appears to have been used as storage, with a large pile of wiring ripped out from somewhere lying in a loose coil on the floor and the remains of an IV 'bot smiling up at the ceiling, the central pole still in place but its blue bottom missing its wheels.

The small galley and wash-fac—each behind their individual doors—are shocking only in their griminess.

With a mixture of relief tinged with something like disappointment, I make sure all the doors are closed—nothing creepier than a dark, gaping entrance in the distance—and return to the first room. It's the only one with a bed, let alone bedding. With the little bit of time I have left before I need to start "working," I should start getting it in order. Starting with washing . . . everything.

When I step across the threshold, I hear a familiar gritty crunch under my boot. Brine.

Confused, I retreat back into the corridor, looking down

at the floor. The bartender back on EnExx17 had seemed to indicate it was someone from there who took this job before, possibly a briner. But for brine *still* to be on the floor, and in such quantities . . .

A fine, almost invisible layer of loose granules is scattered unevenly at my feet, spreading from the doorway and deep into the room. But nothing like the thick coat that clings to everything on the lower levels at EnExx17.

Frowning, I crouch down for a better look. Definitely not brine. This is more like individual particles, more clear than white, except for where it's gathered in small piles.

I touch it, pressing my fingertip to the floor to collect the particles and then lifting my hand.

It's . . . salt. Like processed table salt, I think. As in, the seasoning.

Huh. I stand, brushing my hand off against the side of my pants. *Weird.* Maybe someone here was cooking instead of using ready-made meals like the ones Karl ordered. But why in the room instead of the galley? And why so much of it? This isn't so much a little spill as a liberal pour.

My holocomm gives a warning beep, reminding me of the timer I set before starting my explorations. I'm down to ten minutes before I'll need to go push the button in the SecOffice.

With a mental shrug, I cross into the room again. It doesn't matter. People are strange when they think no one else is around.

Sometimes, even like entirely different people. My mouth pulls into a bitter smile.

At least *this* can be cleaned up with a broom.

I head toward the bed, ignoring the crunch beneath my shoes for the moment, and start to pull the bedding off the mattress. I didn't get a good look at the machines in the washfac; I'm hoping there's a functional sanitizing cycle. I'm not a germaphobe, but—

Something small and dark flies out from the bed, landing on the floor with an audible *click* and sliding to a halt.

Roach. I jump back and drop the sheets immediately. During the campaign, we stayed in several prefab structures established by the Port Lucie settlement on Mars. Roaches were everywhere, having hitched a ride on a shipment from the early days in Florida. And the adaptable bastards thrived in the close quarters of dome life. Some of the residents had even learned to use them as an "alternate protein source," learning from other colonists about old-world recipes from several Eastern countries on Earth. One of our welcome dinners involved a stir-fry that polite custom and Niina insisted we should eat—

I stop, deliberately shoving the memories down. Particularly that she had discreetly scraped my portion onto her plate when she saw I was struggling, all the while carrying on an engaged conversation with our host. Niina was talented, sharp, empathetic. Always looking out for me.

Just not as much as herself, it turned out.

It shouldn't hurt this much. Not still. It wasn't love, not in the romantic sense. But some dense tangling of admiration, joy, a united cause, and being valued. Someone who looked at me as if I were vital instead of a problem to be solved. Someone who counted on me.

And while it makes me feel pathetic to admit these feelings, apparently that doesn't lessen the pain. Or the sense of betrayal.

Absently rubbing at the ache in my chest that won't be soothed, I edge closer, around the corner of the bed, for a better look at the dark . . . thing on the floor.

It's not moving, not immediately skittering for the shadows. A dead roach? I'm not sure that's any better.

It's slender, about six inches long, with a patterned texture visible even at this distance. No legs, though.

So, not a roach.

There's also a tiny burst of bright blue color at one end, with frayed ends sticking out like antennae.

My brain is so fixated on the possibility of bugs and vermin that it takes me longer than it should to place what I'm seeing.

It's hair. Human hair. In a thin, dark braid, with a small blue bead on the end.

Revulsion locks me in place for a moment. Then I instinctively recoil, tucking my hands under my arms. What is *that* doing here?

But after a second, my rational mind kicks back in. *Calm down.* It's just hair, probably synthetic. An extension or an accessory, forgotten and left behind like the boot.

You're letting this place get to you, which is ridiculous. You have a new identity, not an entirely new personality.

With a flash of irritation at myself, I step forward to pick it up—gingerly, with two fingers, because it's still gross. I think I would have rather had the roach, and I'm not sure what that says about me.

But when I bend down, the other end of the braid, the one without the bead, catches my eye.

The strands are coming unwoven, and the hair itself is ragged, poorly cut, looking almost chewed off. No finished edges that would allow for attaching it to . . . well, anything.

I pull my hand back, heart thumping too hard.

Beneath the braid, a bright glint of metal shines up at me from the floor. When I lean closer for a better look, I find a small, uneven cross, freshly carved into the textured metal surface of the decking. Actually, now that I'm down here and the light is at a different angle, I see a series of small, uneven crosses, cut in thin lines into the scratched and worn metal, stretching in both directions, around the bed as far as I can see. Like a perimeter fence.

I stand up immediately. What the fuck?

As I back away, my bootheel connects with something, sending it sliding away. I automatically look down and find that I've knocked the small plush rug out of place. I'm now standing on the curved edges of a roughly carved design. A familiar one. Overlapping circles that form a floral pattern, with the crosses leading from either edge and outward.

No, not crosses. *X*'s.

Relief washes over me in a giddy wave, and I half laugh, half groan, covering my face with my hands. I'm an idiot.

It's superstition. Tradition, if you prefer the polite term. They're protection marks. The *X*'s represent days of safety and the curving floral pattern is meant to distract evil from approaching. In theory, evil entities will try to follow the lines and become caught in the endless circles of the floral loops. It's like breadcrumbs leading up to a trap.

I saw something similar on EnExx17 on the levels where the briners lived and worked. There was a lot of paranoia about disturbing the planet's surface for human purposes, a lot of rumors about angering something that lived beneath the ice, even though scientists had proven, repeatedly, that there was no life beneath the frozen surface. Someone—or several some-ones, more likely—had carved basically the same symbol on every visible vertical support beam.

Same thing on some of the Mars dome colonies, and even the older lunar settlements. Humans straying into the unknown tends to trigger old fears, I guess.

The braid is probably part of that. Wasn't there some ancient Earth tradition about giving a lock of hair for luck or something? That feels right.

Before I can contemplate it further, the timer on my holo-comm gives off a series of chirps. I pull it out of my pocket, the flashing 00:00 appearing in the air in front of me, and tap it off.

Shaking my head at myself, I head for the stairs to the Sec-Office. I stop laughing, though, as soon as I enter the stairway, as the sound is echoey and creepy. But this time I know it's just me.

A low mechanical buzzing starts up in the distance, like a saw or other tool revving up to work. The lights overhead in the stairwell flicker in a series of staccato bursts but remain on. Karl and his repairs, probably.

The power surges—or reductions—continue as I enter the corridor on the lower level and open the door to the security office. Or, as Karl refers to it, the SecOffice.

In the office, the images on the vid screens are staticky, with rolling black bars running through them. Related to the lights probably. I ignore them, focusing on the control board. The indicator above the all-important button—I should probably find out the true name of it, but in my head I'm going to call it the babysitter button—is a dull glowing orange now, a warning of time running short.

I press the button, watching the indicator flip to a bright green with an absurd amount of satisfaction. It feels good to do something as prescribed, as needed, without worrying about hiding, keeping my head down, wondering if I'm drawing attention to myself. This place is what I needed for a break, a chance to catch my breath, and figure out what to do next. The hearings won't last forever, no matter how many delays both sides manage to conjure.

So. Now, rounds.

The lights steady and the buzzing noise stops, thankfully, as I start for the doorway. But it occurs to me that Karl never specified whether I need to check the rooms and corridors on my assigned levels before or after pushing the button, or if it makes a difference.

I stop and contemplate reaching out to him to ask, pressing the button that I assume opens an internal channel to the engine room. But that feels like a little too much Karl, a little too soon. Plus, irritating him this early on—more of a mutual irritation, frankly, but still—feels reckless.

Whatever. If it matters, I'll do it the other way next time. He seemed far more focused on keeping the board off his back and this ship via the timely press of the button than anything else anyway. Besides, I imagine signs of a massive leak or damage would likely be visible on the vid screens anyway. When they're not on the fritz.

I glance automatically back toward the vid screens. The images are clearing, shuddering as they settle into place, except . . .

What is that?

I frown. On a single screen, one row above the control board, there's movement. Separate from the shaking or trembling of the image itself. In a corridor, it's . . . something, long and stretched out. Inching forward, upward on the screen, in a slow, uneven manner. I'd almost call it a blotch or glitch in the feed. It looks familiar somehow, but I can't put my finger on why.

Head cocked to the side, I move closer, squinting to try to see through the remaining distortion.

It's only when I'm a few inches away that my brain is finally able to piece the fuzzy sections together.

Those long portions, jutting toward the camera—those are legs, stretched out, bare feet at the ends. In the middle, a torso that's belly down. Then skeletally thin shoulders that are propped up on spindly elbows. The drooping head bobs with effort as a bony hand reaches across the floor and drags itself forward.

It's a person. Naked. And crawling across the corridor.

5

I jerk back. Is that . . . a tank breach? Am I watching someone who woke up after a century and a half on ice?

Just to crawl to their death on the corridor floor. Jesu.

An abrupt burst of static spreads across the screens, then they go dark, collectively, all at once. Followed by the overhead lights in the office.

Instant blackness.

I freeze, a scream coiled on my tongue.

Before I can release it, before I can even inhale, the overhead lights rev back to life, bringing the screens with them.

Each one blinks on and into place, no static or rolling lines.

I immediately look to the screen where I saw whatever it was I saw.

But . . . there's nothing now. It's an empty corridor, like all the others.

I blink twice, quickly, as if that will reset my vision. The image remains the same, though. No person stretched out on the ground. No hand scrabbling and clawing at forward progress.

It's just the gritty beige of the industrial no-slip flooring of the lower floors and closed doors lined up on either side.

How is that possible? He or she—they weren't moving fast enough to vanish into a room or into the stairwell. The lights and cameras were only off for a few seconds, at most.

I check the screens around that particular one, in case I'm off on the recollection of which it was.

But they, too, show nothing out of the ordinary. More empty hallways with closed doors.

Shit. If a "resident" is out of their tank and on the verge of dying (again?) in a nook or cranny that I can't see, that seems like something I should tell somebody about.

Gritting my teeth, I hit the button to summon Karl. Hell of a first day.

He appears on screen in profile, jaw clenched as he works with something out of sight. Bright sparks sizzle and snap in the air around him. "What?" he demands, without looking at me. "I'm a little busy, if you haven't—"

"I saw something on screen. Someone," I amend. No sense in being mysterious about it.

Karl stills immediately, turning to give me his full attention. "Which entrance?" Then he holds his hand up, cutting me off. "Never mind. If they've made it into the cargo hold, we don't have—"

"Not like that," I say quickly. "I saw someone on the floor in a corridor, crawling. I think it might be a tank breach."

His face contorts, first with disbelief and then deep exasperation. He shuts his eyes. "Not this again."

I stare at him. "This has happened *before*? Why didn't you—"

"You just got here. This shouldn't be happening." He opens his eyes and looks upward in a faux plea to an invisible higher authority. "Why me?" he demands plaintively.

Frustration rises in me. "I don't understand. What are you—"

"Seeing shit, hearing things," he explodes, his shoulders rigid.

A tiny squiggle of fear blooms in me, before I crush it. No, I know what I saw.

"You said you didn't scare easily," he continues. "You've only been here, what, minutes?"

Closer to an hour, but that doesn't seem like the point. "What does how long I've been here have to do with anything?" I ask, working to stay calm.

He takes a deep breath, pinching the bridge of his nose. "Look, I can't deal with this right now. I'll get you a transport as soon as we swing toward Tian Station. Seventeen hours or so."

Panic replaces my frustration. *Where am I going to go if this doesn't work?* I'm out of money. "No," I say, shaking my head quickly. "I'm not asking to leave. I'm just telling you what I saw."

"And I'm telling *you* what you're describing is not possible," he says. "They're dead, frozen through for a hundred years. Even if the system fails, they'll . . . I don't know, fuck, defrost." He raps his hand against a column of metal behind him. "This beam is more likely to move around than they are. They're not going to wake up. They sure as hell can't get out to crawl around on the floor. The muscle atrophy alone—"

"I didn't imagine it," I say, too sharply. "I don't do that."

Karl snorts.

But my determination must show in my expression. Because then he sighs heavily, as if indulging a ridiculous child. "Where?" he asks. "Where did you see this *miracle*?"

I choose to ignore his wording. "On the screen in the second—

"What level?" he interrupts.

I look again to the correct—I hope—screen, trying to find something in the image that might identify its location. No luck. The lower-level corridors all look the same. "Are none of these things labeled?" I demand finally.

"Lower left corner." Karl sounds bored now.

Edging closer, I finally find a label with the number, tiny and worn, stuck where he said it would be. "Fine. SB-3."

"Now, is the escapee still there?" he asks in an overly patronizing tone.

Fucker. I refuse to answer on the grounds that he's being an asshole. And, of course, that he is correct and the corridor is empty. Where could the person have gone? Someone struggling that hard to crawl wasn't going to leap up and run. Or yank open a door and hide inside another room. "Can't you run back the stream?"

"Power surge took the cameras out, you saw that."

"Before that," I insist.

"That's what I'm trying to tell you, even if you saw what you think you saw, which is impossible, you literally couldn't see it. The feeds are super sensitive to interference. They go to static every time this happens."

"I saw the static," I acknowledge. "I also saw *through* the static to—"

"No." He scrubs his hands over his face. "You saw shadows and shapes in the visual white noise, and your brain interpreted them into an impossible scenario. You're new here and a little creeped out by it, like everyone else."

I stiffen, offended. "That's not it."

But the slightest wobble of doubt has now entered the gravity of my certainty. It wasn't a clear picture, not at all. It had taken me a moment or two to figure out *what* I was seeing. Is it possible that I extrapolated something that wasn't there?

No. I'm not that kind of person. I make decisions based on logic, facts, and the desired outcome.

Except I'd freaked out only minutes before, seeing a roach instead of a braid of hair. Granted, the roach would have been the more expected sight, but still.

"When was the last time you slept?" Karl asks, sounding a little nicer.

"On the transport," I say immediately. Just because I want to fight back. I don't need his pity.

"Before that," he persists. "Seems like you're running on empty."

I want to argue. But I can't. Exhaustion has been an ever-present pressure in my head, behind my gritty eyes, for so long now, I'm not sure I remember what it's like to not be so tired.

He takes a deep breath. "Just . . . do the rounds. Keep an eye out. Look for an empty tank. If you find one, by all means let me know. I'll be the first one out of here. Then get some sleep." A shower of sparks rains down behind him, and he flinches. "In the meantime, I'm going back to keeping us alive and the lights on. Okay?"

Before I can answer, his screen goes dark.

I stand there a moment in the security office. Trying to get my bearings. Or maybe trying to work up my nerve. Though now I'm not sure whether the anxious energy coursing through my veins is more about the prospect of finding out I'm right or that Karl is.

The lights flicker a few more times but remain on. I make my way through the main exhibition floor, checking the food court and the gift shop, even peering into the depths of the Winfeld train scene display. And I check every "resident" room, confirming that each tank is occupied.

I try not to get distracted by the ostentatious displays of wealth and infamy. But it's not easy. One of the residents, Amli Browning—a tall blonde actress who looks vaguely familiar— has so many diamond tiaras, rings, bracelets, earrings, and cheek studs piled into glass cases that her room more resembles a poorly organized jeweler than anything else. She even has a jewel implanted on her cheek, right below her eye. It gleams like a tiny blue teardrop. This actress apparently mastered style ahead of her time—that's still a popular look. Though if the rest of her room is any indication, Amli's jewel is real, unlike the synthetics used today. The only other thing in her room is a mannequin wearing a short dress made of see-through netting and tiny metallic strips. That must have caused a hell of a scandal back in the day.

Other residents have literal blocks of gold, statues, carved items with their names emblazoned in the center, plaques, and records. Interesting that these are the items they thought they would most need in the future they awakened to. Then again, maybe it's simply practical. Money—actual paper money—has been gone for nearly as long as they have. Gold and diamonds still have value as currency, even in a credit-based system economy.

I do the same on every level after that. Down here, it's more likely to be preserved copies of legislation they worked on or keys to various cities, some of which don't even exist anymore, mixed with heartrending family images. In a few cases, there are two or three tanks crowded in a room, families or spouses who passed within the limited window that *Elysian Fields* was operating and accepting new "members" or whatever.

But mostly, it's individuals. Alone, forever.

Like little Viviane, who I find in one of the first rooms on SB-3. My memory was wrong—her hair bow is red, not purple. She is as still and frozen as I remember, though. Like one of those old-fashioned graveyard cherubim carved from a warm shade of marble.

Every tank down here, part of the "regular people" section, is full. There are no signs of any disturbances. No cracked tank glass. No tangled wires or tubes. No damp footprints leading to or from a tank.

I look under tanks, peek around display cases, yank back doors to peer in the narrow gap behind. Where could they have gone?

If they were here at all. That's what you're forgetting, Halley.

My heart descends into my stomach. It's certainly not that I wanted to find someone in such dire straits. But the alternative is even less appealing.

To be certain I'm not missing anything, I take the emergency stairwell down to SB-4, steeling myself against the dimness and loud echoing thunder of my footsteps. But there's nothing. Some dust in the corners, a few alarming spots of rust around heavy bolts that look important. No curled-up former corpse.

By the time I finish my rounds one thing is very clear: every-thing is as it should be, on SB-3 and everywhere else.

Apart from me, apparently.

Embarrassment scalds my cheeks. Karl was correct. I must have . . . imagined it. What other explanation could there be?

But just thinking a variation of those words—*I imagined it, you must have imagined it, you're letting your imagination get the best of you*—triggers my fight-or-flight response, heavy on the fight side.

My hands ball into fists automatically and the urge to shout—at no one, mind you—is a hardened ledge in my lungs, a jumping-off point for an argument that I won't win but can't stop fighting. I do *not* imagine things.

That's what people say when they don't believe you and they don't want to bother with fucking listening.

I have a . . . slight hang-up about being believed.

Taking a deep breath, I exhale slowly and then head back toward the elevator.

No matter what Karl says about the probability of a resident waking up, it's always a possibility. Because even seemingly impossible ideas, ones barely worth considering, can be true. This year has taught me that, if nothing else.

But I don't think anyone could escape their tank and crawl on the floor without leaving behind evidence of it. That's the key.

Once I'm in the elevator and it's under way, I close my dry eyes, allowing my weary body to sway with the pull of upward motion. I feel shaky and disconnected, as if I'm hovering over myself instead of operating from within.

That's what happens, I guess, when your perception of the world, including your perception of yourself, is flipped upside down and turned inside out without warning. It takes some time—*more* time—to adjust.

Why should this be any different?

I open my eyes and straighten my shoulders as the door opens on the main exhibition level. I need to get my shit together and make this work because . . .

Well, because, this is all I have.

6

It turns out, three hours go by quickly when that's all you ever have. After the first couple of days, time begins to blur and I start to lose track, between button presses and endless rounds. I was exhausted when I arrived, and somehow I'm even more tired now. I can sleep all I want between rounds, but it's never enough. Something about the repeated interruptions for rounds or the knowledge that I have to get up in a few hours *again* makes it impossible to get any true rest. My eyes burn with perpetual dryness and weariness.

I develop an intense hatred for the sound of my holocomm alarm.

The lights continue to flicker and go out at times, but I learn to wait a second or two and Karl will get them back up. If I happen to be in the SecOffice at the time, I keep my gaze away from the screens. In our daily check-ins, Karl never mentions what happened on my first day—a rare moment of generosity, or perhaps he's waiting for the right time to strike. But we both know. And in my eagerness to avoid another embarrassing incident, I don't give my mind the opportunity to create what I know can't be there. Simple solution.

On day four or five, I realize I've already developed a routine:

Get up, press the button.

Do rounds at a quick jog. Hope that counts as exercise.

Eat something—avoid the sweet and sour chicken dried meal-pak, even though that means I will, at some point, have nothing left but the sweet and sour chicken, which will make for several miserable days.

Download the latest news headlines as text packets on my holo-comm and skim them for updates on the hearing.

Rounds again. Press the button.

Chores that I've assigned myself, including laundry on a regular basis and cleaning one of the shower stalls so I don't feel more disgusting stepping out than I did going in.

Rounds. Press the button.

Watch vids in the SecOffice on one of the screens that someone has set up with access to all the old films, footage, and news coverage of every occupant on the *Elysian Fields*. Likely part of the "lega-cies" donated to the ship itself, I'm guessing. Karl never mentioned it, so he might not know about it, as I only found it with an acci-dental button press. Occasionally, check in on a very erratic feed of SNN, when we're close enough to access it.

Rounds. Press the button.

Sleep.

Rounds. Press the button.

Back to sleep.

Rounds. Press the fucking button.

Over and over again.

Soon, my longed-for safety devolves into something more akin to stir-craziness. I don't have enough to occupy my time, and yet somehow I still have too much to do.

"I'm beginning to see why Karl wanted to hire someone. It's not onerous; it's the sheer relentlessness of it," I say, through a mouthful of Mix-travaganza, stretched out in the ostentatious leather desk chair that's part of former governor John Franks's display in his room.

Franks is a resident of SB-5 and winner of the most egregious eyebrows, if such a contest existed. They're bristly white hedgerows, dividing the smooth backyard of his forehead from the rest of his face, and several inches long, at least.

"You never get a break or a chance to fully relax because it feels like you're just waiting for it to be time again, you know? But also, nothing else is going on. It's like being perpetually caught between boredom and anxiety," I say, rocking myself in his chair, my feet propped on an old-fashioned filing cabinet in some kind of shiny wood. The chair creaks agreeably beneath my weight. He might have been a misogynist jerk, but he had good taste in office furniture. His desk, in the opposite corner, is overly large as well and draped in patriotic paraphernalia. Framed signatures, miniature flags of state, county, and country, a faux version of a bill in actual paper with a pen lying next to it, as if he was in the middle of taking care of important business when he decided to take a cryo-nap.

The former governor is, of course, silent. Behind the lightly frosted glass of his tank, his face is permanently furrowed, deep lines by his thin mouth, a wattle of thin skin beneath his chin that is now eternally skewed to one side. His long, thin arms, speckled with age spots and bruises, cross over his body, out of view beneath the privacy shield. But I imagine his wrinkly hands clutching his equally wrinkly junk in a protective posture.

More than a century ago, he was in charge of one of the

square states in the middle of what used to be America, and according to his display, he's most famous for his opposition to the ratification of ERAII, the updated and revised Equal Rights Amendment. Because of the "protections" it would remove from women, "our most vulnerable citizens, mothers and wives who we are meant to safeguard." In other words, protect us from being treated equally under the law, being paid the same as everyone else, and making decisions about our bodies without his say-so.

I've decided that his version of hell would likely be someone like me—single, career-driven (once), and as much in charge of my own bodily autonomy as anyone with a penis—talking to him for weeks on end without him being able to respond, so I'm fine with making that a reality for him, even if he's not aware of it.

I think this is day nine for me on the *Elysian Fields*. Or maybe ten. That's nine thousand credits, maybe ten, to my name. Only 134,000 to go to earn passage off here. I need to start making hash marks somewhere to count off the days.

That thought immediately summons the image of the protection marks carved into the floor by my bed. I left the rug—which I'm now pretty sure the previous occupant swiped from one of the resident rooms, but I don't know whose—in place, to cover as many of the interlocking circles and X's as possible. But I still know they're there. The hank of hair I threw away, preferring to take the chance of theoretically cursing myself with bad luck than to hold on to it.

A shiver raises the hair at the back of my neck, followed immediately by a jaw-cracking yawn that threatens to split my face open. Completely representative of my experiences on the *Elysian Fields* so far.

Rubbing my eyes, I pull my feet off the filing cabinet and stand. *Time to go.* I need to push the button and then try to sleep.

"See you next time, Governor. We'll have a conversation about paid parental leave. You were already dead when we figured that one out, but I'm fairly sure that would have killed you anyway." I'm delirious enough that I laugh at my own pathetic attempt at a joke—and, well, no one else is going to.

I tuck my bag of Mix-travaganza under my arm, close Franks's door, and make my way back toward the stairwell for my second stop on SB-3 during rounds. That's become part of my pattern, too. A double check on SB-3, and then back up to either the SecOffice or my quarters.

I've never found anything unusual on SB-3. Or rather, anything *else,* after that first day. But it makes me feel better, more reassured to take another look, so I don't lie awake in staff quarters, four levels above, wondering.

It's already hard enough to sleep with the noises. I'm still trying to get used to those.

Some of them are, I assume, normal for a ship of this age. Random popping sounds, like rivets giving way. A series of clicking noises above my head that might sound like sharp fingernails tapping loudly against the floor above but is more likely some elderly apparatus attempting to reboot itself to functionality. Groans, loud and far too human-sounding at times, as the metal walls protest the temperature difference between the warmth inside versus the cold of space. Probably.

That's another reason why I've taken to chatting with the governor and others. To hear something else. To hear something I know is real and not my mind running away with me.

Like now, as I'm trudging up two flights of stairs, between the metal clanging of my footsteps, deep whooshes of air—even and regular—exude from the walls somewhere, echoing around me. Probably something to do with the life-support systems or the ventilation shafts. But another person, one prone to fantasy or dread, might think it sounds like some overly large creature inhaling and exhaling, just out of sight. A perception that is aided by the distant slithering and scraping noises, also within the wall.

Never mind that I know for a *fact* that Karl is working on

the ventilation system, and part of that requires him to actually enter the vents. I asked about that the other day and he confirmed it, but not without a weird look, of course.

Near the landing to SB-3, I have to resist the urge to hurry, the childish feeling that something is on my heels, reaching out for my ankles through the opening between the metal-grate steps.

Of course, it never does.

On the landing, I tug on the door handle, as always feeling a momentary flare of fear that the door will be stuck and I'll be trapped in the stairwell.

But it's not. I'm not.

I step in to find the SB-3 corridor empty and still, and after a quick, perfunctory glance around, I poke my head into my favorite room: Viviane's.

The room itself stands out from all the others I've seen, with their bland institutional beige. The walls in here have been painted a light shade of pink. I don't know if that happened when she was first brought on board or if her walls were painted later, when the ship was turned into an attraction.

But either way, it has the effect of making the room seem warmer, more personal. That, plus the huge portrait of her as a toddler on the left wall, eyes sparkling with mischief as she holds a chubby fistful of birthday cake toward the camera. Then there are the display cases along the walls. In one, a menagerie of stuffed animals lingers, like their live counterparts used to in zoos, their mouths open midsound, their batteries long dead, and their programmed brains obsolete. In another is a three-foot-tall Walk-and-Talk Barbie with her elegant plastic leg lifted, her mechanical knee joint visible in sections, as if she might charge forward from behind the glass, her tangled dark hair still in messy braids with a dozen or more brightly colored barrettes clipped unevenly within. A charging cord still dangles from her back, as if she had been removed from her owner's room and immediately transported here. Which, for all I know, is true.

Viviane's own drawings are interspersed throughout the room, behind protective frames. Most of them are smiling stick figures with overly large heads and joined hands. Her initials, V. P., are bold along the bottom edge of the drawings, in now fading red wax, as confident as any burgeoning artist.

But there are a few of what I assume was her home. A sun holds court in the upper right of the page, above a square box of a house with a triangle roof, and, ironically, a blue circle representing a pool off to the side. Less than two hundred years ago, but such a different world, one in which clean water was abundant enough to be used for recreation and to pose a significant hazard.

Viviane drowned in that pool. Her body was kept alive for months on whatever life support systems were available at the time, but without any hope of her ever waking up. Funding her spot on this ship was her family's best and last chance for her to live again, however slim that chance might be. But brain death is still impossible to overcome, even now. Of course, even if we'd reached that point, the cryo-tech used has made reviving her an impossibility. Winfeld's Lie. That's what that display on the main exhibition level should really be called.

"Just saying hello again," I say softly as I approach Viviane's tank, like I might startle her. It's a hard impulse to break. She still looks so alive; I can easily imagine her opening her eyes and sitting up. Her long eyelashes curve over her plump cheeks. Her chubby hands are folded high on her chest, above the privacy shield, and her little fingernails bear the remains of a pale pink nail varnish. The red bow, resting over her dark bangs, is slightly off-center. A little kid caught in a moment of living her life. Only, instead, it's her perpetual funeral.

The white rocking chair I pulled from the side of the room is still in front of her tank. As if there's anyone to move it back into place.

I sink into it heavily, stashing the snack mix at my feet.

It's probably good that Viviane won't ever wake up again. I

can't imagine what it would be like to open your eyes and find yourself this alone.

Or maybe I can.

Oh, come on. Being a little melodramatic, aren't we? Comparing yourself to a poor little dead girl? At least your situation is temporary.

I grimace.

Another reason I need to get out of here. I'm not really the melancholic type, but limitless amounts of my own company, undiluted by anyone or anything else, seem to have that effect.

My holocomm buzzes with another batch of text updates, finally finishing their download.

I ignore it. It's more of the same. Hearing delays. Missing witnesses. Lawyers bickering. But slow, implacable progress toward an end.

I should be pleased by that.

Once the hearing is over, the committee will probably vote to officially censure the prime minister, but they won't go for criminal charges and they certainly won't overturn the election. Too risky.

Because of you.

I ignore that interjection.

I'll still be a figure of interest at that point, but less so. I have contacts on Lida Station, and given their intense disinterest in involving themselves in anything related to the UNOC, I can't imagine they'll make a fuss about my temporary residency. Once I've saved enough to get there, that is.

After I've been there for a few months, Niina will realize I'm not a threat to the PM. And when that happens, my value to my parents as the ace up their sleeve will vanish. Then, when other news takes over the forefront, I'll be able to work my way back toward the inner colonies. Find a job again.

And then it'll be back to normal, like nothing ever happened. Sort of.

I'll never be an assistant to the prime minister's chief of staff again. Never work at such a high level again. Or in UNOC politics. Everything I've pushed for, the change I wanted to see, all of it gone.

Yes, that's definitely the worst part. Not the people who were cheated, lied to, deceived. The people who died *in the riots.*

I wince.

Even though others were helped at the same time, how do you weigh one against the other? What is the ethical and moral math on that? I still haven't been able to work that out, but I suspect that's why there are rules in place, to keep the playing field level, if not entirely fair.

Rules that I helped break. Or, rather, helped someone else break. But it all amounts to the same thing.

My holocomm buzzes again, and in irritation I tug it out of my pocket and shove it under my chair, out of the way, away from me.

I stretch my legs out in front of me, staring unseeing toward Viviane's tank.

I made the best choice I could at the time, the only logical option left to me, based on what I learned and when I learned it. Sometimes the lesser of two evils is the only "good" choice you have, especially when there's little point in fighting against a no-win situation.

But it gets trickier when the two evils in question are not about degrees, lesser or otherwise, and are simply different flavors of the same foulness.

Beneath my unfocused gaze, Viviane's small shoulders seem to move, rising and falling, almost like she's breathing.

I freeze in place, my gaze snapping into focus on her little body. The movement immediately and utterly ceases, her chest as still as if it was never happening.

Because it wasn't.

I relax. I've seen this before. With Viviane and even a couple of the others. Fingers twitching. Eyes moving beneath lids. Mouths curving downward or upward slightly, just out of sight.

The residents all look so lifelike; it's as if my brain can't handle their unnatural stillness, so it creates the illusion of movement.

It's peaceful, though, in a strange way. They're all immortal here, sort of—memorialized and unchanged even as events unfold around them. A crowd of silent observers to history, with absolutely no concerns about how it will all turn out.

I rest my head against the back of the rocking chair, closing my gritty, sleep-deprived eyes for a second.

In that moment, I'm back in my office at Bierhals's campaign headquarters, trying desperately to figure out where I went wrong on an expenditure packet. The numbers refuse to cooperate, changing every time I look at them. In the distance, someone's holocomm is chiming endlessly, but they're not picking up. It's incredibly annoying.

Sweat drips down my spine. I have to get this form right. Everything is counting on this one—

Why is no one answering that stupid holocomm?

When I look up, the office is empty. My desk is gone. The walls have vanished, and I'm staring out into an empty expanse, the blue carpet unfurling out into dark nothingness.

Fear gnaws a hole at my center. *Something* is down there. In that darkness.

In spite of my resistance, I'm drawn forward, toward the emptiness. Cryotanks suddenly appear on either side of me, moving toward me like they're stationed on an automatic walkway.

Only these tanks don't seem to be housing celebrities, politicians, or CEOs; inside, I see the familiar boots and ragged overalls covered in brine. Briners.

I edge closer to one, and a little face pops up at me. I jump back, hand against my chest. It's the little boy. The one at the paddle cake vendor on EnExx17. His face is turning blue, and his hand scratches weakly at the tank lid.

Oh, God. He's alive in there.

"Hold on, hold on! I'm going to get you out!" I fumble at the front of the tank, looking for the controls. But it's all smooth, with none of the buttons and monitors I'm used to seeing. Damn it.

Screw it, I'll tip the whole thing over. Crack the lid that way. *He's running out of air, hurry, hurry.*

I grip the edges of the tank, but it's much heavier than I expect, impossible to shift even a little. I step back in frustration. This isn't right. Nothing about this is right. It doesn't make sense.

Movement in the darkness off to my right catches my attention.

When I turn to look, *it* skitters toward me out of the black, moving faster than it should be able to on all fours. The naked person I saw before on the cameras, skinny legs bent in rock-climbing position, spindly arms. But it's all wrong. The way it moves is *wrong*. No person moves like that.

Pausing, it rocks itself back and forth, as if waiting for me to make a move.

But I'm frozen, gaze locked on its face. The eyes are gone, leaving indents in the papery skin where they should be, and the nose is a slit. But the mouth is a gaping maw with silvery flashing teeth.

It cocks its head at me, nostril slits flaring, and then it launches itself at me, teeth snapping above my leg—

I jolt awake, scrambling out of the chair and to my feet, panting. The tank in front of me sends an immediate bolt of dread through me, until I realize it's not the little boy within. It's Viviane.

I'm still on *Elysian Fields,* specifically SB-3. I fell asleep on rounds, that's all.

Just a dream. Jesu. Just a dream.

I draw in a deep breath and let it out slowly. My hair is sticking to the back of my neck in a film of cold sweat. Maybe not sleeping is a good thing, if that is the kind of nightmare I'm going to have.

As I stand in the center of Viviane's room, my pulse slows and the rush of blood past my ears quiets enough for me to hear a faint chirping.

It's the holocomm ringing, from my dream.

Except . . . it's here. It's real.

Realization dawns in a horrible instant. It's the alarm on my holocomm, tucked underneath the rocking chair. Not in my pocket, where I would feel its insistent buzzing. And it's reached the muted stage, where the holocomm reduces volume and frequency of the alarm to conserve its charge. Which means it's been ringing for at least ten minutes. Maybe longer.

I suck in a sharp breath. I missed the button. I missed pushing the button!

I bolt for the hallway, running for the stairs as fast as I can. The stairs are quicker than waiting for the elevator. It doesn't seem to matter whether I do rounds first or push the button first, as long as the button press happens every three hours.

Which is not happening this time. *Fuck, fuck, fuck.*

The stairwell doorway is in sight when I hear the faint *pop-crackle* of a vid screen coming to life in the corridor behind me. "What are you still doing down here?" Karl asks.

I stop short, breathing hard and trying to hide it. He doesn't *sound* angry, but that doesn't always mean anything with Karl.

"I was . . ." I hesitate. Better to confess my sin and throw myself on his mercy or keep my mouth shut? I don't know. Commitment one way or another means the possibility of making the wrong choice. Panic flutters in me.

"I don't get why you talk to them," Karl continues in a normal voice, as if this is a normal conversation. "The residents."

Slowly, I turn to face the vid screen, hands sweaty. I don't understand. Is he waiting to attack, to shame me for missing the button? Trying to lure me into believing I got away with it, before he fires me?

Or . . . does he not know yet?

As always, Karl's attention is fixed on something else, so

only part of his face shows on the screen. Metal squeals against metal and he grunts with effort, twisting or screwing a part into place. "They're just meat."

Maybe it's because of proximity of that dream pulsing through me already, but my anger snaps to life.

They're people! Or they were. That's the argument he's waiting for me to make so he can smirk at my relentless naiveté or compassion or whatever it is about me that irritates him so much.

"Aren't we all?" I ask instead, jaw tight, daring him to correct me.

He stops what he's doing and looks at me directly, cocking his head to the side as if seeing me for the first time. "Fair enough," he says after a moment, with something that sounds like grudging admiration.

What is happening here?

"So, listen, we're coming up on New Kazan, and we're expecting visitors momentarily," Karl says.

"Board members?" I ask, dread coiling in my stomach. "I thought you said they hardly ever came out here."

Unless you fuck up and miss a check-in.

Am I *that* late? How would they have gotten here so quickly? Surely they would have tried to reach Karl first before making the trip out here. Unless one of them happened to be on New Kazan already. But even still, that's fast.

"Someone put a bug in their ear," Karl says with disgust. "So, they're going to want to poke around, be officious, and rub their authority in my face . . . the usual. I need you upstairs and out of sight. No noise, nothing." He points at me. "You don't exist, remember? And we don't want to give them any reason to stick around and question things."

"Right. Yes." I nod.

"Now?" he asks pointedly, eyebrows raised. "They're already on their way."

"Okay." My heart throbs frantically in my chest as I turn away from the screen and back toward the stairs.

I climb up toward the main exhibition level as fast as I can, trying to ignore the clatter and clang of my steps on the metal stairs. They're not here yet. I don't have worry about the noise until they are.

If I push the button before their arrival, what are the odds that the delay could be written off as an equipment malfunction? I mean, Karl surely wouldn't admit to being late in front of them.

The thought stops me in my tracks momentarily. That would be . . . dishonest. Manipulative. Both things I'm trying to avoid at the moment.

But it's not as if Karl is being honest about my presence here to begin with.

Sometimes you don't have the luxury of doing things the right way. I grimace. That sounds like something Niina would say.

Fuck it. I'll push the button and then see what happens.

I step out onto the main exhibition level and immediately pivot toward the right, hustling toward the far end, where the SecOffice is located.

But then motion catches my eye.

I spin back around, searching for the source.

The Inspiration scene I just passed is still dark, motionless. The door to the pop star's room and the others nearby are closed, as I left them earlier.

Then I see it again, in the distance. Motion in the form of shadow and light shifting and dancing on the wall opposite the auditorium doors.

It's on. The quick pulse of dread and anticipation is automatic, ingrained after so many years of thinking about *that* moment, from the first time I visited *Elysian Fields*.

Oh, come on. Not today. I shake my head. *Not now.*

As far as I know, everything inside the auditorium should be shut down. And besides, the "show" is triggered to start—or continue—by sensors inside that detect the heat of human presence. That's what I learned after digging around for information the last time.

So one or more of the sensors has probably deteriorated. Since there's no one on this level but me.

I hesitate. I should let Karl handle this. This is his problem, after all. And, obviously, I know nothing about repairing sensors of any kind.

And I need to push that fucking button.

But . . . the button is already late. And that won't be the worst of it if these visiting board members see an obvious malfunction and decide to look around more thoroughly. Karl firing me is one thing. I would still have my freedom and a little money. A board member finding me here and calling in the IEA is a whole other. I can't take that risk.

Gritting my teeth, I turn on my heels and hurry toward the supposed-to-be-darkened space.

7

The show aspect of *Elysian Fields* started back when the ship was still a private (and mostly eccentric) venture. Right before Zale Winfeld vanished for good and his family died as part of that tragic shuttle crash.

It was, I think, meant to serve as a welcome to new members of *Elysian Fields*, those who signed up and paid a lot of money to be "saved" by cryo at the time of their deaths. By the time I saw the presentation, though, it was more of a historical document. A moment in time, preserved.

The AI holograms of the Winfeld family—the three adult children, at least, Ianthe, Bryck, and Aleyk—were truly beyond state of the art, not only for the time period, but even now. One of the highlights of a visit was being able to talk with them, ask them (carefully moderated questions) about their lives and the time when they lived. They responded in real time, with thoughtful, funny, or brusque answers, depending on who you were speaking to. They talked over each other, even seemed to get annoyed when, say, Bryck interrupted his older sister to insist she was wrong.

It truly felt like you might be able to step backstage afterward and find them chatting among themselves, wiping their brows with fresh towels, or sipping tiny glass bottles of expensive water post-performance. The novelty of it was what helped keep visitors—and historians and tech wizards—coming back to the ship. At least for a while.

But as soon as I get within a few feet of the closed doors, the shifting shadows and light from within stop, the theater growing dimmer.

Not dark, though. It's almost like . . . someone's waiting.

Blood rushes through my ears, drowning out everything else.

Half expecting the doors to be locked, I reach for the closest handle, with its sculpted metal grape leaves and vines twined around the base. But the door opens silently at my tug, and I step across the threshold.

A thick, creamy silence envelops me, my footsteps muted on the still plush carpet inside. In here, it's all very much gilded walls and more frescoes, mixed with the smooth tech-black on the faux stage up front, an uneasy combination of old and new that doesn't quite work.

Speaking of the stage, which is more of a ledge than a full-fledged performance area . . . There's a spotlight on, shining down on . . . nothing.

The knots in my stomach tighten. But I ignore them and head toward the stage, hoping for a control panel or some well-marked Off button. Wine-colored velvet ropes held by brass stands block the audience off from the stage, and in the event that this is not warning enough, faded yellow-and-black-striped caution tape lines the edge of the stage. Theoretically, both are to protect the hologram projectors. I still have my doubts, which is probably most of my problem.

When I'm about halfway down, Ianthe appears on stage. Startled by the suddenness of her arrival, I stumble, my foot catching against the runner edge. Normally, the holograms "walk" from around the edge of the curtains draped on the side, for a more realistic effect. But instead she's suddenly there, not quite in the center of the spotlight. Off to the right slightly. She looks just as I remember: a statuesque blonde in a white sheath dress with a high collar and capelet around her shoulders. Her hair, with darker streaks at the part and the ends, as was the fashion at the time, is piled high on her head, with pearl bobs hanging at her ears. She's represented at thirty-seven years old, roughly the time of her death.

Her gaze drifts over me, unseeing.

"Ianthe." My voice comes out in a whisper, which sets goose bumps off along my skin.

She doesn't respond.

Their names are meant to act as triggers, a signal to whatever programming that they're being addressed. So I clear my throat and try again. "Ianthe," I say, moving forward, toward the stage again.

This time, her attention dips briefly to me.

I hesitate, not sure what to say. "You need to stop. Uh, end program. Turn off."

She looks down her long, elegant nose at me with utter disdain as I reach the edge of the stage, but she says nothing. Which is odd. We must be outside the formal show program, because she normally does most of the talking, including the intro to *Elysian Fields*.

I keep moving toward the stage.

Up close, the illusion of her solidity and reality is ruined; her form flickers slightly and her feet, shod in matching white boots, float slightly above the surface of the stage, not actually making contact. In someone else, it might raise the childish temptation to slice a hand through her holographic legs, but I fucking know better.

From the audience side of the velvet ropes, I look up and down the front of the stage, searching for buttons or controls. Nothing. I even reach out, making sure to stay on the safe side of the caution line, to press on the wooden lip of the ledge, as if a panel might appear. But no.

How the hell do you turn this thing off?

"Ianthe," I say, forcing the tremor out of my voice. I used

to work for the fucking prime minister. I organized crowds of journos, called security on protesters, even helped escort one of them out the door. *Real* people. Not this bullshit. "I need you to—"

Her attention shifts over her right shoulder, and the fine hairs on the back of my neck rise in response, sensing a presence before the rest of me.

"Hello," he says. The voice is gentle, smooth, with the faint lilt of musicality. And familiar enough to send recognition like lightning through my veins, stealing my breath. "Rather, I suppose, hello *again*."

I step back automatically even as my gaze shifts, following Ianthe's.

He's here.

Aleyk Winfeld, Zale Winfeld's youngest son, is standing behind and to the right of Ianthe.

A tremor runs through me, my hands shaking at my sides. Immediately, I'm twelve again, caught between the excruciating embarrassment of being noticed and such fear that cold sweat is already forming under my arms.

The rush of anger, though, that's new.

Holographic Aleyk looks the same. Forever trapped in his early twenties. Handsome, of course, a masculine version of his mother, the singer and artist. He has her blue eyes.

Unaged, unruffled. Completely nonglitchy, if such a term exists.

His loose white shirt is wrinkled at the elbows and rolled up at the wrists. It has too many pockets of varying sizes to be practical, but that—and the mandarin collar with wide neck—must have been a style at the time. His hands are stuffed into his pockets, dark trousers a shade between khaki and brown, tucked into loosely laced boots. It might seem like disrespect, given how his siblings are arrayed in expensive finery. But it's practical. At the time the holos were made, he was working with an aid organization helping refugees from what used to be Southern California relocate in the middle of an extreme heat wave that was killing thousands.

His dark hair curls at the ends, turning blond where it has been exposed to the merciless sun. Dirt streaks up one arm and across his back, which can be seen when he turns. A rumpled blue bandanna, white with salt from sweat, dangles around his neck.

Supposedly, he had wanted to help. Not just by sending money but by being a pair of hands and feet on the ground, where needed. I read that in an archived press release from his father's company, back when I was trying to figure out what had happened. Whether I was losing my mind.

Aleyk grins down at me now, with that dimple showing forth on one side. "Thank you for your continuing interest. If you wish to find a seat, the presentation will begin momentarily."

Exactly what he said the last time.

At first.

I wait, watching him, waiting for the slightest twitch, a hint, a betrayal of his true motives.

But he continues beaming at me, showing no sign of fatigue (of course not; he's not alive) or impatience.

And the longer it goes on, the longer he remains in harmless mode, silent and "normal," the more my doubt—in that black hole in my gut where I had stuffed the whispers of uncertainty, every one of my misgivings, over the years—grows, consuming from the inside out.

I feel like I can't breathe. If it was a glitch or even the AI system hallucinating—the old ones sometimes do—why isn't it doing it now?

Aleyk's smile slides off his face and I catch my breath.

Here we go, finally. I can't figure out if I'm relieved or more pissed.

"Thank you for your continuing interest," he says again. "If you wish to find a seat, the presentation will begin momentarily." His smile, utterly innocuous and once, perhaps, charming, returns.

"Really?" I demand, anger boiling off all the fear. "That's all you have to say to me?" I throw my hands out. "I was a kid and fucking terrified! Had nightmares for weeks. And I couldn't tell anyone what you said."

Dead, dead, dead. We're all dead. You'll be next. He walks here still. I shiver at the memory. I can still feel Aleyk's grip on my wrist, an agreed-upon impossibility that still somehow managed to occur.

My parents would have thought I was lying. A twelve-year-old kid making up impossible stories for attention. Because fabricating facts to achieve a certain end was second nature to them, as easy as breathing. Their careers depended on it. Plus, rogue AI was one of their favorite "angles." That sort of malfunction—AI acting independently—was rare, but the cautionary tales circulated frequently enough that it was a convenient excuse for all-too-human misdeeds. Like when diary excerpts accusing their client, a prominent colony governor, of abuse appeared everywhere. Obviously, it was AMI, the artificial intelligence program in the daughter's journo-friend, creating events that never happened. At least that was the story they spun. I don't know how many people bought it, but it worked well enough to keep most of the heat off the governor until the next election.

My parents never would have believed me if I'd told them what happened with the Aleyk AI holo. Never.

I probably should thank him. It. Whatever. It was a formative experience, one that brought a new, sharp-bladed reality to what my parents had been saying for years: *the truth doesn't matter, only what people will believe.*

"Hello. Rather, I suppose, hello *again*." Aleyk smiles. "Thank you for your continuing—"

"Oh, shut up, Svalbard 6.2."

His gaze narrows, seeming to *see* me for the first time. It's an illusion. Probably. And the dimple in his cheek flickers, wavering in and out of existence.

Triumph lights up my insides, victory presumptive. "Yeah, I know that's you. Not Aleyk Winfeld. Not Ianthe or Bryck. They've all been dead and dust for a couple centuries."

At one point, I studied Aleyk, this ship, everything I could get my hands on. Treated it all like a subject I needed to pass in order to graduate from . . . something. Absorbed every detail I could, from my memory, from the information I could find in various postings, historical records. Trying to make it all make sense.

Svalbard 6.2 is the mysterious AI program behind the Winfeld siblings' appearance and personalities in this sales pitch. The one that so intrigued outside programmers at the time; the one they were never allowed to take apart and analyze.

"You're just malfunctioning tech. That apparently likes to torture children," I say, pushing a little harder.

His smile drops abruptly.

"Something to say? More 'secrets' to share today?" I press. "Why me? How about that, huh?"

A distant, ominous rumbling starts beneath my feet. Automatically, I look down, half expecting to see the carpeted floor tearing itself apart under my worn boots.

But when the sound continues, smooth, mechanical, and even in intensity, I realize what it likely is: Karl is extending the bridge.

Shit. Our visitors are here. And I'm out of time.

"You hear that?" I point down. "That's board members arriving for a surprise inspection. Keep this shit up and maybe they'll shut you down for good. And you can enjoy talking to yourself forever."

He moves closer to the edge of the stage. I step back automatically. For a moment, a split second, it feels as though he's going to respond. And my pulse jumps in anticipation.

But then the edges of his form flicker to nothingness. "Th-

th-the only secret is how *Elysian Fields* will tr-tr-transform the future for a s-s-s-s-s-select few who . . . who . . . who . . ." His face contorts in a grimace before his mouth drops wide in a silent, gaping scream.

As I watch, his features melt away—nose, mouth, and eyes vanish, leaving behind only the suggestion of something human as movement writhes beneath drooping skin, like fingers trying to poke out through his cheeks, along his forehead.

Jesu. I think I broke him. It. Svalbard.

Then the flesh splits, right where his mouth had been, and a hand emerges, followed by an arm, draped in the same white fabric as his other . . . two arms.

Nausea rises in the back of my throat, and I clap a hand over my own mouth, as if the same might happen to me and I can prevent it with the pressure of my palm.

He raises his hands, fingers pulling at his face and that extra arm, stumbling back from the edge of the stage.

Chills rise along my skin. It's not real. Just Svalbard throwing a tantrum. But the horror of it looks real enough.

"Stop, Svalbard! End presentation!" A command that's only slightly undercut by the stressed fracture in my voice.

For a moment, nothing happens. The Aleyk hologram continues staggering around the stage, even as the arm emerging from his mouth flails, as if trying to pull itself free. I can see the glimpse of a shoulder now. The white shirtsleeve is damp and streaked with pink and red foam as if this new limb is tearing him apart from the inside to escape.

I grimace and turn away. "Stop!"

Then, a moment later, the room darkens slightly.

I look over my shoulder cautiously . . . to find the stage empty. No Aleyk. No Ianthe looming in the distance.

No one.

Relief washes over me.

The flickering light show has stopped as well. There's nothing to attract the visiting board members' attention now.

In fact, the stage is quiet and still, the theater's thick silence coating everything like the untouched dust in the other staff rooms upstairs.

As if nothing had happened. As if it was all in my head, like when I saw the residents "breathing" in their tanks or someone crawling on the corridor floor—

"It was real. I saw it," I say defiantly, loudly. Too loudly.

The responding silence makes me shiver.

Below me, the bridge machinery grinds to a halt with a muffled groan, having reached its full extension.

Move, Halley!

My heart trips in my chest as I pivot away from the stage and charge up the slightly slanted floor toward the doors at the top.

Hurry, hurry, hurry. The chant in my head is urgent and relentless, even as I reach the doors.

But not quite loud enough to drown out the other voice that follows.

"Be careful, Katerina." Aleyk's voice. Soft, but clear through the darkness behind me.

Goose bumps launch themselves into existence on every inch of my skin. I pause for a second, my hand on the cool metal panel of the door. Is that a warning or a threat? I can't tell.

A distant high-pitched whine shimmies through the corridor outside—the cargo bay doors opening below.

Fuck. I don't have time to ponder it now.

I shove through the theater door, and I'm five steps down the corridor before it clicks.

He called me Katerina.

8

I freeze as the theater door swings shut behind me.

Be careful, Katerina.

The swirling sensation in my head feels like falling, even though I haven't moved.

How is that even possible? Malfunctioning or not, AI doesn't have memory like that, especially AI as old as Svalbard. It doesn't *remember* people or faces; it obeys commands, triggers. And I no longer have anything on or in me that identifies me as Katerina Weiller. I made sure of that.

Karl. It could be Karl. Some kind of prank, like when I first boarded and he made me think I was hearing someone gasping for air from Chessley Max's room. He suspects my name is fake, clearly, but he's never said anything about who I am. And I have a hard time imagining him holding back on that information when instead he could gleefully dangle it over my head, like a sharpened guillotine blade hanging by a bit of unraveling rope.

I half turn back toward the theater, hand reaching for the handle, to find out. But a dull thud echoes through the ship, indicating we're locked and latched, open for business. If I stick around too long in the theater and the board members come up to this level first, to check out the SecOffice . . .

You might run into them in the hall. Go! Now.

Following the rounded corridor, I bolt past Winfeld's Inspiration and the former food court. As I pass the dry fountain, still filled with a few dusty plastic tokens that visitors could buy at the gift store and toss in for a "wish," based on an old Earth tradition, I automatically check to make sure I've left no sign of my presence. I've taken to sitting out here, underneath the skylights emitting faux sunlight, where there's better signal—when there's any at all—to download the news packets to my holocomm at the start of my rounds.

I reach for my pocket, to pat it for the reassuring bulk of my holocomm. But my pocket is flat and empty.

Panic brings me to a stuttering halt, along with a horrifying realization.

I left my very modern, very out-of-place holocomm in Viviane's room. With my stupid snack mix. Under the chair that's sitting in the middle of her room, right next to her tank, not along the wall where it's supposed to be. In a room we're not supposed to be spending time in, except to check for leaks or whatever.

I squeeze my eyes shut.

I have no idea how detailed this board inspection is going to be, but if they even peek into Viviane's room, they're going to see it. Or possibly hear it, if the holocomm alarm is still going.

Fuck. It seems I am determined to fail today, in every way possible. Sleep deprivation is destroying my brain.

Okay, first things first. Get out of sight.

I open my eyes and rush the rest of the way to the end of the corridor, trying to hurry while also working to land as lightly on my feet with each step as possible. No point in hiding if your pounding footsteps give you away beforehand.

At least this ship is full of weird noises, so maybe the sounds of my movement will blend in.

Shoulders tensed and heart pounding, I reach the threshold of the stairs to the staff quarters, push through the door, and

ease it closed after me with a quiet *click*—all the while antici-
pating a shout of discovery at my back.

But the corridor remains as silent as ever. I made it.

Except . . . now I'm stuck. I suck in a breath in dismay. The
metal stairs are not quiet. And I have no idea where the board
members are. If they're taking the stairs instead of the elevator.
If they're still in the cargo bay or on their way up.

I press my ear against the door, trying to hear something,
anything. The clatter of footsteps, overlapping voices, yelling,
boisterous fake laughter. Or even the sound of the ancient lift
machinery kicking in.

Nothing.

Even the ship seems absurdly quiet for the moment. No clicking, tapping, rustling, or scraping. Of course. The one time I
need the creepy sounds.

After a moment, I edge the door open a fraction of an inch
to listen.

Still nothing.

I frown and pull the door open a little wider.

Where are they? If they were concerned about the button,
you'd think they would start up here.

I suppose it's possible they began their tour on SB-5, the
lowest residential floor that's not under extensive repair, and
they're working their way up.

But that means they're that much closer to catching my boo-
boo in Viviane's room on SB-3.

I hesitate for a second, then slip through the door, cutting a
direct path to the SecOffice. I need to know where they are. If
I have a chance of fixing my mistakes—all of them—without
getting caught, all the better.

Though my parents would be the first to point out that it's
usually not the crime that gets you. It's the cover-up.

On the control board, the indicator next to the babysitter
button glows a threatening amber. Holding my breath, I press

the button and watch with relief as the amber bleeds out to green in silence. No alert, no automated announcement about a system reset. Thank God.

Next, I scan the screens, looking for movement. On SB-5. In the cargo bay. On this level, if they're somehow stealth operatives *and* board members. Somewhere, anywhere.

But everything is still. And empty.

I wait and flip through all my available feeds and angles. Maybe they're around a corner or in a room I can't see.

But no.

Where did they go?

Scowling at the screens in front of me, I find the appropriate keys to run the camera feed back on the cargo bay. And sure enough, in reverse, a trio of figures dressed in dark suits—with formal cloaks, even—retreat from the far edge of the camera's range near the elevator and scurry backward on the screen.

Except . . .

I pause the feed, squinting to make sense of what I'm seeing. One of the members—the tallest of the three, and thin in an almost skeletal manner, like I can see the shadow of his skull through the skin at his temple—appears to be swaying on his feet, steadied by the two shorter figures escorting.

I run the feed forward again and they vanish out of sight near the elevator, but they don't reappear. Anywhere.

Maybe they took the stairs up to meet Karl on one of the floors he's working on. That makes sense if he's hoping to demonstrate need and rustle up more funds or to show off the repairs he's already done.

I frown. I thought it was too dangerous for anyone down there, except in an EV suit, which these people are definitely not in right now.

Not my problem, I suppose.

If they're touring the work in progress on the lower levels, SB-8 is the one directly above the cargo bay, then it'll probably take them a while to work their way up.

It's a risk, but one I think I can manage.

I creep back out into the corridor and into the stairwell again, moving down the steps as quietly as possible and keeping my ears perked to the sound of voices, machinery, anything.

As before, it is deadly quiet. So weird.

I make it to SB-3 and Viviane's room without issue. After grabbing my holocomm and my snack mix and stuffing both in my pockets, I wrestle the chair back into place along the wall.

With one final glance back to double-check that everything is as it should be—as best as I can remember, anyway—and that there are no major screaming signs of interference, I duck back into the corridor, close the door after myself, and hurry back to the stairs.

My return trip to the main exhibition level is much the same. No shouts of alarm or even snatches of conversation drifting through the air vent.

I hesitate in the stairwell, behind the closed door. The smart bet is to keep going up. Go up one more floor to my quarters, shut myself in, and wait until Karl gives me the all clear.

But . . . I chew on the inside of my lip. Something about this is odd. I can't shake the feeling that I've missed a connection, a detail of some kind, and that it matters.

Or it's boredom. I've never been very good at being still, ignoring my gut, and staying out of things. It's one of the qualities that made me excellent at my job. A little too excellent, unfortunately.

I dip back into the corridor and into the SecOffice.

I'll watch on the feed and listen for the elevator. Eventually, they'll come out somewhere, and when I see them, or when the elevator moves, I'm close enough to the stairs that I'll be able to duck out in plenty of time.

I shake my head as I settle into the cracked leather chair behind the console. I'm pretty sure that this is nothing, just a bunch of official people being officious. It seems like a coincidence that they showed up around the same time I missed pressing the button. Though maybe the distraction of their visit is why Karl hadn't noticed my mistake.

Either way, I think I'm as safe as I've ever been here. So I'm not even sure why I care, other than keeping myself out of it.

But I reset my holocomm alarm for the next button press and wait, nonetheless.

And wait. Forty-five minutes pass.

Then an hour. An hour and a half.

What the hell? What are they doing down there?

"Come on, come on," I whisper. My eyes burn from staring at the unchanging—save the occasional bursts of static and interference—screens. Probably Karl should think about adding "fix whatever is wrong with the security system" to his endless list.

Then, finally, movement.

My gaze snaps to the appropriate screen. The cargo bay again. Huh. As I watch, the visitors emerge from the shadowy region near the elevator.

I frown. That's weird. I never heard the elevator machinery kick in. Not going up or down. But what else is on the cargo bay level? Just the empty prep rooms. Why would they want to see those?

Also—I lean closer, squinting at the screen gone fuzzy again—why are there only two of them now? The tall, cadaverous-looking one isn't with them. Maybe he stayed behind to ream Karl out about something?

I keep my focus on the two figures. The women—that's clear now from this angle—hunch together under their cloaks, arms wrapped tightly around each other. But even with that additional support, they stumble and sway on their slow progress across the cargo bay toward the extendable bridge and their own ship.

Have they been drinking?

No. My stomach plummets toward my boots. Not drinking. I've seen behavior like this before and recently. The empty expression, the staggering clumsiness.

Fuck. Daze.

9

I *knew* it. I knew Karl was up to something. I even thought it might be drugs—along with some less likely schemes involving ransom and abduction. But I never dreamed he would be this brazen. Inviting people on board to, what, sample his wares directly?

That's way riskier—not to mention morally shittier—than simply off-loading some "mislabeled" crates at a station somewhere.

If he hasn't already caught the attention of UNOC authorities, I'm betting he will soon. Which puts *me* at risk. He should have told me before I came on board.

But, of course, it's become clear that honesty is *not* his policy. Not when he can get away with a shaded version of the truth, at best.

"Motherfucker," I mutter, jabbing at the lit-up floor button, as if that will make the ancient elevator move any faster.

As soon as I heard the bridge being retracted, which presumably meant any departing visitors had left the ship, I charged out of the SecOffice for the cargo bay. Karl and I were overdue for a chat. My tardiness in pushing the button hardly seemed like the biggest issue now.

In fact, I half expect Karl to be waiting when the door finally opens. Given the ungodly amount of noise the lift machinery makes, there's no way he wouldn't know I was coming.

But the cargo bay is empty. Of people, at least.

Pivoting, I turn my attention to the darkened junction to my left, the one leading to the prep rooms.

Except it's not as dark as it was before, the first time I saw it. Now light spills out from somewhere farther within the corridor. Not quite enough to illuminate the entire space comfortably. More like a forgotten night-light left on. Or a slash of brightness coming from underneath one of the closed prep room doors farther down.

I hesitate.

Good God, woman up. Let's go. It's just Daze. It's not like you haven't seen it before. Niina's voice is loud in my head.

"She" is right. And it's not only my EnExx17 experiences, either. One of our campaign stops was a UNOC-sponsored re-hab facility on one of the struggling Europa stations. The need for beds was so great that Daze addicts were lined up outside the door, waiting for a spot to open up. And using while they waited.

But . . . the tall guy hadn't left with the others. And while Daze users aren't typically violent, anyone threatening the availability of their next fix might find themselves in a bit of a tough spot, staring down a blank-faced zombie incapable of feeling pain. Plus, I'm still not a hundred percent certain that those visitors *weren't* board members. Just because they're using doesn't guarantee that. Maybe that's Karl's gig—selling to the high-and-mighty so they don't have to sully themselves by buying from the usual dealers.

Of course, if they are board members—and high as fuck—they're probably not going to risk ratting me out. Probably.

I move away from the elevators cautiously, rounding the corner to the corridor, and sure enough, one of the prep rooms about halfway down is lit up. A cool bluish-white light shines through the frosted glass panel.

"Karl!" I whisper-shout. "Karl!"

No response. Not even a flicker of shadowy movement

inside the room. But the irregular rustle-thumps—routine ship noises I've grown accustomed to—return suddenly overhead, at a louder intensity than before. And this time, they're accompanied by the clickety-clack of something sharp, followed by that hollow whoosh of air, almost like breathing.

That tells me Karl's likely not even down here anymore. He's working somewhere on something, making a racket.

Probably.

Fuck. Fuckity-fuck.

Sometimes you've got to take matters into your own hands.

Yes, yes, mental Niina. Great advice. Except you wouldn't like if I did that in every circumstance, would you?

Still, I creep toward the door, ready to dart backward at the first hint of movement inside or the lever doorknob lowering.

But nothing happens.

I pause outside the door, listening. It's quiet inside, except for the faint hum of something running, which is probably coming from below or behind the room rather than inside. Maybe Karl took his "customer" with him to let him sleep it off. Maybe that's what all the levels "under renovation" are about.

I grip the cold metal knob and push it down. There is no resistance, and it offers a quiet *click* as the tongue retracts. Unlocked. Absurdly cold air slips through the gap, nipping at my knuckles.

Pushing the door open slowly, the first thing I see is a pile of neatly folded fabric—a deep aubergine velvet—on a chair inside. This close, the carefully stitched glyphs and symbols in shiny gold thread on the edges are now visible. I frown. That's one of the cloaks the visitors were all wearing.

Except now that I can see the cloak in person, I recognize it as more than simple formal wear. This is a Benadrian ritual cloak. The Benadrians are a small but vocal environmentalist sect, worshippers of the Living Planet. Most of them reside under the dome on Mars. They're very firm—and loud—believers in no waste, following a very ascetic lifestyle. Everything returns to the planet. These hand-stitched cloaks are reserved for their most sacred of ceremonies—the joining of two households or the "departure" of one of their members. Weddings and funerals, basically.

Why would Benadrians be *here*? And why the fancy getup for an illicit visit to a closed museum? Addicts come from any and all backgrounds, but this combination is . . . odd.

Never mind that the precious cloak—along with the suit and a set of well-worn but highly polished black boots, tucked neatly beneath the chair—has now been discarded. So . . . there's a tall, skinny, naked guy running around on the ship? What is happening here?

I push the door open a little wider, holding my breath, waiting for a shout of confusion mixed with annoyance. I am not, after all, who the possibly naked Benadrian might be expecting to see.

But instead of hearing a cry of alarm, I see feet. Bare feet, with long skinny toes pointed upward, floating in midair and surrounded by a thin white mist.

No, not floating.

Contained within translucent walls . . . a tank. A *cryotank*, with the hinged lid open, locked in the Up position.

Oh shit.

I shove the door open the rest of the way.

The cryotank dominates the small space, in the center of the room. With my gaze, I follow the bare feet inside it to the thin legs, past the discreet privacy shield still folded off to the side, to the scrawny, bony chest, where tubes attach to a port over the heart with white medical tape. Next to the open tank, what looks like a revamped IV droid—patched together with spare parts, including the upturned neck of an old clothes hanger as a bag hook—hums busily to itself as it dispenses a viscous-looking clear gel through the tube. More of that white mist hovers over the body, thickening and thinning in waves, evaporating above the tank itself, turning the air frigid.

Maybe without the folded robe on the chair I would have thought it was simply routine maintenance on one of the current residents. Maybe there are such requirements to keep the residents in such good condition, all these years later. A refreshing of the protective fluids. How do I know?

But with the robe, and that tall, skinny body, this is *clearly* the Benadrian I saw walk onto the ship a couple of hours ago. All stretched out and, what, being prepped for a permanent stay? Through a process that was proven not to work, decades ago.

Confused, I edge closer to the occupant, half expecting his eyelids to flutter open. For this to be some kind of prank or, God help me, really bizarre role-playing game.

But his eyelids and frail eyelashes are coated in very real frost. And . . . now that I'm standing over him, looking down at his face through the shifting mist, I can see what I missed before on the camera feed.

First, that skinniness, where his bones seem to show through the translucence of his skin, is not natural or due to aging. He's been ill. Prominent purplish half circles under the eyes and his overall grayish tinge scream long-term illness. So do the faint but precise scars on his bony ribs, signs of previous medical intervention. Lungs, it seems.

Second, he's young. Very young. Based on the wispy mustache on his upper lip and the angry spray of acne across his forehead—how cruel that his complexion continues to rebel even while he's fighting a larger bodily battle—I'd guess maybe fifteen or sixteen. At that stage where he's reached adult height but hasn't filled out yet.

Hadn't.

I wince. But it's true, and it's not as if he's going to have a chance now.

In short, he's a child.

A very *sick* child.

Suddenly, the random pieces of information I've been trying

to put together rise up and rearrange themselves in a different order, presenting an entirely new picture.

Those women, the ones who left. What if they weren't high or drunk but struggling under the weight of grief, of losing their child?

Or, more accurately, of leaving him behind while still clinging to a shred of hope?

A wave of horrified realization washes over me and I stagger back a step, everything feeling off-balance and wrong, like the ship's gravity generator reversed its horizontal and vertical vectors without warning.

This has nothing to do with drugs, Daze or otherwise.

I turn and leave the prep room, gently closing the door behind me, and then storm out to the cargo bay. Fury buoys my speed. *He couldn't. He* wouldn't.

I center myself in front of the screen, the very vid screen from which Karl greeted me upon my arrival on board.

"Karl," I bellow, no longer fearing being overheard. At the same time, I mash every button, touch every display indicator I can find on the old tech. "Karl! Answer me, you fucking asshole!" To my surprise, my throat is tight with the threat of tears—rage tears—and I have to work past the lump to speak.

Don't cry unless you can use it.

I grit my teeth. *Shut up, Niina!*

"Karl!" I shout again.

The screen flickers for a moment, displaying rolling horizontal bars, then comes into focus with an image of the man himself. "What? What? I'm a little busy here," Karl says breathlessly, finally answering. He's pale and sweaty, as if he's run a great distance. Or he's been doing something he shouldn't have, something for which he likely has no skill set or experience. Something for which *no one alive* has the skill or experience.

"I bet." I fold my arms across my chest. "I just found your latest *project*."

He stills instantly and seems to notice for the first time that I'm not in the SecOffice. His face goes white, except for two splotches of bright color rising above his beard. "What are you doing in the cargo bay? You're supposed to be upstairs in your quarters!"

"Please tell me you are not offering false hope to desperate people by using tech that never worked in the first place," I say. "Please. Tell me that."

He glares at me. "This is none of your business. And if you were caught—"

"I stayed in the SecOffice, watching the feeds until they left. Two of them, anyway," I say. "And bullshit, those weren't inspecting board members. Not even close."

He raises his chin. "They are. Well, friends of board members. Friends of friends. Look, it doesn't matter. Don't you have rounds?"

"In forty-five minutes." Give or take. I didn't have my holocomm with me the last time I pressed the button, so the next alarm is set for my best guesstimate.

Karl frowns, as if he knows that doesn't sound quite right.

"And trust me when I tell you it most definitely matters," I continue, before he can say anything. "You lied, taking advantage of desperate people by—"

"I'm not lying!"

"Uh-huh. So the Winfeld Trust is all okay with this? They're totally fine with what you're doing?"

Karl says nothing.

I snort. "Of course not. But those people, the ones with the sick kid, looking for any kind of hope, their money's good, right? So what does it matter, as long as the board doesn't find out." I can see it so clearly now. The parents were probably already searching for miracle cures before Karl found them, on a message board or through a mutual contact or whatever. The Benadrians would never condone spending excessive resources to keep a child alive rather than letting him "become one with the Living Planet." Dying, in other words. Without resistance. It was meant to be a badge of honor rather than a fate to be feared. So, coming here, paying Karl to "save" their child, would have to stay a secret on their side as well. Perfect for Karl's purposes.

"You don't understand," he says quietly. "They don't have anywhere else to go when they come to me. No other hope."

My eyes nearly bulge out of my head. "Wait. You've done this before?" There aren't many childhood diseases/afflictions that can't be cured or at least treated to provide some quality of life. But the ones that remain are vicious, harsh, and terminally unfair.

Karl ignores my question. "If they've tried everything else, what harm does it cause to put someone in cryo-stasis? We have all the equipment, and it's mostly automated, so it's not that hard to—"

"Because it doesn't work!" I shout. "You're offering them a fantasy." I'm horrified at the thought of those women returning here, year after year, to visit their child, always hoping, always grasping for that thin thread of possibility that doesn't even really exist. It's cruel.

"You don't know that," Karl snaps. "It's only that one part of the process, the unfreezing. And I'm sure scientists could easily figure out—"

"Karl." I scrub my hands over my face in frustration. "We're not even studying it anymore. No one's even trying to figure out cryogenics. It's a . . . relic. Like petroleum-based fuel or cooking with microwaves." *That's the whole fucking point of the ship/museum*, I want to shout.

"How many times have you done this?" I ask.

His gaze skitters away from mine. "I don't answer to you. You work for *me*, remember?"

"Oh, God." I clap a hand over my mouth. "That's not . . . Those lower levels, they're not all full of—"

"No, of course not!" Karl sounds almost offended. "I'm

repairing damage, I told you." He straightens up, then, and seems to gather himself. "Listen, this is not relevant to your work here."

I gape at him. "My work—"

"Therefore, this conversation is pointless," he says, narrowing his eyes at me. "I'm not going to stop, when I deem it necessary, and you're not going to say anything."

A harsh laugh bursts out of me before I can stop it. "Excuse me?"

"You, my dear, are on the run from something. You don't want to draw any more attention to yourself than you have to." He leans back with a smug expression.

Fuck. My heart sinks. He's . . . right. If I turn him in, I'm bringing myself into a high-profile story, which is the last thing I need.

I want, more than anything, to reach out and smack that smirk off his face. "Anonymous tips," I counter. Those are still a thing, albeit much rarer these days. Even if you can manage true anonymity, the news streamers are reluctant to trust anything from a source they can't identify. Same, if not worse, with government officials or regulatory bodies who might be interested.

"Which would surely lead them to me, but then I have so much information to share with them. First, that the parents consented to this procedure and I have the records to prove it. Second, that their informant might be a bit unreliable. No UNOC credentials. A false name. 'She fled here in the dead of night, unfortunately. But I have so much footage of her, surely you'll be able to find her in no time.'" He leans closer to the camera, his face growing larger in my screen. "If you try to take me down, you're going with me." He grins.

And suddenly it's very clear to me why Karl chooses the people he does for this "job." My problems and false identity aren't impediments for him; they're assets. To be manipulated and used as he sees fit.

The realization must show in my expression, because Karl shakes his head in mock sorrow. "Don't make me take steps I don't want to take."

Yet being the implied threat.

"Back to work, Halley *Zwick*," Karl says, and the screen goes dark.

10

I stand there for a long moment, wrestling with my fury at both Karl and myself.

He's right. I'm stuck.

I turn away from the screen and head back toward the elevator, legs moving woodenly.

This was why I went into politics. To help people escape from systems and organizations taking advantage or abusing their power. To *believe* people.

And now . . . I can't.

I push the Up button, my eyes burning with unshed tears. Under my ribs, there's a burgeoning scream locked away so tight that it feels like the bones might peel away from the force of trying to contain it.

Fuck you, Niina Vincenzik!

She showed up one day without notice, appearing on a dirty, poorly lit station cargo dock like a misprojected SNN hologram. Jet-black hair cut to her chin, clothes ruffled a bit from whatever transport she'd stepped off, and smaller than she appeared on screen, but with an energy that pulled your attention straight to her. She seemed to be missing something without a podium in front of her. The white stem of a nicotine sucker stuck out from one corner of her mouth.

"You're doing good work here," she said, pulling the sucker

out and leaning back casually against the old desk that we used more for temporary storage than anything else.

I was in my second year of working for H_2OPE, a cobbled-together nonprofit organization with the goal of clean drinking water for every kid on every station. Starting here on Mar-Dow-12, one of the poorest Mars residential satellites. Theoretically, my job was in marketing and fundraising, but in a small, struggling organization, you did whatever was needed on a particular day. On that day, I was exhausted and dirty from unloading crates of individual servings of boxed water from yet another damaged "donated" shipment.

"You could be doing more, though," she added, gesturing at me with the glistening red candy.

My shoulders ached, my back throbbed, and I was annoyed. I'd recognized her immediately, despite my best efforts to stay out of my parents' world and anything related to it. She was the campaign manager for Mather Bierhals, the one and only candidate in the running for prime minister who seemed to have any moral code, or at least one where the first tenet was *not* "Thou shalt be a hypocrite if the money is good and the clicks are high."

But she was here, and that could only mean one thing.

With a sigh, I straightened up, brushing my hands together in a hopeless attempt to remove the embedded grime. "Listen, I have limited contact with my parents and absolutely zero say in which clients they take on or what stories they . . . interact with."

My parents—Weiller and Ivanova Consulting LLC—are infamous in the political sphere. Despised in public, beloved in private. They're the people you call when you "forget" to pay taxes for a couple dozen years. Or when you're caught "accidentally" sleeping with your housekeeping 'bot. (No judgment, but the vacuum attachment holes aren't really meant for that.)

They make troublesome facts, scenarios, and ideas go away.

Or bury them under a thick layer of "whataboutism" until they suffocate. They work on both sides of the aisle and across the platform. And for anybody else who could pay.

Niina laughed, a raspy delighted sound. "I'm not here for your parents. I'm here for *you*."

I stared at her. In the silence, the quiet but steady *drip, drip* of water hitting the metal floor from yet another leaky carton somewhere in the stack of contaminated crates seemed to echo through the space.

"You've done an amazing job drawing attention to your cause with limited funds. You even got Van Arsdale to back the passage of a station gray water bill, and that man probably takes a shit in vintage Cristallo." She sounded impressed. Niina Vincenzik, impressed with me? I tried not to be too flattered.

(Also, Representative Van Arsdale was an easy get when you knew what I knew. That housekeeping 'bot example was not a hypothetical one.)

"What do you want?" I asked Niina warily.

She returned the sucker to the corner of her mouth, where it seemed like it comfortably lived. "I could show you Math's water reclamation and treatment plans."

Math. She meant Mather Bierhals.

"I can also tell you that one of his campaign promises is for a more equitable distribution of essential resources, including water. But I don't think that's going to matter. Not until you decide."

"Decide what?"

"Whether it's more important to make a difference or to make a point by telling your parents to fuck off. In not so many words, of course."

I gaped at her for the second time in as many minutes.

She grinned at me, white teeth gleaming. "Look, I get it. We're more alike than you realize. I grew up on New Vegas, one of eight kids. My dad wanted me to marry his boss's daughter so he could get a promotion and bring home more money for my siblings. My mom told me that if I kept my legs shut and a smile on my face, she could probably land me a job in the laundry and get herself a bonus. My parents didn't give one fuck about me unless I could do something for them. Something I think you might know something about," she added lightly.

My mouth opened automatically in protest, but the words wouldn't leave my throat.

She nodded, as if she understood. "To them, I was useless, a mouth to feed. Proving to my parents that I wasn't wrong for believing I could be more was job one. And then I realized that wasn't enough. I didn't want to work my way up in the system, I wanted to break through it." Her eyes shone with fervor, her cheeks were flushed feverish pink—she believed in what she was saying.

Chills rose along my arms and at the back of my neck. She got it. Niina knew. For the first time in my life, someone understood. Someone alive, anyway.

She shrugged. "You're smart, resilient, and you've got the right moves. But we can help you learn more. *Be* more. Instead of wasting your time in this"—she waved her hand toward the leaking crates—"well-intended but ultimately pointless endeavor." Her mouth twisted in a moue of distaste.

"And if I join you, my pedigree doesn't exactly hurt," I pointed out, unable to resist. Because of my parents' relentless nonpartisanship—"The only *-ism* we follow is capitalism" was one of my father's most famous quotes—my name attached to Bierhals's campaign would cause a stir, providing the attention and maybe even the additional legitimacy his fledgling campaign needed. At least temporarily.

In the brief seconds before Niina responded, I found myself holding my breath, like this was the make-or-break moment, the test to be passed. I wasn't even sure why; it wasn't as if I'd asked a question.

But then she'd tipped her sucker at me with another red-lipped smile. "I knew I liked you."

And that, somehow, was the right answer.

Rage at my blindness then, and consequently my impotence now, rises up in me until I feel like I can't breathe. How did I fail to realize that someone so skilled at manipulating others was doing that very same thing to me? The answer—because I didn't *want* to see it—is no less infuriating.

In front of me, the elevator door finally rolls back and I stare inside without seeing the empty space, a vague idea beginning to form in the back of my mind. Something clatters and rattles in the shaft, the cargo blankets lining the walls wave in a faint breeze. God, sometimes this ship sounds like it's seconds away from collapsing in on itself. Or like it's infested with some kind of creepy-crawly with too many legs.

I step inside, still thinking. I may be stuck, but I am *not* helpless.

Instead of returning to the SecOffice or my quarters, I press the button for SB-7, at random. Right in the middle of the floors I'm not supposed to visit.

But the button refuses to light. Same for SB-6 and SB-8. Teeth clenched, I select SB-5 from the available options. That is the last of "my" levels.

When the doors open, I make my way through the corridor to the stairwell. The door there opens without difficulty. Then it's an easy climb down. I descend the steps at a jog, making no attempt to silence the clattering of my bootheels on the metal steps. If Karl wants to stop me, he'll need to come himself. And he won't.

I reach SB-6, the first of the floors outside of my responsibility, without any impediments. No bars, no barricade, not even any caution tape.

Just a regular door, set into the wall, like the others. Only this one is metal, less showy than the ones on the upper floors.

The window set into the door is . . . foggy.

I frown and step closer. No, not foggy. It's draped in plastic sheeting, the kind that indicates construction of some type in progress. As Karl said.

So maybe this isn't the right floor, or maybe it's window dressing, literally, for what's really going on.

There's only one way to find out.

I reach out for the handle. It twists easily under my hand. Not locked.

But I hesitate. Whatever I see on the other side, I won't be able to unsee. What made the whole Bierhals thing so stupid was how ridiculous it was—I saw something, questioned it. That's it. That's all. Then I signed my name—and my life— away. I didn't find any proof of conspiracy, no espionage, no secret files, just one severance payment that seemed too high.

Bierhals was going to lose the election; even the lowliest staffer knew that by the end. It was absolutely crushing, but what could be done? Rober Ayis was making promises about colony and station independence, about breaking away from legacy Earth government influences in UNOC, that he absolutely could not keep. But it didn't matter. People believed him because they wanted to believe him.

Other staffers—some of whom had actually fled Ayis's campaign to begin with—wanted Bierhals to go low, to drag Ayis through the mud, but Bierhals—and more importantly, Niina, my mentor, my friend—refused. I remember feeling so proud of who I'd chosen to work for. We might lose, but we were *honorable*.

We were proof that politics could be about the people instead of power.

Then the riot on Nova Lennox, a station with pending approval to vote in the upcoming UNOC election, Ayis's home station, changed everything.

The New Independents yelled and screamed about Bierhals's operatives inciting the violence that ended their probationary membership, eliminating their chance to vote. And yes, one of

Bierhals's staffers, Jamez Ildris, had been found in the crowd, allegedly working up the protesters.

Ildris had come to us from Ayis, had spoken out against Ayis. But he'd been fired weeks before for pushing those same radical tactics in the Bierhals campaign. I watched him leave, escorted by Jahn, our head of security. I remember it vividly because his severance payment came to me for authorization. Niina was delegating more and more tasks to me in those days, "training you up for bigger and better things," she said.

Her belief in me and my ability to make a difference was a fucking narcotic. I craved it. Didn't bother questioning it.

When I checked with Niina about the severance payment—it was way higher than it should have been, according to what I knew—she brushed it off. Part of his employment contract, a golden escape hatch. She told me not to worry, to go ahead and sign it.

So I did.

A perfect story.

Except . . . oh, except.

I was at the office late one night, after Jamez was fired but before the riots, catching up on our voter outreach results. And who did I see but Jamez Ildris? Going into Bierhals's office. My parents would have roasted him alive for having that meeting in a campaign office, just asking to get caught. But that was Bierhals's sincerity again, or his idiocy.

After rumors started circulating about Jamez being an operative for Bierhals and the riots being a form of election tampering, I had to tell someone what I'd seen. If I had witnessed it, someone else might have as well. I didn't want Bierhals facing a scandal so soon in his term.

"I'll look into it," Niina had said with a grimace. "I'm sure it's nothing. Probably Math trying to help Jamez find a new job before he went all vigilante. Mather is too softhearted for his own good sometimes."

But even after talking with Niina, I couldn't get that meeting out of my head. And then, one night, the two separate pieces of information—Bierhals's meeting with Jamez and Jamez's excessive severance payment—bumped together in my head and exploded in a bright light of revelation. Had Bierhals and Jamez . . . conspired? If Jamez had agreed to go to Nova Lennox to trigger the riots, Bierhals couldn't risk that blowing back on him. Jamez would need to be fired. But Jamez, if he was smart, would expect remuneration for taking that kind of chance.

But I told myself that Niina said it was fine, and I *needed* to believe her. To be fair, it also felt incredibly outlandish, like some kind of spy plot from a vid series. I couldn't even voice my suspicions out loud to myself without blushing. It sounded so paranoid, complete conspiracy theory territory, like something my parents would have cooked up as a distraction from a real news story. And working for Bierhals was the first time in my life I felt useful, valuable. I trusted Niina. She was my friend, my mentor. She believed in me. More importantly, she believed in a government that served the people instead of the other way around.

Niina never mentioned anything about Jamez again. Until the subpoenas started and the committee investigation revved up.

On the day the search warrants were activated on our offices, Niina pulled me aside. "Keep your mouth shut and this will be over soon," she said softly. "Rober Ayis would have ended up hurting more people than he helped, destroyed all the progress we're trying to make."

That was it, the moment burned in my brain, forever frozen in time. It felt like falling and being trapped in an endless moment that I couldn't escape.

I could smell the sweet cherry of her nicotine sucker, though it was nowhere in sight. Her perfume, warm and familiar, drifted over me as she smiled and nodded at the officials meandering through our space.

She knew. She knew. The phrase kept echoing over and over in my head.

And she'd lied to me.

"It was Ayis's supporters who started the fire, metaphorically speaking," Niina continued, under her breath. "They could have simply ignored their opposition at the protest. But they didn't, and it cost them the vote." She gave me a sidelong stare. "That's self-inflicted damage. Don't let your overactive conscience get the better of you."

Self-inflicted damage? This was election tampering on an almost unimaginable level, far worse than anything my parents could have dreamed of. A gaping hole struck in the side of democracy.

And I had signed off on it. Out of ignorance, certainly. But that was no excuse.

But the worst part was . . . Niina was right. Ayis's proposed One Station program—designed to make each station independent by stripping away UNOC aid and taxing the hell out of imports—would have left thousands unemployed and potentially starving. *If* he'd succeeded. *If* he'd managed to convince New Parliament to follow his lead. But he'd never gotten the chance. And at what cost? In short, who is the greater evil? I didn't—still don't—know.

In the end, it doesn't really matter. Bierhals will most likely come out of it clean—Jamez really had been fired, and Bierhals and Niina will continue to claim ignorance on the payment—and Ayis's paranoia, justified as it is, is not playing well with the public. Crazy loyalty tests, unhinged behavior, and dictator-like qualities are dragging his numbers down like a broken satellite plummeting through atmosphere.

That's the thing—it would be my word against Niina's. I have no documentation for our conversations. And I'm the perfect scapegoat, an idealistic junior staffer given too much responsibility and too little supervision. Either I'm a political manipulator who gave Jamez the idea and paid him accordingly or I'm the naïve nepo baby who had no clue what she was doing and signed whatever was in front of her, depending on which version of the story you want to believe.

I can't help but wonder now if that's the real reason Niina showed up that day to recruit me. If she knew how useful someone so desperate for approval and belonging could be. She owned me. Still does.

Unless, of course, I speak up. Out myself while trying to stop Karl from his bullshit. Then it's all over.

No more career, no more chance of helping people, potentially no more freedom if I'm indicted, and quite possibly no more *living*, depending on who finds me first.

The metal handle grows warm in my hand, the longer I stand there.

Karl says the parents are fully informed, that they know "slim hope" in this case is overstating the situation by a large margin. Do I believe him?

I don't know.

He is, in a messed-up way, trying to help people. If his "clients" or whatever are already certain to die, then what difference does it make if it's in a few months, in a hospital, or in a decade, when the powers that be decide to scuttle *Elysian Fields* permanently?

Either way, it doesn't change what's on the other side of this door, what's on the other levels. There's no way to undo what's been done.

Except that it's *wrong*. I grit my teeth.

And if I look now and find something when I can't do anything about it, I suspect I'll be haunted by the peaceful and serene faces, each with the unexpressed hope of waking up again one day.

I let go of the handle, without opening the door.

"Fuck. Fuck!" I shout. My voice echoes in the stairwell, carrying upward, like there's a mini me shouting on each level. The skittering and scraping sounds in the walls resume, having followed me up here, closer and louder than ever. Sometimes I wonder if there are rats.

Besides me, obviously.

I duck my head in despair, arms winging out to either side to cover my ears, as if hiding will change anything.

I hate this. Hate myself.

But once the trial is over, I'll no longer be in such "demand." To testify, to keep quiet, to not exist.

Eventually, I'll be able to find another job, to work again in trying to help people. And before I leave here, I'll get every fucking detail of who Karl has conned. He *will* pay.

But not now. Not today.

I force myself to lower my arms, straighten my shoulders, and then walk back up the stairs.

11

The light is on in the theater again. The spotlight most likely, shining down on what I hope is an empty stage. The brightness pours out of the crack between the doors and the gap underneath them, like heat radiating off a smelting furnace.

My whole body aches as I drag myself off the elevator, glaring at the theater doors. I do not feel like dealing with Svalbard today. Or ever again.

The fucking light has switched on every time I walk anywhere near the theater on rounds in the last two days (fifteen button pushes, fifteen sets of rounds). I have no idea how Svalbard knows where I am in the ship. But I don't care.

I haven't slept well at all, even worse than usual, since my discovery of Karl's little side business. More dreams of people screaming, trapped inside their tanks. Of tiny children wandering around the ship on fragile limbs, crying out for their mothers. *Jesu*.

In every case, I try to help in my dream. I work to free the people from their tanks, only for them to run out of air right as I manage it. I coax the children to come to me, to let me get them back to their parents. Except they always run away. And I'm chasing them until I get lost and can't find them, or my way out.

My subconscious is not subtle.

Even so, I just want to go back to bed, for the next two

hours and seventeen minutes, preferably without any REM-generated nightmares, until I have to be up again.

I step out of the elevator and turn away from the theater and the light beaming out from it. I should tell Karl, make him deal with the malfunction *and* Svalbard, assuming they aren't one and the same.

But Karl and I aren't really on speaking terms, except for necessary communications. Like today, when he warned me that he was replacing a whosit with a whatsit—I honestly wasn't paying attention to that part—and it would be noisy. Noisier, I would add, than usual.

Which is accurate. Metal screeches on metal with an almost humanlike cry. Crashing sounds, bellows from drills tightening something or other, alarming thuds that seem to shake the entire ship. If I didn't know better, I would have assumed the ship was coming apart at the seams.

Not that Karl had communicated this information to address my peace of mind. He didn't seem to give a shit about that. He'd chosen to express his disapproval of my discovery of his side business by stalking outside my room the last couple of nights, with dragging footsteps that were loud enough to wake me up.

And then, for God's sake, there was the "present." Tiny, white, oddly shaped pebbles on the floor in the corridor outside my room. I assumed they were decorative stones from somewhere in the Roman villa display downstairs, or even clumps of salt I had somehow missed, until I picked one up.

Nope. They were bones. Finger bones. I have no idea where he got them from. My guess is that there's lots of weird leftover human debris on this ship somewhere—organs in preservation flats, sample slides, the odd vial of blood that rolled into a corner and was forgotten—left from when it was the *Clara Barton*, or perhaps even from whatever failed processes might have occurred during Karl's efforts or when Zale Winfeld was in charge.

But either way, message received. I get it. We're all mortal, and he's trying to preserve life for as long as possible.

Another interpretation: *Keep your mouth shut or else.*

I should probably be on guard for him giving me up, in an effort to save himself, before I can turn him in. But for the moment I have nowhere else to go, and no ability to tell on him without exposing myself, and he knows it. So I suspect I'm safe for the time being. Safe-ish.

With a sigh, I keep moving in the direction of my quarters. I'll deal with the theater later. Tomorrow, maybe.

The murmur of noise is lost, at first, in another squeal from belowdecks.

But then I hear it.

"Kat."

"Uhhhh."

"Ree."

"Nah."

It takes me a moment to piece it together, as choppy as the broken bits of words are. And in that time, it repeats, growing louder.

"Kat."

"Uhhhh."

"Ree."

"Nah!"

Katerina. But formed of syllables seemingly cut from other sources. Like one of those ransom notes from the old vids, only with sound.

My name, my *real* name. One that Svalbard should not know. One that I definitely do not want Karl to know. Karl doesn't seem to pay a whole lot of attention to the theater—and he's preoccupied at the moment—but I'm pretty sure that will change if Svalbard continues shouting my name, especially in this weird-ass way.

I pivot and charge toward the theater, irritation fueling my burst of activity.

"Kat."

"Uhhhh."

"Ree."

"Nah!"

Louder still, as I yank open the door.

"Hey!" I demand in a hushed voice. "What is wrong with you? Stop it!"

But the stage is empty. Except for . . .

I stop midway down the aisle with a frown, trying to figure out what I'm looking at.

A projection, obviously. But not a hologram. It's flat, 2-D. A scene from a film, on the back wall of the stage, almost faded to nothing with overexposure.

Two women frozen in dancing positions, arms extended toward each other. A blonde and a brunette.

As I watch, the film kicks into motion. The sound is awful, distorted, and the jumpy images aren't much better.

Clearly the file is corrupted. It's an old film, not properly restored, or damaged in an upload.

That's when it clicks with me. I've seen this. I *know* this. It's one of the films stored here, as part of a display for a "resident." Amli Browning, the former movie star on the main exhibition level. The tall blonde who'd seemed familiar, the one with all the diamond jewelry in her "room" and the scandalous dress made of netting and metal bits.

I tried to watch this movie on, I don't know, my first or second day here. Before I realized most of it was damaged.

What is it called? *Gentlemen Prefer Blondes*, I think, or something like that. A remake from a movie originally made a century before that, during a time when musicals were all the rage again. Amli is playing the Lorelei Lee character, though she looks vastly different than her actual body in the tank does—older here, and shorter even. As limited as films were back then, they could do amazing things with their rudimentary generated effects and makeup, I suppose.

I turn my attention away from the crackling, jumpy mess. "What do you want, Svalbard?" I ask, aiming my voice toward the left side of the stage, where I'd last seen Aleyk. A human thing to do, but I couldn't help myself.

The movie continues.

"Svalbard!" No response. No Aleyk, no Ianthe, no Bryck.

Okay, fine. I start toward the doors, and the movie grinds to a halt behind me.

"Kat."

"Uhhhh."

"Ree."

"Nah!"

I whip back around. "What do you want from me? Show yourself at least."

Aleyk appears suddenly around the edge of the drawn curtain, walking toward the front of the stage. My heart trips in my chest, in an odd combination of anticipation and fear.

The movie, which should cut through him, does not. He is solid. As solid as he can be, which is more than most expect. His hands are stuffed in his pockets. His bandanna is tied still at a jaunty angle. Hair still flopped forward over his forehead in that careless mussed fashion, which must have driven the girls mad back in the day.

"What do you want?" I ask, moving cautiously toward him. I don't particularly want an encore of him seeming to regurgitate himself onto the stage. What was the point of that, anyway?

Aleyk arches his eyebrows in that polite *Are you stupid?* fashion, and then jerks his head toward the now stilled film.

"You want me to . . . watch a movie. With you."

He holds his hands out, as if to say, *What else?*

But he doesn't actually say anything.

"Why aren't you talking?" I ask suspiciously. Back in the day, he certainly had the ability to carry on conversations that were not clips from other stored media sources.

He gives me an exasperated look, then waves me forward. Closer to the stage.

"Oh, hell no." I'm not a child anymore, but that does not mean I feel any safer. That moment when I crossed the caution line, when he reached out and gripped my arm, it was like that moment when a dream shifts abruptly into a nightmare.

They used to have these primitive robots that would sing and dance to entertain children in mini theaters and restaurants. I've seen vid clips. They were utterly terrifying. And then someone—probably a child who'd grown up into an adult and recognized the horror for what it was—made a collection of films about those robots taking on a life of their own . . . and killing everyone.

That. That's what it was like. The moment that your doll blinks her eyes and grins at you with her pointy little teeth, even though her charge is dead. When your My-T-Bear whispers in your ear that maybe your family would be better off if you hung yourself with his tie in the closet.

Fucking messed up. Not just deception but something akin to betrayal.

"How do you know my name?" I ask now, edging a little closer.

He smiles, then. "We're all friends here, aren't we?" It's a portion of his prepared greeting at the start of the presentation.

"No, we're not," I say flatly, but my face is flushing.

That feeling of a bond, of being understood, that's why I stepped closer that day. To be fair, it might also have been a little bit of a crush. Aleyk's holo was—is—handsome, dashing, charismatic. And I wasn't the only one who thought so. During the presentation, the older girls in the row in front of me were whisper-arguing about where Aleyk would fit in a round of FMA—Fuck, Marry, Airlock.

But it was different for me. Aleyk rolled his eyes when Ianthe talked about the importance of their father and his work. The muscle in the back of his jaw went visibly tight when Bryck claimed that their father was a genius and would be remembered for centuries. Aleyk said nothing aloud to contradict them, but even at twelve, out in the audience, I flattered myself that I understood what he was not saying. Because I *knew* those feelings.

Aleyk and I were the same. I thought.

But Aleyk is not real. Or rather, the real Aleyk is dead, and this AI imitation, fueled by Svalbard 6.2 and a nasty sense of humor or a desire for inciting chaos, is nothing like me.

"Did you hate your father for loving his work more?"

I suck in a sharp breath at the sound of the young voice, a memory brought to life in the echoing auditorium. Except it's not in my head; it's *my* voice from more than a decade ago.

At the end of the presentation, I'd wandered up to the edge of the stage to speak to Aleyk directly. My holocomm lenses were still full of messages back and forth from my parents.

My parents had either forgotten that I was on that chain or they didn't care.

—Not my turn. I did it last time. I need to be at this fundraiser to keep my guy from shoving his foot down his throat again.

—Are you joking? Who takes care of everything else for her, Declan? ME. And I need to get these talking points massaged and out before this sex-holo thing blows up.

—Never should have blitzed the nanny droid. You were the one who couldn't handle it when she wanted Maritizka instead of you at the photo op.

They were arguing back and forth about who had to pick me up from the field trip. It was not a secret that my parents weren't interested in me except as an obligatory accessory. I had been produced out of a lingering societal pressure, a brief weakening in their resolve against interfering family members.

I'm pretty sure my grandmother, my mother's mother, even told me that once, directly.

I knew all of that, can't remember a time when I didn't know that, but something about seeing it in shimmering blue letters hanging in front of my face made it impossible to ignore that day.

"For always putting work first?" my younger voice continues, sounding so lonely, so isolated that I wince.

For loving work more than you. For putting work first instead of you. Back then, I thought I was being discreet. I was trying to survive the situation, adapt, and learn from someone else—who was, ironically enough, already dead—how to do that.

Obviously, Svalbard detected that vulnerability easily enough and decided to take advantage.

"How are you doing that?" I demand now. More important, why? But asking that would seem to imply that I care, and I would not let him have that win.

"We're all friends here, aren't we?" Aleyk says, with that same beneficent smile.

"Fuck you." I fold my arms across my chest. "What do you want?"

He gestures exasperatedly toward the frozen film clip.

I hesitate. Negotiating with a maybe broken, possibly insane AI program is not a great idea. But not negotiating seems like a quick way to make things worse.

"Fine. I'll sit here"—I point to a chair safely in the middle of the theater—"and you shut up with my name." *That you're not supposed to know.* I know I didn't tell him my name back in the day. I never got the chance to.

Aleyk bows his head and extends his arms theatrically, as if in a grand gesture of agreement or thanks. The loose curls pushed back from his forehead flop forward, giving him more of that roguish charm.

I shake my head. "Whatever." I slip into the row nearest me and settle into one of the caramel velvet–covered chairs. A plume of dust emerges, and I wave it away, coughing.

In spite of my intention to ignore the film, with its flat, fake appearance and shaky presentation, I can't help but be drawn in. The sound is still for shit, but the costumes are gorgeous. Brightly ornamented and designed to stand out, so different from our films. Otherworldly compared to the suits in the prime minister's office, coveralls on EnExx17, or worn clothes from the exchange. These were clearly bespoke, made for the performers. Probably worth a ton, if still in existence. Silk hasn't been around in close to a century, and sequins and glitter went away after the microplastic bans—and for the better. But still, pretty.

The images skip and stutter; the whole thing only lasts about fifteen minutes before the credits roll. Amli Browning being the first name to appear.

"Okay, it's done," I say to Aleyk, who's been waiting quietly off to the side of the stage. I stand up. "Satisfied? I—"

I stop abruptly as my brain processes what I'm seeing on the screen. The name Amli Browning, next to an image of the absolutely stacked brunette in the film. Gorgeous, pixie-like in height, and frozen in a sassy wink.

AMLI BROWNING AS DOROTHY SHAW.

The letters are half a foot tall and unmistakable.

"That's not right," I say. "Amli is the blonde, she—"

Aleyk lets the film roll on for another frame.

NORA BAKER AS LORELEI LEE. And next to that, the image of the blonde woman blowing a kiss.

Wait. Who the hell is Nora Baker?

Then the film flips back to Amli's screen, with her image, and I squint at it more closely.

It's not only the dark hair color, obviously. That can be changed. No, it's her shape, her height, even her age. This woman is too old to be the young woman in the room down the hall, who died—was preserved—in her early twenties or late teens. It doesn't match.

This actor is not Amli Browning.

Or—I sit up straighter, as my next thought sinks in—*whoever is in Amli Browning's room is not Amli Browning.*

12

Staring down at the woman in the tank in Amli Browning's room, I'm very sure of one thing: this is not Amli Browning.

As I thought, she's too young. And too tall. The dress on display, shiny metallic strips on a fine netting, would be a shirt on her.

But she still looks vaguely familiar for reasons I cannot put my finger on. She kind of resembles me, in my old life. Same hair color, a similarly long nose, but I don't think that's why.

I scowl at my own reflection in her tank lid, bleary-eyed and too pale. *Come on, think. Work, brain, please.*

All right, the simplest explanation is usually the correct one, right? So maybe it's a mix-up. Maybe Karl pulled the tanks out for, I don't know, cleaning or maintenance in the rooms. The tanks do have their own individual power packs, in the event of temporary shipwide outages.

Then, when he put everyone back, this girl ended up in here while Amli is elsewhere, and he didn't notice.

That . . . does not seem right, mainly because I have a hard time imagining Karl giving enough of a shit to clean under and behind the tanks. But it would explain the nagging sense of familiarity. I saw her on my first trip but in a different room, under a different name.

I shake my head. That doesn't *feel* right, though.

Still, I take a quick look for Amli through the other rooms

on the main exhibition floor and then on SB-1, but it doesn't take me long to realize very quickly that there are two problems with this idea. First, I have no idea what Amli looked like when she was preserved. How old she was. Second, I don't know if *any* of these people are in the right place without the hologram clips and explainers turned on.

This old guy could be Hugo Stevens, world-famous vid director. Or he could be some random old guy that Karl stuffed in this room.

The only ones I know for certain are those I remember from the field trip. Viviane. The pop star Chessley Max. Even good old Governor Franks. But everyone else? It's a mix of ages, genders, gender identities, and ethnicities. The only thing they all have in common is money.

But why does any of it matter? Who cares which tank is in which room? Amli is probably here somewhere. Or maybe her tank failed, her body had to be disposed of, and Karl put one of his "clients" in the room, hoping the board wouldn't pay that much attention as long as there was an occupied tank.

That seems as likely as anything.

What I cannot wrap my head around is why Aleyk bothered to bring it to my attention. Assuming, of course, that was the point. That he even *had* a point.

I return to the theater, but I can tell it's dark before I even pull open the doors. The silence is loud in my ears, the muted rustle of my steps on the carpet the only sound.

"Aleyk? Hello?" I call, sticking close to the doors. At this point, I'm prepared for him to pop up on stage, out of nowhere, scaring the shit out of me.

But he doesn't.

"What was the point of that?" I ask, a little louder. "Amli Browning isn't there. That's what you wanted me to see, right?"

Still no response.

"Why? What does that matter?"

The theater remains dark and quiet. My anger flares, white-hot at first but quickly cooled by simple exhaustion. Really, what did I expect? I know this thing likes to play games.

Like using a physicality it's not supposed to possess to take hold of a kid and tell her that everyone on board is going to die.

Yeah. Games.

"Okay, if you're not going to answer me, I'm done here." I turn toward the doors, half expecting him to call after me.

But no.

Fine. Good. All the better.

I head toward the end of the corridor and the stairs to my quarters. If I fall asleep right away, I still might get a solid hour before I have to start rounds again. *Motherfucking Aleyk. No, motherfucking Svalbard.* It's dangerous to assign personality and intent to what is essentially glitchy code.

But as I pass the SecOffice, I slow.

The SecOffice has records on the residents. Incomplete now, after so many years. Files deleted by mistake or corrupted by time and an aging operating system. In my downtime—read: boredom—I've nosed around a little. Information is power, one of my earliest lessons in life. But there are lots of gaps.

I might be able to piece together some details, though. At least confirm a few identities.

With a groan, I stop and turn toward the SecOffice. It's not like that hour is going to make that much of a difference in the massive sleep debt I'm accumulating, but I'm not even sure why I'm doing this. The residents of *Elysian Fields*, the *real* residents, have been frozen for more than a hundred years. They would have died of natural causes long ago. So what if Karl is pulling a slightly larger scam than I thought and replacing some of them with his newer clientele?

Because it's wrong.

Because they are people. Or were.

Because it's possible that Karl is up to something even worse that I haven't figured out yet. Like, I don't know, selling off preserved celebrities to private collectors as relics or something equally horrific. How much money would someone pay to "own" Amli Browning? I do not love that idea or my certainty that he could find a buyer, easily. An unscrupulous scientist hoping to study the long-term effects of cryogenic preservation. Or someone with more . . . niche interests.

And maybe because I'm still bothered about the sick kid down in the prep room and his parents.

"All right, all right," I mutter. "I'll check. Ten minutes, tops."

An hour later, I slap at the timer on my holocomm and press the button for the next round of, well, rounds.

My back aches from hunching over the control board, and my eyes are gritty and dry from squinting at screens and ancient flat images.

The records, as I suspected, are a mess. But even worse than that, it seems *someone* (*cough* Karl) has gone through and removed photos, holos, anything that would at a glance identify any of the residents. So unless I'm planning on getting up close and personal with birthmarks and scars, I'm sort of out of luck.

The only place where I've had some success is in the tucked-away file with all the old vids, films, and news footage. The problem is only some of the residents—usually the original participants in Winfeld's great experiment—were famous enough to be included, and only some—like Viviane—generated enough controversy and interest in later years to be covered by the news.

I have a list of forty-seven names. Forty-seven residents out of 456 that I might be able to identify. Except all their faces and names are blurring together in my mind now. Amli is the only one that stands out. An elegant and dignified woman in a turquoise wrap dress with an ornate closure at the neck and a silvery bob cut short at her jaw—that's what she looked like when she boarded the *Elysian Fields* for the first . . . and last time. Dying of pancreatic cancer that no one caught in time, back when it couldn't be cured past a certain point.

At least humanity's outlook had improved somewhat in the intervening years, if only in certain medical areas, ones that happened to coincide with a fuckload of money for investors.

"Okay. Rounds, then we'll start fresh tomorrow." I frown. "Or later today." I had completely lost track of standard station time.

A quick glance at the display tells me it's three a.m. Fantastic. Can't tell whether it's night or day anymore. Or, frankly, what day it is. Only that it's one day closer to me getting out of this place. That reminds me . . . I need to check the balance on my hard chip. *Only a hundred-and-some thousand to go!* Probably. I stopped checking daily after the first couple of weeks because watching the infinitesimal progress sent me into a depressive spiral.

I move quickly on each of my designated floors, opening and closing doors as I go. Nothing out of the ordinary. Except I can't help noticing I haven't seen anyone who could be Amli. At least not at a glance from the doorway.

I finish the abbreviated version of my rounds—I don't even double-check the rooms on SB-3, just wave hi to Viviane's tank as I pass—and then I drag myself upstairs to my quarters.

The light outside my teardrop-shaped window is brighter than usual. We must be turning, ever so slowly.

That brings to mind the image of that eerie captain's wheel, moving by itself, that I saw on my first day. I honestly haven't paid much attention to that screen since then. It's on the floor above my quarters—the bridge and the incomplete special exhibit, whatever that is—and not part of my rounds.

I pull my boots off and flop back across my bed. I should get up, clean my teeth, shower, put on something else to sleep in, given that I only have a couple changes of clothes that are suitable for "work." As in, ones I feel comfortable with Karl spying on me in.

At least his clanging and crashing noises from the lower levels have stopped. I frown up at the ceiling, suddenly noticing the quiet. I wonder when that happened. I was too involved in what I was doing, I guess, to notice at the time.

With an effort, I push myself around on my bed so my head is on the flat pillow and my feet are toward the bottom. I toe off my socks—can't stand my feet being too hot—and shuck my pants without even getting up. And that's about all I've got left in me. The rest will have to wait.

Once I'm comfortable—pillow adjusted, covers up to my chest, and one leg out on top of the covers to regulate body temperature—it doesn't take long for me to slip into that in-between state where sleep lingers just out of reach and strange thoughts circulate.

That's when it dawns on me that I have one more place I could check. The special exhibit, up on the bridge level.

That's probably where Amli is. It's not finished yet, so her stuff is still down here. And Karl being Karl, never one to miss an opportunity, stuck one of his clients up here in the meantime.

Relief floods through me. Problem solved. I hadn't realized how much it was bothering me. I still don't know why Aleyk thought it necessary to draw my attention to Amli's relocation, but entertaining himself by fucking with me seems a distinct possibility.

Then a yawn takes over my whole face, stretching so wide that it cracks my jaw painfully and threatens to make my dry lips bleed.

I roll over onto my side, hugging the covers up to my chest. Tomorrow—no, later today I'll check upstairs to confirm my suspicions. If I can get in. Karl said it was closed off, but does that mean locked? Sealed?

Who cares? That's a problem for future Halley. Three-hours-from-now Halley. Present Halley is going to sleep.

I deliberately close my eyes and think of nothing, which

rarely works, and then I run through UNOC-member plane-
tary colonies and stations in the order they joined, which always works. Europa-1, Mars BP-3, Tranquility City, New
Valles Marineris, Tycho, Mare Nubium, MetaLuna-1, Earth,
EuAma . . .

The first thing that wakes me is the slip of cold air over my
exposed arm. Prickles of goose bumps rising from shoulder to
wrist. I should pull my arm under the covers, readjust, but that
feels like so much effort right now, with my limbs heavy with
sleep. It's not quite cold enough to be worth it.

I ignore it until I drift back off into a dream about stores of
grain that turn rotten as soon as I open the metal doors and a
riddle-like dilemma on how to get the grain out without opening the doors.

The second thing, though . . .

A soft, snuffling sound from somewhere nearby. Not the
banging or clicks or any of the other noises I've gotten used
to. This is different. More like breathing. A terrible congested
sort of inhale and sputtery exhale. Coming from near the foot
of my bed.

I open my eyes, suddenly alert. In the dim light, I can't really
see anything; I'm facing away from the window.

But my heart immediately kicks into high gear, and I'm
caught in a flashback to the break-in on EnExx17. A fist wrapped
painfully in my hair, holding me down on the gritty ground.
The broken ribs that still ache when I move suddenly in one
direction or another.

Before I can decide whether it's better to stay motionless and
pretend to be asleep or to jump up, the sound stops.

But then . . .

On my leg outside the covers, hot, moist air coasts over my
bare toes, followed by the delicate scrape of sharp and jagged

edges across the skin. Then the first ounce of pressure, those edges digging in.

It all happens in a fraction of a second, before I can even process what's happening.

I jolt upright, jerking my legs toward my chest.

In a decomposing face surrounded by scraggy strips of white hair, eyes stare back at me, reflecting the starlight in yellow metallic disks. Arms—corpse thin and blackened in places—support its thin pale body at the foot of my bed. The hands, closer to me than anything, are skeletal, with flesh standing up in dry pale hunks, waiting to flake off. Black patches show through on them as well.

The crumbly lips pull back, revealing broken and jagged teeth in a smile that makes me question my sanity. A loud buzzing starts in my ears.

Then it lurches toward me.

13

I scream, a hoarse, maglev train–whistle of a noise.

Yanking my legs up and away, I scramble to my hands and knees and then upright at the head of the bed. The bed itself shudders and shifts under my movements. Of course the wheels aren't locked.

I slap a palm against the wall to keep myself steady, my feet pressed into the unstable surface of my pillow, and try to listen for the sounds of anything beyond the panic buzzing and blood rushing in my ears.

Farther away, the same old clatter and clicking, the things I hear all the time on the ship. But nothing in the room. No breathing sounds, no whispery movements of decaying flesh against my sheets.

But the mound at the base of my bed is still there, unmoving.

Keeping one hand on the wall and my gaze on that *thing*, I crouch down and fumble in the sheets for my holocomm. It has to be here, somewhere. *I fell asleep with it last night, every night, why can't I find where it—*

My fingers close over a familiar curved shape, and I snatch it up, flicking it on in the same motion.

Bright blue text floods the room with pale tinted light, the headlines I last downloaded acting as illumination.

I shift the holocomm down, tensing in anticipation when it reveals . . . a clump of blanket, in a distorted shape.

I shake my head involuntarily. No, no. That's not what I saw. It had eyes, shiny reflective ones, like an animal caught in a ventilation shaft, and those nasty tangles of white hair.

But could the "hair" have been twists of the white sheets and my imagination? And my brain simply filled in the gap, with the eyes? Humans are trained to find faces in anything and everything. Pareio-something.

I slow my breathing, trying to convince myself to relax.

Just a dream, Halley. Another nightmare, more accurately. One that I was slow to wake from completely. I am, it seems, prone to this blurring of dreamscape and reality in high-stress situations.

Once, at a campaign stop, after anti-UNOC protesters threw simulated blood at us, I woke up Niina and two rooms on either side of us by turning on all the lights and shrieking about the bloody boy in the corner. (The protesters, speaking out against UNOC's decision to reduce military expenses, had shouted about more casualties, and clearly my mind had latched onto that, right quick.)

And right now, my whole life is one big stressful lie.

Plus, I'm on this ship. Talking to Aleyk and surrounded by the almost-dead. Not to mention my worries about what Karl is up to. My little extracurricular project before bed, trying to find Amli and conjuring up all sorts of dark and frightening explanations for her absence, probably didn't help, either.

"Okay, okay," I whisper to myself. "So, we're fine."

According to my holocomm, I still have an hour and a half to sleep before my next set of rounds. I should try to take advantage of it. Sleep deprivation might also be no small part of this.

My legs shaky from the adrenaline, I carefully step off my pillow and away from the wall. Part of me expects that . . . creature to leap out at me from nowhere. But it doesn't. The room around me remains silent and still.

And "creature" probably isn't even the right word. It had

humanlike qualities, if humans could somehow survive that level of rot and remain functional.

Clearly my subconscious is extrapolating, combining the idea of all these long-dead bodies with my own fears of death and dying before my time. Or something.

I lower myself to sit on the mattress, hating the immediate increase in the feeling of vulnerability.

Get over it. Go back to sleep. Just a dream.

With reluctance, I turn toward my pillow, my lit-up holo-comm still in hand. I'm not ready to give up my night-light yet.

But when I reach to pull my pillow closer, a thin, dark streak on the pale, worn-out fabric catches my eye.

I touch it, and it smears. Still wet. And when I lift my finger-tip away from the pillow, it comes away red. Blood.

Not a lot. But still.

A nosebleed, or maybe I scratched my face while trying to get away from the *imaginary* decaying corpse creeping up on me, that's all.

But something about the blood makes it feel all too real, once again.

My heart, slowing to something close to normal, speeds up again, thumping in my chest like it wants out.

Suddenly I feel all too aware of the dark and shadowy corners of the room. And the giant void under my bed. At least, I hope it's a void. It is the only possible place something could hide.

There's nothing in here.

I'm *almost* sure of it.

Damn it. Feeling foolish but unable to talk myself out of it, I brace myself and bend over the edge of the bed with the holocomm to take a quick peek underneath.

The unevenly carved protection marks from my predecessor shine up at me, bright and fresh as if cut today. But there's nothing else. Not even a lost sock. Just dust. Undisturbed dust, even.

I pull myself upright, pausing for a moment again at the protection marks. There, if anything, is the proof I need: this place will make you a little crazy. If it's not the isolation, it's the sheer creep factor.

No more. I'm done. I start to push myself back upright, the light from my holocomm shifting and bouncing as I move. *I'm going to focus on counting down the days until I have—*

I freeze. Pale blue light lands on the far wall, across the back of the door and into the V-shaped slice of dimness of the corridor beyond.

The door, *my* door, is wide open.

Ghosts don't need to open doors to get to you. But then again, neither do nightmares. I don't believe in ghosts or ghouls or creatures of the night, anyway. And it's entirely possible I left the door open myself. I was tired and thinking about going to clean up before bed. I just didn't.

So I might have walked in and collapsed on the bed. Leaving the door gaping open behind me. That's not so crazy.

That's what I keep telling myself as I drag myself through rounds the next day. Later that day. Whatever.

I still haven't slept beyond that little bit . . . before. I couldn't.

Instead, I turned on all the lights I could find and searched my room, the corridor, and all the rooms on this level, including the wash-fac. But everything looked as I remembered it. Nothing out of place.

Then, by the time I was ready to try closing my eyes again, with everything I owned piled up against the door to make noise in case someone or something tried to open it from the outside— Why had I never noticed there was no lock?—the alarm on my holocomm was beeping again. Time to go.

Now, on SB-5, I push the button on the elevator to take me

back up to the main exhibition level. Normally, I would stop off at SB-3 again to double-check everything.

Not today. I'm feeling too thin-skinned. Too vulnerable.

You're fine. Everything is fine. It was a dream, possibly even triggered by your subconscious awareness that the door was open.

That, or it was a prank by fucking Karl.

The possibility has not escaped me, but it doesn't ring true even in my own head.

Mostly because I can't stop thinking about what I saw. Or thought I saw. It looked like what I caught that first day on the security cameras, the naked body crawling along the floor. Which makes sense, if it's my mind conjuring it both times. But less so if Karl is responsible. How would he have known what to re-create to scare me? I hadn't described it to him, not in that kind of detail. Detail that I myself was fuzzy on until last night, because of how shitty the resolution is on those cameras at times.

And I've been here long enough now to recognize that the idea of a tank escape is as ludicrous as Karl suggested when I first mentioned it.

But then there's the third thing: the blood on my pillow.

When I checked my face in my holocomm cam—didn't quite feel safe enough to cross to the wash-fac—I found no sign of a nosebleed or scratch. It wasn't until I was getting dressed for rounds that I found it: a jagged little cut on the top of my foot, right at the base of my toes.

Something I might easily have done to myself when I was rushing around the corridor barefoot or piling up my belongings in front of the door.

Except . . .

How would the blood have ended up on my pillow? Unless I was already bleeding before my panicked retreat to the head of the bed, when I was standing on said pillow.

The visceral memory of that hot, moist air against my bare toes makes my stomach clench.

No, not air. Breath. From a mouth. Possibly with sharp, jagged teeth sticking out right over my vulnerable flesh and . . .

Okay, enough. I shake my head, dismissing my imaginings with a shudder. *You have a hundred and three days left.* I had caved and checked my hard credit balance last night when I couldn't sleep. *Focus on what needs to be done. Forget everything else. No more random research projects. No more chitchatting with Aleyk.*

If he even shows up again.

When I exit the elevator, though, the light flicks on inside the theater again.

He's back.

I should keep going, walk right past, go upstairs to my quarters for very needed sleep.

But I hesitate. Blame it on the isolation and Aleyk being only one of my two options for conversation, perhaps even the better option of the two. Or maybe it's my annoyance at his disappearing act yesterday and wanting to let him know that I know he's playing and *I don't fucking appreciate it.*

I scrub my hands over my face. I need sleep. My patience is always stretched to the breaking point when I don't get enough rest.

So is my better judgment, apparently.

I turn and stalk toward the theater doors, yanking one open.

"What—" I begin, but the rest of whatever I was going to say is cut off, the words lodging themselves in my throat like oversize stones.

On the stage at the front, it's not just Aleyk. Ianthe is there, too, and Bryck, for the first time, has joined them.

The three of them are facing one another, Aleyk on the left in his normal spot, Ianthe closest to the front of the stage on the right, but pivoted so she's angled toward her brothers, and Bryck at the back in the center.

They are staring at one another with an intensity I can *feel* all the way from here. The silence is eerie and thick, like there are whole conversations going on but at decibels I cannot hear.

I edge a couple rows closer but it feels like I'm intruding, and I have absolutely zero desire to draw attention to myself from . . . whatever this is.

But Aleyk's gaze shoots to the side, catching me, pinning me in place.

Ianthe and Bryck turn simultaneously to do the same.

Shivers dance along my skin. At the same time, a cold sweat breaks out at the back of my neck. "Like something out of my nightmares," I mutter. Okay, not my most recent nightmare, but still.

Aleyk cocks his head to one side, and the image of Amli from the vid reappears behind them. Actually, it appears *over* Bryck, covering him partially in the letters of Amli's film credit, but he doesn't seem to even register it. His gaze is vacant and distant, still focused on me, but also past me. Like I'm not even there.

I grimace. Something is not right with him, even more so than his siblings. He looks okay, still dressed in that pristine dark blue suit that I remember, with a gray tie loose at his throat. His mustache is that perfectly tidy brush line across his upper lip. But he seems *emptier* somehow. Like there's no spark of humanity remaining in him, which is ridiculous because it's an AI illusion to begin with. It's a *manufactured* spark that Aleyk and, to some degree, Ianthe still seem to have. So maybe Bryck is caught up in another glitch?

The image of Amli flickers and then returns, and Aleyk raises his eyebrows in question at me.

Irritation rises in me. "No, I didn't find her. You were right that it's not her in her room, assuming that's what you were trying to tell me. I'm not sure anyone out there is who they're supposed to be, actually." I pause, as I remember my earlier conclusion. "Amli is probably upstairs in the special exhibit."

"No."

"No!"

"No. No. No."

Though none of their mouths are moving, and the clipped word is clearly pulled from elsewhere, it feels like all three of them are shouting at me.

I hold my hands up, palms out. "Okay, okay!"

Ianthe turns her attention back to Aleyk, and they silently communicate again.

"Why does it matter?" I shake my head before he can respond. Wrong question. Of course it matters. Amli matters, they all do, and if Karl is up to shady shit, it's wrong even if I can't do anything about it. "Why does it matter to *you*?"

Aleyk raises his hand and points at Amli's image, with clear exasperation.

I grit my teeth. "Yes, I get it. You want me to find her. Why?"

He just stares at me, as if waiting for something.

I move farther down the aisle. "Why aren't you talking to me? Like before?"

That's the thing. When I was a kid, hanging around after the presentation, it wasn't that he listened to me (or seemed to) or even that he understood. It was what he *said*.

And not in chopped-up bits of other people's words from a decades-old script.

Did you hate your father for loving his work more? That's what I'd asked him.

Aleyk crouched down on the stage then, waving me closer.

I remember feeling like he saw me, not as a kid asking a question but as a kindred spirit, another person trapped in that eternal battle of being "good enough."

I felt *special*, chosen, for once in my life. I hadn't even hesitated, drawing right up to the edge of the stage, stepping around the end of the velvet ropes to get to him.

"Sometimes people don't know how to love you the way that they should, even if they're family," he said after a moment.

"*Especially* if they're family. It's not your fault, and it doesn't mean you have to forgive them. But it does help to know that.

"All right?" he asked gently. Those blue eyes were bright with emotion, even as my own eyes stung with (mostly) unshed tears.

I nodded, scrubbing at my eyes with the back of my hand. I was so tired of feeling lonely and not enough.

"Come here." He'd urged me closer, holding his hand out right at the edge of the caution tape.

If I could have launched myself onto that stage, I would have. Instead, I reached out for him . . .

And that's when he grabbed me and whispered all that crap about danger and being dead.

Exhaustion catches up with me suddenly. "Look, I can't do this anymore. I don't know if you're playing games to entertain yourself or if you're broken, if you're Svalbard or some twisted version of AI Aleyk. All I know is I have months to go, and I'm tired. I'm being chased by creepy decaying people in my dreams now, and it's not worth—"

The three of them move simultaneously. No. That's wrong. Move would imply taking steps or shifting positions. This is not that. One second they're spread out on the stage, watching me, and the next they're gathered on the far right of the stage, the closest point to me, overlapping one another and leaning right up against the caution tape. As if they've gone from three individual entities to one, with three heads and a random assortment of limbs. Bryck's jacket shows through Ianthe's white dress; Aleyk's hands on his hips bleed through so it appears his elbow is poking through his brother's chest.

"*What,*" they demand. The word booms in the theater. And it is a demand, even though it doesn't have the sound of a question following it.

I jerk back, stumbling in my haste to put a little more distance between the stage and myself. Then I catch myself. I am not afraid of them. Any of them.

Anymore.

"What *what*?" I ask.

Aleyk separates himself from his brother and sister. Another silent conversation among the three of them ensues before he turns his attention to me.

"Dream," he prompts.

"Oh." Embarrassment makes my cheeks flush hot. "It's nothing, really. I'm not getting enough sleep, and let's face it, this place is fucking eerie—"

"See. Him." Aleyk persists, his expression urgent, even if his borrowed words and tone don't match.

I hesitate. "I saw something. I don't know. I think it was maybe a night terror or stress or something. It's nothing, I—"

"Dead," Aleyk says flatly.

"I . . . yeah. I guess?" If what I saw on the vid screen and what I saw in my room are the same thing, then definitely. But that doesn't mean it's *real*.

Without another word, Ianthe and Bryck blink out. Just gone.

I stare at the place where they were. "How did they—"

"Leave," Aleyk says.

I jerk my attention to him. "I'm sorry, what?"

"Go. Now. Please." If a hologram can look tired, worn-out, Aleyk does. "Danger."

My mouth tightens. "Is this the *Dead, we're all dead, you're next, he walks at night* thing again?"

"Thank you for attending our presentation on the wonders and opportunities of *Elysian Fields*. We wish you safe travels home and one day hope to see you again."

"I don't understand—" I begin.

His body contorts and spasms, and he bends at the knees, trying to keep himself upright.

The impulse to rush up to the stage and help is almost overwhelming, but I keep it in check.

And it's good that I do. A moment later, Aleyk's "face" splits wide and once again that arm in a white sleeve, covered in shiny red and clear goo, emerges from his mouth. Then a shoulder, and finally—after the distorted and broken face shreds away with a final gush of fluid—a head.

Aleyk's head, the hair plastered to his face, his bandanna dripping and stuck up around his chin.

"Katerina, you need to go. As soon as you can." He coughs and sputters. "He—" The internal Aleyk slips back, as if being pulled back inside, as the Aleyk on the stage staggers and shudders. The other head dangles back over its shoulder blades, like a discarded and incredibly disturbing hood. "He . . . *consumes*."

Before he can say more or I can ask what he's talking about, the Aleyk inside, the one who *knows my name*, vanishes back within the Aleyk on stage.

Then the theater goes dark, and I'm alone again.

What the fuck *was* that?

14

I wait a few minutes. But the space stays dark except for the dim emergency lights, high above on the sidewalls.

"Aleyk?" I whisper. I don't know why. It seems inappropriate to shout in here. As if the dimness itself is listening.

"Hello?" I ask.

But there's no response.

Finally I turn and head out of the theater. *He consumes.* He *who*? The thing that I saw? Mentioning it certainly seemed to freak them all out. Though I'm still not sure it's anything other than my messed-up subconscious.

The door was open. The cut on your foot.

I shake my head as I push open the door to the corridor. I don't believe in fake spooky stuff; people are much more frightening.

It could simply be an elaborate ploy. I can't imagine how bored a sophisticated AI system like Svalbard must get with no one to speak to, no one to entertain, after decades of doing just that. It's not unheard of for them to glitch by telling stories. Lying, is what we would call it in a human. Also, what is going on with that whole Aleyk-inside-Aleyk deal? It's like a hologram version of matryoshka dolls; it makes no sense.

I frown. But it seems like the second Aleyk, the one who emerges from inside the other, can speak more freely. He is the one who used my name. Both times, I suspect. And his speech isn't chopped-up pieces of other audio files.

It occurs to me then that maybe what I'm seeing on stage isn't *just* a representation of Aleyk and his siblings. Yes, they're programming. But maybe I'm seeing *other* programming at work as well. Something that doesn't want Aleyk, or a version of him, speaking freely.

It wasn't an issue when I was here before. But then again, maybe that is *why* it is an issue now. Could someone have put restrictions on his ability to—

"What were you doing in the theater?"

Lost in my thoughts, I jump at the sudden intrusion of a voice in the corridor.

I spin around to find Karl on one of the display screens outside a room. Amli's room, or the one assigned to her anyway.

His hair is ruffled, sticking up stiffly as if he hasn't had time to wash it, let alone comb it, and he looks agitated.

"What do you mean?" I ask as I approach the screen, stalling to give myself more time.

He cocks his head to one side. "Halllley," he says, drawing out the name in a disapproving tone. Like I'm a child caught with the good scissors in one hand and a clump of hair in the other. "You're spending a lot of time in there."

The best defense is a good offense. "Yeah? When was the last time you were in there?" I demand, folding my arms across my chest.

He frowns at me. "Why does that matter?"

"Isn't taking care of this place supposed to be *your* job?" I press. "The emergency lights are glitching. On and off. All the time. I see it when I walk by. I'm supposed to ignore that?" I raise my hands, as if in surrender. "I mean, that's fine, but how old is the wiring in this place, anyway?"

I'm not even sure why I'm lying, other than a hunch. Something deep inside me telling me to keep quiet about Aleyk.

Karl scowls, his glare fixed on me as if he doesn't quite believe me.

That's fine. I came up in politics, baby. He can glare all he wants. I know *this* game, at least.

I wait patiently, eyebrows raised in question.

Karl's gaze shifts to something behind me, his frown deepening. Instinctively, I turn to look over my shoulder.

Under the closed doors to the theater and in the small gap between them, light flickers unsteadily. Not as bright as when Aleyk is on stage, but certainly not as dark as I left it either.

Holy shit. The emergency lights are glitching. Flaring with brightness and then stuttering to near nothing. I'm glad I have my back to Karl so he doesn't see my surprise.

"See?" I ask, facing him once I have my expression under control.

"Fine. I'll add it to the list. I'll see when I can get to it." Tension is thrumming off him. Not angry. More . . . anticipatory. As if he's stressed but looking forward to it. "Today's another busy one," he adds.

"Replacing the whosit with the whatsit," I mutter.

Karl grins widely, revealing perfectly white, even teeth in the mess of his untidy beard. It's . . . disconcerting.

"So glad you're paying attention," he says. "If there were ever an emergency, you could save us by finding the whatsit and turning on the whosit." He laughs a little too loudly, on the verge of mania.

I shift my weight uncomfortably. I don't like this. "Are we done here? I'm finished with rounds, and I want to try to get some sleep." *Right.*

"Sure." He gives me that unsettling grin again. "Making some good progress down here. You'll be excited to see it."

"Uh-huh." Progress on repairs or his fucked-up side business? For a moment, I'm tempted to ask, to knock him off-balance, but I'm not sure I want to witness an even more off-balance Karl.

I turn away and start to head toward my quarters.

"Do try to stay out of trouble," he calls after me.

I toss a salute in his general direction. "Always."

"I don't know, sometimes it seems you find trouble without even meaning to, right, *Katerina Weiller*?" His voice, louder than before, carries past me, echoing down the empty corridor.

I go still, a rabbit frozen in place in one of the protective pens at a preserve, sensing danger on the other side of the glass.

I can't breathe, and my heart is fluttering unevenly in my chest like it might give out at any second.

Karl waits for a bit, as if waiting for the echoes of the metaphoric explosion to fade before continuing. "That *is* your name, isn't it?" he asks. Knowing full goddamned well that it is.

I whip around and stalk back to the screen. "What did you do?" Suddenly, his earlier excitement makes sense. He knows who I am. Even worse, he knows why I'm here. Nausea swells in me; I feel like I'm going to be sick all over the corridor floor.

"Me? Nothing." He holds his hands up in a mockery of innocence. "Sounds like you, though, might have done quite a bit, eh, *rypka*?"

"Fuck off," I snarl.

"Easy . . . easy." He laughs. "As long as you mind your business, your secret is safe with me."

For the moment. That part goes unspoken.

Back in my quarters, it takes only a few seconds for me to determine how Karl figured it out.

My parents. They're all over the news streams again. Only this time, it's so much worse.

MISSING BIERHALS STAFFER SPOTTED ON ENEXX17; PARENTS PLEAD FOR HER RETURN

My heart plummets to my acid-filled stomach.

Settled on my bed, I manage to download a recording of the earlier live feed. We must be close enough to . . . one of the old lunar resupply stations? Or Earth? I've lost track of where we are on *Elysian Fields*'s predetermined course. Not that it really matters. Either way, I'm piggybacking off someone's communications signal that's strong enough to give me the vid. It's pixelated and still weakly attempting to buffer, but I can see enough.

My parents stand alone in a bright center of light, dozens of streamers focusing cameras on them. My father's graying hair seems even grayer than before; red splotches of irritated skin stand out on his cheekbones from stress or drinking. My mother is as sharp-eyed as ever, but she's still in her crisp, form-fitting jacket and trousers, her work clothes that scream *Do not fuck with me.*

"We're grateful for confirmation that our daughter is alive," my father says. "We just want her to come home. EnExx17 is no place for someone so young and alone."

It certainly isn't now. Somehow my former presence there leaked. The hostile hostel manager, if I had to bet. Which means my fake name and ID are now probably tagged, too. *Shit.*

"She would come home if she could," my mother interjects. "She is frightened, of course. Who would not be? Her life has been threatened by the very people she thought she could trust."

I grimace. Never one to pass up an opportunity to strike at your opponent, that's my mother.

"If you could get a message to your daughter, what would you say?" one of the on-site streamers shouts.

"Katerina," my father begins.

"*Rypka.*" My mother interrupts, staring directly at me. ["It's good to visit, but better to come home."]

I flinch. It's innocuous sounding enough, on the surface. If you don't know my mother. She loves me in her own way, I think; they both do. And she's not cruel. But she is eminently practical. If she can save her daughter and boost her career at the same time, all the better. I'm worth more alive, in both scenarios.

So this is not only a plea to come home, it's also a warning that I've been exposed. And a lecture that I should have known better.

I hate that fucking nickname.

Rypka. Little fish. It's an endearment, but also, I can't help but think, utterly symbolic of my relationship with my parents. Little fish, much less important than the big fish, their clients, their work. Also, what are little fish best used for?

Bait.

Like I said, practical.

"Please, reach out, Katerina. We can help you," my father adds.

"What do you have to say about your firm's connection to Rober Ayis?" another streamer calls out, this one female. "Is it true that he has contracted with your firm?"

That question catches me off guard. *Finally*. Someone is paying attention.

"Our client list is confidential, and we are not here for business," my mother insists. "We are here for our daughter."

Also business, if she can get away with it.

If I come crawling back to them, tell them what they already suspect, Rober Ayis will be the first person in history to overturn an election. God only knows what he will do with that power.

Going home is not an option. But now, I'm not sure if staying here is, either. How hard can it possibly be to track me from EnExx17 to *Elysian Fields*?

Then again, I didn't give my name to the transport and I paid in hard credit. And it's not like they have updated images.

The vid cuts away from the press conference to a simulated anchorwoman on SNN. "That was Tatiana Ivanova and Declan Weiller, speaking out about their daughter, the former assistant to the chief of staff for embattled UNOC Prime Minister Bierhals. The twenty-six-year-old was reported missing approximately eight weeks ago. The circumstances surrounding her disappearance were unclear, though with the release of today's video from an anonymous source, it appears to be voluntary."

They have video? I sit forward.

Sure enough, a moment later, a scrubby image of my face appears on my holocomm. I'm wandering—limping, actually—through what appears to be a midlevel floor on EnExx17.

Realization slowly sinks in. This is me trying to find the auto-doc. The fucking auto-doc. It probably reported my injuries since I wouldn't give it all the details. Not a big deal, normally, but clearly someone was keeping an eye out and tracked me back from there. The UNOC agents I saw on EnExx17, perhaps.

The bruises on my face are dark and still fresh. My chin is tucked down and my sweater hood is pulled up over my head. But it's not enough. The angle of the camera catches not only the change to my eye color but also the new cut and dye of my hair.

My parents, assuming they didn't release the video themselves, are letting me know that it's out in the world.

Helpful, except holding press conferences and shouting about it only draws more attention to me from people who would rather I disappeared . . . permanently and not of my own volition.

I know what my parents are doing. They're gambling that the pressure will send me back to them and their relative safety. Even if it is at the cost of my soul. Bierhals may have murdered democracy, but Ayis is fucking dangerous.

His money spends, though, and I'm betting there also are high-level positions in the offing for anyone who helps him.

I shut the holocomm off.

It could be that more attention on me might actually keep me safer, make Niina hesitate to send someone after me.

Again. Send someone after you again. *Come on, time to stop kidding yourself.*

Yes, the New Parliament investigatory committee has IEA agents searching for me, and Rober Ayis's team of lawyers has probably unleashed the hounds, metaphorically speaking. But in both cases, those people want me alive.

There's only one side—rather one person—for whom it would be much easier if I simply disappeared.

That tattoo I saw on my attacker on EnExx17: *Mors mihi lucrum.* Death is my reward.

It's a motto for one of the Spetsnaz; in this case, a former Special Forces unit under the combined EuRuso Space Forces.

I know because I asked. Because only one person I've ever met has that tattoo: Jahn Cerny, Mather Bierhals's head of security.

I've eaten meals with him. He's kept me safe from protesters. But he also broke my ribs and fractured my eye socket without hesitation.

Despite the mask and the attempt to disguise his voice, the distinct rough lines of that tattoo made him immediately recognizable. I pay attention.

But Jahn doesn't act on orders from just anyone. Even if Prime Minister Bierhals commanded him directly, I suspect Jahn would make a stop by Niina's office first before doing a damn thing.

It's Niina.

The woman who looked out for me, who *believed* I could be more than my parents' kid. That I could be my own person and make a difference.

Yeah, make a difference to Niina by taking the fall for her scheming.

The betrayal shouldn't hurt anymore—she would remind

me that you have to look out for yourself first—but somehow, it still does. Maybe because even though I hate what she did, I understand why she did it.

Maybe in another universe, another version of myself, I would have done the same thing.

Not killing someone or threatening them, but cheating the system to get the outcome I thought was better for everyone.

Dropping my holocomm, I scrub my hands over my face. How did this get so complicated? I just wanted to help people. Isn't it supposed to be easier to figure out which is the lesser evil and then choose that one?

A high-pitched screech pierces the silence from somewhere below, making me jump.

My breath catches in my throat. The bridge extending? Is someone here already?

But after a moment a grinding noise follows, and I relax. It's Karl, working. For now. But that doesn't mean that Jahn—or whoever Niina has tagged with the task this time—is *not* coming. She'll need to make sure she tracks me down and gets to me before anyone else, or it's all over for her.

Okay, okay. I stand up and start pacing. *Options.* I have them. I need to think them through.

Obviously, I can turn myself in to UNOC directly. There's a formal summons with my name on it from the New Parliament committee investigating the origins of the riots on Nova Lennox. I'm sure they would be more than happy to collect me.

But that is no guarantee of safety. Everyone would know where I was. If politics of centuries past is anything to go by, "accidents" can be had quite easily. A shuttle malfunction. An unfortunate encounter with a mugger or Daze addict. The public will be suspicious, but if there's no proof, it'll remain a conspiracy theory that's whispered about and never pursued officially.

No. I shake my head. Turning myself in, that's too risky, at least for now.

But—I eye the room around me, mentally picking out my belongings—I can take what I've earned and get out of here. Schedule a short-run transport when we swing close to the next station. Which, when I consult our position on my holo-comm, happens to be Amster-York. Fuck. Very close to Earth and not nearly far enough from Bellaterra Station, where all things UNOC are based. Including New Parliament and their investigative committees.

I don't have enough credits for transport from Amster-York to somewhere more remote, and definitely not enough to buy a new identity. That means I'll be stuck, nowhere to run or hide. How long will it take for the wrong person to notice me and report it? With as much press coverage as the trial and my parents are generating, not long I bet.

The problem is, the qualities that made *Elysian Fields* the best of a lot of bad options are still present. The ship has mostly slipped out of everyone's collective awareness—the idea of it as a destination would be a stretch. Plus, there's no one here. No one can sneak up on me. I don't have to worry about someone dropping a bag over my head on a lift and abducting me on my way to get food.

In fact, no one can even get on the ship without us knowing about it. Without Karl letting them on, even.

An idea begins to coalesce in my mind.

With Karl's little entrepreneurial side venture, he's not going to want UNOC IEA agents on board. If they show up, we're both cooked. I may have run from a subpoena, but I'm fairly sure Earth has some pretty stringent regs on, oh, call it free-lance cryogenics.

But the other parties—Niina or Ayis's team or my parents—they might try to bribe or bully their way on. If Karl has good reason not to let them on, though . . . If there was a scenario in which hurting me would hurt him . . .

I stop pacing. I don't need to leave. And I don't have to sit here and let him dangle threats over my head. I need leverage. It doesn't have to be complicated, either. Just enough of a threat to make sure he knows our fates are tied and he better keep his mouth—and that cargo bay door—shut.

To do that, I need information, as much of it as I can get. Documented proof of his "clients," about the potentially missing residents, like Amli Browning. I still have access to the relay I set up, a series of networked comm accounts, from when I was getting my new name. I can schedule a release of all the information I collect to, well, everyone. Unless Karl plays along.

The gritty thrill at finding a solution—one that puts power back on my side of the chessboard, at least for the moment—sends waves of relief through me, followed by a sickening swirl of dismay. If I was who I thought I was, who I would like to be, I would probably turn Karl in for what he's doing, without attempting to use it as blackmail.

But apparently I am still my parents' child and Niina Vincenzik's mentee. Practicality above all. That all three of them would be proud of me for taking this step is almost enough to make me reconsider. Maybe it's time, though, to accept that I will always be both more and less than who I want to be. Halley *and* Katerina.

Another crash sounds from levels below, followed by a loud scraping like furniture being shoved around. I frown. Karl says he's making repairs, but I have no idea what he's actually doing down on those lower floors.

Seems like now might be the perfect time to find out.

15

The door to the bridge level, the floor above my quarters, is not locked. The lever-like handle lowers easily when I apply pressure. And while the edges of the doorway are sealed, it's not the way I imagined. Rather than rivets punched through the door into the frame or a jagged seam of melted metal from being soldered shut, it's . . . taped.

Yellow-and-black caution tape, the kind that is used to warn people away or make it clear whether an opening has been breached, clings to three sides of the door, the top, right side, and bottom, avoiding the hinges.

All I have to do to break through, I think, is pull.

But I hesitate. For some reason, the door being unlocked and not barred in any way, other than by a mechanism that will show if it's been tampered with, makes me uneasy. It feels more ominous than if the door was simply locked. Locked is normal, this is . . . not.

Or maybe I'm in my head too much.

I crept up the stairs from my quarters, moving as quietly as I could, though I was fairly sure Karl wouldn't be able to hear me over the bursts of noise he was making. The bridge level wasn't my first choice, but I didn't know where Karl was downstairs, and popping off the lift to bump right into him would complicate matters. So I decided that I might as well get what I could from up here first.

Plus, something about the way Aleyk, Ianthe, and Bryck reacted when I mentioned Amli being up here—simultaneous denials, all rapid and emphatic, in their borrowed voices—it was odd. Maybe they wanted to make sure I wasn't misled. Or maybe they're messing with me—I'm still not entirely sure I should trust anything that comes from Aleyk, or any of them.

But that reaction, in combination with this door, I don't know. It has me feeling itchy. Like I'm missing something important.

No. More like I'm about to walk into something I won't be able to get out of.

I square my shoulders and shake off the creeping sensation. Okay, enough of this overwrought *I have a bad feeling* crap. It's just another floor on the ship.

I reach out, turn the handle, and pull. As expected, the tape gives way with a little extra effort. But the adhesive releases from the frame with a horrendously loud and shrieky stutter, accompanied by the random pops of the tape pulling free or splitting.

Like pulling duct tape off a roll into a megaphone.

I freeze, the door open only a few inches.

Below me, the industrious noises from Karl's efforts have stopped, and the abrupt silence makes me all too aware of my rushed breathing.

But then a resounding clank and a softer whirring noise emerge. He's still going.

Letting out a soft breath of thanks, I turn my attention back to the door. I yank it open wide enough to allow me through. There will definitely be no getting this tape back to normal. It's all rucked up in some places, dangling in long strips in others. It will be very clear that I've been through here.

All the more reason to hurry your ass up, Halley.

I slide through the narrow gap, wincing as the metal edges scrape my skin, and into a dim corridor on the other side. No emergency lights in here. The only illumination comes through the doorway from the stairwell I've left behind.

But it's enough for me catch some detail. First, the floor is . . . carpeted. Not the metal or tile of the lower floors. It's hard to tell the color. At first, I assume gray. But then, as I step forward, my foot disturbs the tight nap, revealing a lighter cream color beneath the gray streaks. Dust. The gray is dust. How long has it been since someone has been in here?

On the wall ahead of me, a pale expanse marred by my shadow, I catch the gleam of something metallic.

Moving closer, I pull my holocomm out of my pocket and flick it on for light.

The simulated anchor returns, beaming at me with too many teeth. "That's right, Rian," she says loudly, and I fumble for the touch controls. "Forecasted projections include a water shortage, thanks to the excessive rain on—"

Her artificially perfect visage vanishes, and the corridor in front of me now appears in a smaller, holographic form. I'm not recording yet, but I want to be ready. And the illumination of the projection makes it easier to see.

I hold the holocomm out in front of me. Metal reflects brightly back at me from the wall and then falls into familiar shapes.

Letters. They, too, are coated in a thick layer of dust— maybe that failing air filtration system that Karl mentioned— but they're still readable.

BRIDGE, then an arrow pointing to the right. QUARTERS, with an arrow pointing the opposite direction.

I know for certain that Karl monitors the bridge—I even have a screen showing it in the SecOffice—so best to avoid that for the time being. And besides, given that we call the people on this ship "residents," I'm guessing that "quarters" is more likely the location for any kind of special exhibit.

I move in that direction, holocomm up and in front of me, the faint light illuminating a few feet ahead. My steps are sound-less on the carpeting, and it occurs to me that I can no lon-ger hear Karl working. Because I tripped some silent alarm and he's pounding up the stairs to confront me? Or . . . because this place has been soundproofed? The dense silence around me, almost like a physical presence, a membrane blocking all sound, leads me to believe it's the latter. Or to hope so, anyway.

The corridor opens into a wider space to the right. A large skylight in the ceiling above reveals a star field and a pale blue line-light, glowing around the circumference of the opening. That must serve as the only form of regular lighting in this space these days.

I frown. It looks . . . old. Those lights were all the fashion a long time ago. Until someone figured out that (a) a view of stars on its own was magnificent enough to not require further adornment and (b) even the small amount of heat wasn't great for preserving the seal on the window, aka the only thing keeping you from being sucked out into space.

The cream-now-gray carpet continues throughout, but it looks like mine are the only footprints. Light-colored sofas with sharp edges and cushions that appear more geometrically accurate than comfortable dominate the space. Three of them of varying lengths are arranged in what might have been considered a conversation area, before they went fuzzy with dust and deterioration. Ornately carved side tables in what looks like melted gold sit on either side, with an enormous monstrosity of a coffee table in the center. A darkened fireplace, with actual stones and a gleaming obsidian mantel, waits in the far wall.

Everything about this screams expensive and vintage. And weird. It's like someone set up a period-appropriate living room and then, what, abandoned it?

I frown. This could be the special exhibit Karl was talking about, but it doesn't look at all like it's been set up for visitors. Not like the food court downstairs, or even the theater. This is . . . private.

There are two doors on either side of the fireplace, and then two more directly behind the longest sofa, across from where I'm standing.

They're all slightly ajar, revealing a section of dimness in the rooms beyond.

As if someone just left and will be returning shortly.

Or as if someone is waiting inside.

I shake my head impatiently at myself. *Come on, Halley. Stay focused. Amli or anyone else up here. That's what we're looking for.*

I stride toward the closest room and push the door open without hesitation. It creaks and pops, like a cliché out of every haunted house vid I've ever seen, and to my chagrin, I find myself bracing for something to rush out at me.

But there's nothing.

Well, not nothing, I realize, as I bring the holocomm up for a better look.

It's a bedroom. A large bed, covered in a black-and-silver fabric and a veritable harem's worth of matching pillows, takes up most of the room. But holo-stands, dark and empty, decorate nearly every square inch of the walls. None of them trigger as I move closer. They've been left here for too long without charging. Fortunately, several flat displays are mixed in. Paper photos, magazine covers, even an actual newspaper page—in pink, for some reason—are framed, each of them with one thing in common: Bryck Winfeld's face or name or both.

In some of them he looks younger than he does in the theater downstairs, but it is clearly him, including his very stylized mustache.

The articles all appear to be about his business acumen, how he's following in his father's footsteps with great success—on the management side rather than invention, but still.

An open closet to my left contains a jam-packed collection of storage bags hanging from a rod. When I move closer, though, I can see the bags are deteriorating, falling apart in shards and pieces sprinkled on the floor. Their contents, dark-colored fabrics now sporting various patches of dust.

Suits, I think. Like the one Bryck is wearing in the presentation.

This is his room, or is meant to be, clearly. Maybe his father intended to have him live here, before the shuttle accident that killed Bryck and his siblings. And Zale kept the room preserved?

Zale Winfeld never struck me as a particularly sentimental type. Then again, it might have been less about having a reminder of Bryck than of his former power over him. Who knows.

I back out of Bryck's room to the central living area and head for the next door, on the other side of the fireplace.

About halfway there, as I put my foot down in a step, a *pop-pop-pop* sound explodes into the room, down by my legs. It's followed by a loud hissing.

I jump back, startled. My holocomm slips out of my hand, landing on the floor with a muffled clatter and turning itself off in the process.

I'm alone, in the nearly dark room.

At least until the flames flick to life in the fireplace.

I close my eyes in relief. The fireplace. The sound was the fireplace activating; it must be triggered by movement. I'm surprised it still works. The flames feel real enough, hot and crackling, but they must be contained or artificial in some way. No one would be stupid enough to allow real fire onto a ship.

Opening my eyes, I bend down to retrieve my holocomm, and when I straighten back up, I notice small objects on the mantel that I missed before.

A variety of awards in crystal, glass, and metal glint in the firelight, all of them with Zale's name and dates that read like a history book. They're cluttered together, these trophies, from one end to the other. But jammed on the end closest to me, three miniature paintings. Not photos; actual paintings.

In heavy, carved, gold-leafed frames that look like something from three or four centuries ago, it's Ianthe, Bryck, and Aleyk.

In a line with the rest of their father's accomplishments. At the end.

Maybe that's my own cynicism showing through, but I'm not a fan.

Without thinking, I reach out for Aleyk's, lifting the frame from the mantel. The carved edges are smooth beneath my fingers, and as I expected, it's heavier than one might think for such a small piece. The paintings are good representations, as far as that goes. This depiction of Aleyk looks only a little younger than his form in the theater. Early twenties or late teens, even.

He's got that eyebrow cocked in a very familiar sardonic look. In this case, it seems he's asking *Are you about done?* He is smiling, technically. But it's thin, doesn't seem to reach his blue eyes, though that could be the dim light or the medium—paint on a flat surface.

That being said, sadness somehow radiates from him. Sadness and *loneliness,* like he doesn't want to be there but he also has nowhere else to go.

It makes my chest ache in empathy. My fingers tighten on the frame, and the urge to put the miniature in my pocket, to take *him* with me, is overwhelming.

Projection, Halley. Thinking that someone you don't know, someone who died a century and a half ago—even worse, an AI imitation of said person—feels how you feel. That's how you got yourself in trouble last time. Only this time you're not twelve.

And it's not what I'm here for.

With careful movements, I put Aleyk's miniature back on the mantel, lining up the corners into the exact dust-free spots left by its absence. Then I step back and make myself continue through the suite.

In the next room, I find another bed, this one draped in

silver and white, now gone dingy. Beautiful clothing hangs in those same rotting storage bags I noticed in Bryck's room, except Ianthe's contain a plethora of formerly bright colors and fabrics, including a disintegrating pile of silk and fur on the floor that appears to have been a garment once.

The walls are bare in here except for a large oval mirror set over an empty dressing table. At first I think it's one of those old communication screens, but when I step closer, I can tell it's missing the depth. This is just a giant mirror, oversize by anyone's standards. And yet it shows no sign of use. No products on the dressing table, no brush or hairpins.

It occurs to me, then, to wonder whether Zale set these rooms up for his children. They both seem to contain sly insults that I have a hard time imagining Bryck and Ianthe establishing for themselves: Bryck unable to escape his father's shadow, Ianthe relying on her beauty.

Could Zale have been that cruel? That certainly isn't part of his public-facing legacy, but then again, because the three of them died before he did, it's not as if anyone had time to write a tell-all book or give an interview that they would then backpedal and deny, as is custom.

I leave Ianthe's room behind and start toward the next door. My heart is beating a little faster now. If my guess is right, this will be Aleyk's room. I can't help but be curious about what the room will reveal about him. Or about what his father thought of him, anyway.

But the answer, it appears, is nothing.

The bed is covered in a simple white sheet. No pillow, no blanket or duvet. In the closet, a single suit hangs on the rod, not even wrapped in one of the storage bags. The space is both more barren and less welcoming than even a guest room would be.

I raise my eyebrows. That's certainly a statement, though I'm not entirely sure what it's saying. Aleyk *was* the only one not to work with his father. And in the presentation, the holo version of Aleyk often spoke with a slightly bitter tinge to his voice whenever the subject of Zale came up. That's partially, I think, what drove me to talk to him all those years ago.

Is this contrast in his room related to that, to Aleyk's obviously unhappy relationship with his father, or is his father's treatment of Aleyk why he was unhappy? It's impossible to know. And it doesn't really matter, not anymore, but I want to linger, to check under the bed, to search in the pockets of the suit, to search for some clue that I'm sure doesn't exist.

I want to know Aleyk, as strange as that sounds, to know if my assumptions about him are even close to accurate.

But the longer I'm in here, the greater my chances that I'll get caught. Karl does keep tabs on me, I don't know to what extent.

Backing out of Aleyk's space, I head for the last door, assuming that it'll be Zale's bedroom. Which I have mixed feelings about. He was an iconic figure, controversial, interesting. Call me a prude, but I really don't need to know if he preferred strawberry-flavored lube or nipple clamps in the privacy of his boudoir. Both of which would be fairly tame compared to the rumors that drift through the political field. For some, it seems the more power you attain in life, the more complicated your tastes become.

Fortunately, it's not a bedroom.

In the far wall, a vast expanse of the stars. I step back instinctively before logic kicks in. It's not an open bay door but a ridiculously large window. Dangerously so. There are no supports through the center, and it runs almost the entire length of the room.

Directly in front of it, a conference table in oval glass, with chairs. To my right, a conversation area similar to the one in the living room, only it's a collection of chairs instead of sofas.

On the opposite end, a massive configuration of glass and formerly shiny metal forms an L-shaped desk that holds court in front of matching bookcases that run the length of the wall.

This is *Zale Winfeld's* office. Study. Whatever you want to call it.

Holy shit. Regardless of my personal opinion of the guy, there are historians who would likely kill—or die—to be here. Maybe *this* is the special exhibit.

In spite of myself, I edge closer to his desk. Centered behind it, taking up the space of several would-be shelves, hangs an enormous oil painting behind protective glass. The wooden frame, carved in curlicues and dusted in gold, looks heavy and shines in striking contrast to the darker image it surrounds.

I squint, trying to understand what I'm seeing. The canvas appears slightly burned on one side, but the two central figures are still intact. A naked man—very muscular—wrapped in a strip of red fabric grapples with another, while a river bubbles, furious and foamy, behind them.

And the other figure in said wrestling match is . . . well, it looks like he was *once* a match for the muscular man, taller and clearly dominating, with extended wings coming from either side of his back like a traditional depiction of an angel. The original outline of the wings and the being itself are still faintly visible, as are a few loose feathers still scattered on the painted foreground. But most of the paint in that specific area seems to have been stripped away, revealing instead a lithe but misshapen figure under the remains of the angel, with black tentacles wrapped around the man's arms.

A little metal plate beneath the painting says it's called *Jacob and the Angel*.

Huh. Creepy.

I move on to the rest of the bookcase. Several temperature-controlled display cases hold crumbling and charred scrolls, with unfamiliar symbols still visible in some places. Actually, they sort of resemble the symbols on the metal plate set into the floor downstairs in the welcome area. Another of the cases holds a similar scroll, only in a green that suggests some kind of corroded metal. The message, whatever it is, appears punched into the surface. Next to that . . .

I frown. I have no idea what I'm looking at.

It's a small holo display and still functional, which means it must be connected to power. From a smooth black base, it projects what appears to be the depiction of a cave—rough walls of yellowish rock, with a mix of stalactites and shallow pools of water. A dark, tight space, except for two glowing orbs set into the far wall. They look like fist-size opals, if such a thing exists.

As I watch, the light shifts, like a flashlight beam, and the opals seem to move in response. It's beautiful, but also eerie somehow. Maybe it's simply the contrast between the darkness and the brightness of the orbs, I don't know.

A shiver skates over my skin. It's probably another Zale Winfeld priceless collectible. Creepy didn't seem to faze him.

Moving on, I skim past old books in leather and folios with flaking pages before turning my attention to the desk. It's empty, except the embedded touch screen keyboard that would likely activate a holoscreen somewhere, and a small item made of glass and wood. The glass is wide at the top, narrows in the middle, and then widens again. White sand fills the bottom half of the glass, with wooden disks on either end. When I reach out and touch it tentatively, a few grains fall down into the lower level.

It's a . . . I frown. I can't think of the name for it. What people used to tell time or time passing.

After a moment, the term pops into my head: *An hourglass. That's it.*

That's not the only thing that's odd in here. The desk chair is out of place, turned to one side and covered in white scaly flecks of . . . something, and on the desk, the thick layer of dust is disturbed. Not wiped clean; more like certain areas have been touched or brushed against.

I hold the holocomm up for a better look. Clean streaks appear on either side of the embedded touch screen. But then they stretch out in either direction as if someone was reaching for something or flailing. At the edge of the desk, five perfect smudges, crunched together. Fingerprints? Except the shape that follows looks more like the start of a foot. What the hell?

Instinctively I look up, hunching my shoulders in defense— against what, I have no idea. But the ceiling is empty, except for an environmental system vent, dangling by a single screw.

And all these weird holes around it, like gouges or puncture marks. But they're rough, more like torn into the metal rather than made by a machine or a tool.

I shudder.

Okay, enough already. This is a waste of time. What I'm looking for is clearly not up here.

As if on cue, the timer on my holocomm beeps, reminding me that I need to press the button and start rounds.

I leave the office, taking care to step only in the marks I've already made. I'm not sure why, only that it feels less disre- spectful. Not that I'm super concerned with what Zale Win- feld would have thought of me, but more that it feels like a crypt in here and I have no interest in desecrating it.

Back in the living area, I turn toward the door and debate crossing between the sofas because the fireplace has turned itself off, and I don't want to trigger it again.

Standing there, however, I notice for the first time a narrow corridor that continues on to my left, *past* Zale's office. And in the silence, made extra loud by the absence of the flickering flames, a faint, even hum.

The galley, I tell myself. That's all.

But even as I head down the corridor toward the open door- way at the end of it, I know that's not it.

I recognize this sound. I've been living with it for weeks now.

At the end of the corridor, the room opens up into what might have been a bedroom at one point. A headboard with royal-blue and silver drapes hanging above it is still attached to the wall.

But the four tanks arranged in a vaguely square outline take up most of the space. The tank farthest from me, forming the top of the rectangle, is open, seemingly awaiting an occupant.

The one closest to the doorway, however, is sealed up and has that faint iciness etched on the glass that indicates it's on and working.

Dread pools in my stomach as I inch toward the head of the tank. I'm not even sure why. This, finally, is Karl's special exhibit. Amli Browning and probably a few others who . . .

A familiar face, serene and peaceful, floats beneath the tank lid, her hands clasped over her chest, in a mockery of death. Her blond hair is loose and arranged around her shoulders, as I've never seen it.

My breath catches in my throat. Not Amli Browning, no.

Ianthe Winfeld.

16

Ianthe. Oldest child of Zale Winfeld. Who supposedly died in a shuttle accident with her brothers but appears perfectly intact here. No burns or signs of traumatic injury. She looks exactly as she does in the presentation, except she's naked, of course, her heavy golden hair is loose around her shoulders, and a thick metal band rests on her forehead.

What the fuck?

I leave Ianthe, dashing past the empty tank, to the sealed one across from her.

Bryck Winfeld. Also not nearly as dead-looking as he should be. Cryogenically frozen, yes, but seemingly whole, with all his limbs intact. Same metal band on his head. I don't understand this. Fatal shuttle accidents in space usually involve complete disintegration, or at the very least a short but very bright fireball.

I try to remember what I know about the accident. The three of them were going to meet their father on *Elysian Fields*. But the shuttle suffered a mechanical failure almost immediately on departure from New Amsterdam Station, something to do with a faulty fuel intake valve.

The debris from the explosion shattered windows on a passing transport, killing three others and injuring a couple more.

But here they are. Ianthe, Bryck, and . . .

I turn toward the final sealed tank.

Aleyk.

My heart trips over itself in my chest as I approach, in both fear and anticipation. As if it might be someone else who happens to be in here with the rest of his family.

But it's not.

I clamp a hand over my mouth to stop a gasp at the sight of him. His hair, normally flopping over his forehead, has been ruthlessly shoved back, held in place by that same type of metal band. A vicious bruise in an ugly shade of purple lines his cheekbone. His lower lip is torn in the corner, with dried—and now frozen—blood collecting above his chin. His hands are not folded neatly over his chest but are cast off to either side, with a disregard that registers as cruelty. On the hand closest to me, several fingers are red and misshapen, as if they're broken. I recognize the dark pattern of diamond marks on the pale skin of his ribs as something I've seen before, but it takes me a moment to realize where and why: it's a boot print, in the form of bruises. I had something similar on my back and ribs after my attack on EnExx17.

Tears sting my eyes in empathy. *Oh, Aleyk. What happened to you?* This looks more like a fight, one in which he tried to resist his attackers, than any kind of accident.

I lean down for a better look, and it's only then, taking in the long eyelashes and high cheekbones, the strange braided-looking red abrasion around his neck, a faint bump in his nose that I never noticed before, that I finally pay more attention to the band around his forehead. It's thicker than I first thought, black foam poking out from the underside, possibly for the wearer's comfort, though I can't imagine that helped much.

I frown. None of the other residents have these bands.

A fine mesh of hair-thin wires, barely visible, extends from the top edge of the band and disappears into his dark curls, the silvery lines glinting in a mockery of what Aleyk might have looked like with a few grays.

The wires, small as they are, look invasive. Like tiny predatory centipedes slinking upward and digging in. I can't think
of any reason why Aleyk, Ianthe, and Bryck would have them.
Not any *good* reason.

My breath condenses on the cold surface, fogging my view
temporarily, and when I wipe at it impatiently with the side
of my hand, dust comes away with the moisture, giving me a
clearer view inside for the first time.

Faint lettering on the band catches my eye for the first time.
Only a few letters at first. An *S* at the beginning and a *d* at the
end. The letters in the middle are too hard to make out, except
maybe . . . is that a *v* next to the *S*?

Svalbard. I go still, ramifications dropping into place like
boulders into a too-small pond.

Oh, fuck.

Fuck, fuck, fuck.

I rush down the stairs, past the second floor and onto the main
exhibition level, pausing at the SecOffice only long enough to
press the overdue button.

But I'm too preoccupied with the burning-hot-coal possibility
at the forefront of my mind to worry about being a little late.

What I'm thinking, it's not *possible.* That technology never
worked well to begin with. Early experiments were a mess,
and it's been illegal for . . . forever! Before Zale Winfeld even
started *Elysian Fields,* or else *Elysian Fields* probably wouldn't
have existed.

Breathless, I reach the doors to the theater and stop, my
hand on the twisted metal vines of the handle.

What am I going to say?

What if Aleyk doesn't know? It would be torture, cruel and
unusual punishment, to tell him.

I shake my head. He has to know. That's part of why the

tech ultimately didn't work. The self-awareness was essential for maintaining sentience, and yet it drove them mad.

I draw in a deep breath, hold it for a moment.

It's possible Aleyk won't even respond to me. That he won't show up. It's happened before. And if my guess is right, he'll know I was upstairs and he might well be pissed about it.

Pissed. Yeah. Not playing at it, or creating the appearance of it, but actually angry.

I let out the breath and pull open the door. I have to know. The thought of someone trapped like that . . .

The stage is dark, but I head down the aisle anyway, the door swinging quietly shut behind me. The sound is muted in here, like upstairs in the living quarters.

I'm about halfway to the stage when the spotlight appears, highlighting a section of the empty ledge. My steps stutter, and I stumble to a stop, hand on the back of the nearest chair while I wait.

Aleyk ducks around from the edge of the curtain, hands stuffed in his pockets, his gaze fixed on me, with that one wayward lock of hair dangling over his eye.

He looks both weary and resigned, his mouth a tight line.

Any thought of a more indirect approach evaporates from my mind. "It's you, isn't it?" I ask. The words sound too thin, too high-pitched.

"Thank you for visiting us today," he says flatly. "We wish you safe travels home."

It's the script, from the presentation. He should go on to say something like "And come see us again soon," where Bryck would interject with "But not too soon!"

But Aleyk doesn't. He cuts it off early. Pointedly.

I ignore him. "This isn't some AI program based on questions you answered or emails you wrote or even recordings of you back in the day. Svalbard, it's an upload mechanism. You're . . . *you.*"

The idea of the singularity was around even at the turn of

the twentieth century. That computers would reach a point where they would match or even exceed human thought potential. That people would one day be able to shed their frail mortal shells for a form of immortality—uploading their memories, ideas, personalities into a computer designed specifically for that purpose.

All the arguments about playing God, the existence of souls, and disrupting the natural order were made by philosophers, theologians, and *some* scientists. But in the end, the possibility was too tempting to resist. You know that old saying, "Fuck around and find out"?

A consortium of scientists from what used to be the People's Republic of China found out.

Pygmalion, that's what their upload system was called, worked. Sort of. The problem is people aren't just memories, ideas, personalities—we're not only brains. We're bodies, too. A smorgasbord of sensory input. Pygmalion could not accommodate it—the electronic version of senses, details in binary, was not enough.

Like going from three-dimensional reality to a flat, thin world controlled by others, one that existed only in shades of gray and offered concepts of sensation rather than the real thing. It is its own version of hell, being aware of what you're missing but unable to change it. Trapped forever, in a liminal existence.

"Jane," one of their first volunteer subjects, suffering from a degenerative muscle condition, was uploaded. Her mind was thoroughly mapped, documented, and engaged, allegories for all five senses were established, and enrichment activities determined, before the upload.

It drove her insane in less than a year, and they had to shut it down. The rest of the world would probably never have known about it, given the secretive nature of the project, except that she took down a massive chunk of the electrical infrastructure in her rage after her keepers tried to prevent her from accessing what was then called the internet.

Laws prohibiting uploads went into effect, banning it in much the same manner that human cloning had been banned before it. But there were always rumors about secret groups, organizations, even individual scientists pursuing the work. Even UNOC recently had to issue a reaffirmation of their stance against human experimentation, after a corporate-sponsored space station was found to be collecting data illicitly from its residents, including confidential, locked DNA profiles, for . . . reasons. Ones they never really wanted to specify. There's always money to be made if you can promise people a way to cheat death.

I move closer to Aleyk, and it's hard not to stare at him in awe. Yes, it's a digital representation, but he's in there. The real Aleyk. A living, sort of, figure from history.

I was right. The realization dawns on me belatedly. All those years ago, when I was sure that he'd spoken to me directly, that he was different somehow, I was right.

The relief feels like an uncoiling of something permanently twisted tight and knotted in my chest. A small laugh, halfway to a sob, escapes me before I can stop it. I clamp a hand over my mouth, my vision blurring with tears. *I was right.*

Aleyk glares down at me. "Challenging. Death."

"Yeah, I guess they did," I say after a moment, sniffling and dabbing under my eyes with my sleeve. I've never heard of Svalbard as an upload system, but then, why would I? Zale would have had to keep it quiet. But if he mastered this, why bother with cryofreezing? It was legal but that doesn't strike me as the type of thing that would have factored into his decision-making process.

"No. You." He points at me and crouches down at the edge of the stage, one knee on the surface.

I shake my head. "I don't understand."

He rakes a hand through his hair in frustration, looking up at the ceiling as if asking for patience from some higher power.

I step closer. "Are you okay?" I reach across the caution tape–marked line and touch his knee.

It doesn't feel like touching someone, not like that. I can't detect the texture of the fabric or the heat and substance of a body beneath it. More a sense of pressure against my palm. And that *is* something that is new and revolutionary, a development I'd never heard of before. Exactly the kind of thing Zale Winfeld was known for willing into existence.

Aleyk's gaze jerks from that skyward point to my hand and then to my face. His blue eyes radiate intensity, a hunger, enough to make me remove my hand and back up.

A quick look of chagrin flashes through his expression before he returns to his normal impassiveness. I wonder how long it's been. Touch is a necessity for humans. The need for that sensory input wouldn't go away.

"Why did they do this to you?" I ask, my voice breaking, as he stands and moves back a step or two from the edge of the stage.

He crosses his arms over himself, and the bandanna around his neck shifts as he visibly swallows. "My father's company."

I nod. "I figured, but why did they—"

He shakes his head. "My father's. Company." Those blue eyes meet mine again, as if willing me to understand.

I repeat the words silently, trying to put them together in a different way. Then, images of the bedrooms upstairs flash into my mind. Individually designed for each adult child. Three tanks, three kids. One empty, left open for Zale himself.

"To keep your father company," I say softly.

He gives a curt jerk of his head in a nod.

"So, Zale . . . his people, they manufactured a shuttle accident to cover . . ." I stop, trying to piece it together. To cover *what*? Aleyk, Ianthe, and Bryck were all here, uploaded. They hadn't died. So it was to cover their absence, their disappearance from public life. Because their father wanted them here to keep him company, even though none of them were sick or dying—

Oh, Jesu. The marks all over Aleyk's body.

"Did they take you?" I can barely force the words out past the nausea curling up in the back of my throat.

He arches an eyebrow at me, as if asking what else I would expect.

I feel sick, dizzy, and reach out to grip the stage. They *murdered* him. That's what it's called when you fucking cryofreeze someone against their will. Even worse, it was presumably on his father's orders. "And then he didn't even end up here," I whisper. It's repulsive. I don't even know what to say.

Aleyk shakes his head firmly. "Here."

It takes me a moment to follow. "Your father?" I frown. "No. He's not . . . he never—"

"Here," he repeats, with extra emphasis.

I open my mouth and then close it. There's no point in arguing.

What do I know? Only that the tank upstairs, seemingly designated for Zale, is empty. The story is that he committed suicide after the death of his children, but since his children weren't actually *killed* in that shuttle accident, I have no idea what to believe anymore.

"I'm sorry," I blurt, unable to stop myself. "For what happened to you, for not understanding before." My eyes sting again as I imagine what it must have been like to fight so hard and then to "wake up" in this altered form, his whole life gone. And no one would listen to him, because they thought he was AI, and his ability to communicate was restricted.

I *know* that feeling. That sensation of words spewing forth and people staring right through you as if you don't exist. No, as if you don't *matter*. A tear overflows, despite my efforts to blink it back. Damn it. I'm not usually this soft.

Aleyk tilts his head to the side, giving me a rueful smile. "Regret."

"No." I laugh, the sound clotted and thick. "Don't do that. Don't be nice . . . It makes it harder."

His expression softens, and he kneels back down on the

stage near me. His hand hovers in the air, above his knee, and for a moment I think he might turn it palm up, an unspoken request to take my hand.

But then he straightens up abruptly, gaze fixed on a distant point, as if hearing something I can't. "Death." He taps his nose, once again looking at me with that silent intensity that screams *Understand, please!*

"Death nose?" I try.

He gives me that arched eyebrow look of exasperation.

"Oh! Death smell."

Aleyk points at me.

"I smell like death?" *Ouch.* In spite of myself, I feel my cheeks go hot. Honestly, charades is something I've never been good at it, and playing with my semi-crush, who happens to be almost two hundred years old, makes for less than ideal gameplay circumstances.

He starts again. This time, when he touches his nose, his chest rises in the motion of a deep inhale.

"Death smells . . . me?"

He nods rapidly, and then points up. Then his hands flash in a quick series of motions, one flat and then other about three inches above. Then he pulls his bottom hand out and put it above the other. Showing . . . layers.

Or levels.

Ah, I got it! "Death smells me . . . upstairs?"

He nods again. "Cat. Uhhhh. Ree. Nah. Believe."

But before I can tell him, first, to call me Kat, because though I hate the nickname, it'll serve us both if he does, and second, that I do absolutely believe him, he shakes his head and tries again.

"—lieve." His mouth moves with the first portion of the word, but no sound emerges until the second syllable.

It sounds a lot like . . . "Leave?"

Relief floods his face and he stands. "Yes. Thank you for visiting us today." He pauses. "Amster-York." The voice is not his but a mechanical-sounding female. A sample pulled from an old audio file, likely a listing of the *Elysian Fields* route.

"Oh, trust me, I'm getting out of here," I say flatly. But now . . . now it's more complicated. How am I supposed to walk away from *Elysian Fields,* knowing all that I know now?

"Now," he insists, in his own voice. His gaze shifts past me again, only this time in the direction of the doors.

I automatically spin to see for myself, half expecting to see Karl lounging against the doorframe, watching.

But the doors are still closed, and no one is there.

I bite my lip, facing Aleyk, who is still watching the entrance over my head. How much of this is part of the inevitable degradation he must be experiencing? Not just the loss of sanity but also the actual breakdown of the components containing the code that makes him *him.* Like dementia in a person, tiny misfiring or blocked connections. Svalbard, no matter how sophisticated, is old. Half the shit on this ship doesn't work anymore. I doubt Aleyk is immune to that. I wonder if that's why he's the one who speaks instead of Ianthe and Bryck—neither of them seem as "alive" as he does.

But then it occurs to me that I have no idea how long I've been in here. How long Karl may or may not have continued working and being distracted. Aleyk is right. I should go, at least for now. Let Karl see me working and not doing anything out of the ordinary, if he's bothering to check.

"I'll do rounds, and I'll come back," I say, backing away from him.

"No," Aleyk says sharply.

"I'm not leaving you here." The words are out of my mouth with the sincerity and intensity of a vow, before I can think better of it.

Good job, Halley. And how are you planning to do that?

Aleyk regards me wearily. "Death. Escape."

"Yeah, I'm going to work on it," I say grimly, as I turn to head for the doors.

"No," he calls after me. "Death. Is. Escape."

Once again, I don't know what he means. Except possibly in the most literal sense of wanting to die to escape this fucking ship. And frankly, if that's what he means, I don't blame him. But we are going to find another way. *I* am going to find another way.

17

I hustle down the corridor of the main exhibition level, opening and closing doors. Trying *not* to look like I'm hurrying. Loud crashes reverberate through the ship from whatever Karl is doing on the lower levels.

There's always a deal to be made. You have to find the right person and apply the appropriate amount and type of pressure.

That is chapter and verse from my mother—the Book of Tatiana.

The issue is that Karl isn't that person. Not for something this big. And reporting all of this anonymously, once I'm away from here and hiding elsewhere, is not going to work. This needs a face in front of it, someone who is furious about what's going on now and back when Aleyk and his siblings were killed.

I slow down as a thought occurs to me belatedly. Aleyk's body is the only one that shows signs of a struggle. Ianthe and Bryck appear absolutely pristine. Which means . . . Aleyk figured out what was happening fast enough to fight and they didn't? Or—a stomach-churning possibility dawns—they knew and went along with it voluntarily.

Ianthe and Bryck, they *worked* for Zale. Were they in on these plans?

Imagining the moment when Aleyk must have realized, seeing them already in place in the tanks, or waiting for him to arrive and join them—by force. That level of betrayal and hurt, it makes me flinch. I don't have any siblings, but I always wanted one. Maybe better that I didn't have one, or else it might well have been them turning on me instead of the auto-doc.

Aleyk is the only one to reach out, as far as I know. And yet Ianthe and Bryck were there when he was telling me—in his own way—about Amli. So, if they were once in alignment with Zale's plans, perhaps they aren't anymore?

I shake my head. It doesn't matter. They're all stuck here now, and that is not acceptable. Neither is Karl's stated intent to keep "saving" people with desperate families. It's just *wrong*. My motivation doesn't have to be any more complicated than that. Though it's morphed into something else, public service is supposed to be about serving the public. Helping those who have no one to look out for them. Keeping the downtrodden from being further mowed down by those who have more money, more power, and fewer ethical qualms.

Someone needs to speak up for them, the voiceless.

But it can't be me.

The second I poke my head up from hiding, they—Niina, IEA agents, Ayis's people, my own parents—will be all over me. And that'll be the end of it. Possibly the end of me.

I need to find another way.

Still mulling, I pass Winfeld's Inspiration again, aiming for the lift, when a shadow moves at the edge of my vision. *Inside* the display.

I freeze, hands clenching into fists automatically.

My breath shortens as I inch around to look, heart galloping so hard I can feel my pulse in my fingertips.

The darkened window looks the same as always. The train car, the seats, the tech on the table, the window with its false drizzles of rain. But in the far corner, where the fake train car continues, with scenery painted on a backdrop and the blurry, faceless forms of other passengers, that corner seems *too* dark. As if there's someone back there, behind the scenery, and that motion I caught a moment ago was them sliding into place.

Against my better judgment, I edge closer to the display, gaze fixed on that corner, looking for any hint or flicker.

In the protective glass barrier, I catch my own reflection, wide-eyed, pale, too thin, with raggedy, chopped bangs. I barely recognize myself. I look scared. Frail. Alone. Nothing at all like the defender of the public I think—or thought—of myself as. More like the frightened junior staffer that the news reports keep referencing.

Behind me, light flashes abruptly, and I jolt and spin around. The overhead light in the corridor behind me is seizing in a bout of frantic flashing. Another thing to fix.

When I turn to face the display again, the light still blinking, I see that same motion in the corner again—only this time, it's clear. It's a reflection, the shifting light shining on and off again in the glass, creating the illusion of movement.

I let out a breath, the tension in my shoulders easing.

All of Aleyk's weird, ominous talk—not to mention my own nightmares—is getting to me. What did I expect? Karl crawling around behind the display to jump out and scare me? Or maybe the ghost of Zale Winfeld?

Rolling my eyes at myself, I head for the lift. I'll stop on each of the levels in my designated area, perform a cursory check.

But I can't shake the dilemma of what to do, turning the problem over and over in my head as I check SB-1 and SB-2.

Reporting Karl and/or the situation on *Elysian Fields* in general to UNOC authorities might help, but it's also possible that the remnants of the former Winfeld Corporation might have enough power to make the problem "go away." Earth, as a legacy government, still holds seats within New Parliament. It is sometimes a problem.

Unless, of course, I sweeten the deal by offering myself in exchange.

Dumb, Weiller. Where is your leverage? How do you enforce the deal once you've made it and given yourself up?

Niina again. Though in this case, my mental version of her raises a reasonable point.

With a sigh, I keep moving, onto SB-3 now. Maybe I'll stop by and visit with Viviane while I'm here. From the consistent racket on the decks below, it sounds as if Karl hasn't noticed my absence. Metal shrieks against metal at a goose bump–inducing level, and I flinch.

As I pass the darkened vid screen outside Viviane's room, my altered reflection catches my attention again, drawing me in. Her face, my face, is shadow and light, bare glimpses of outlines and shapes. Her eyes, my eyes, are dark pits of emptiness.

What are you hoping for? Waiting for, even? she demands. This version of me seems to stare right into my soul, demanding answers that I don't have or don't want to give. And for once, it's *my* voice in my head and not Niina's.

No one is going to rescue you. No one is coming to pull you free from this mess, clean you up, and set you on your feet again. You made a choice. And running set it in stone. Just because you didn't want to be at the center of everything, telling people what they don't want to hear, what they cannot believe.

"I did it to save people from Ayis," I argue. "My options were limited. Bierhals was the better choice. For everyone."

Please. Can you just accept that you were a big fucking coward? There is no moral defense here. You know it. Is this who you really want to be?

"Fuck you," I snap, then clamp my mouth shut. Jesu, I'm losing my mind, arguing with myself. Even worse, arguing with my own reflection. I don't know how, but that's definitely worse.

Enough. Shaking my head, I push through the door to Viviane's room.

The normalcy of its abnormalcy—a child's room preserved down to the last detail, including said child in a preservation tank—is oddly soothing, more from the routine of visiting here than its actual contents.

I'll figure out what to do, eventually. I just need more time.

I go to drag the rocking chair away from the wall to my usual spot by Viviane's tank but then stop dead at the side of the glass enclosure, my mind swirling.

The little body within is as quiet and motionless as ever. Her slender fingers—bare, with polish-free nails—rest motionless on her upper chest, seeming to reach for a gold locket around her neck. Her black hair, cut in a precise bob with thick bangs, splays out on the pillow on either side of her sunken cheeks. But that red bow is still on top.

"No, no, no," I breathe, releasing the rocker and rushing for a closer look, as if that will change what I'm seeing. Where are the little fingernails with chipping polish? The long brown curls? That locket—that was never there before.

Instinctively, I scrub my palm over the tank's surface to clear it, but there's no dust, no frost impeding my vision. It's not Viviane.

Who is this?

18

Okay, okay. Just breathe.

I crouch down beside the tank, wrapping my arms around my folded knees. My whole body is cold and hot all at the same time, sending shivers racing along my skin while sweat dampens my upper lip.

How am I supposed to "just breathe" when I am obviously losing my mind?

Six, eight hours ago, maybe a little more—I've lost all track of time—I was in this room. And Viviane was . . . Viviane. Not whoever this is.

Except, I didn't go in, then, did I?

I was rushing to get back to the SecOffice to do more poking around. I waved from the corridor, paying absolutely no attention to her tank, other than to see that the tank itself was there. I would have noticed that absence.

How long has it been since I've seen Viviane, since I remember seeing her for certain?

Oh, fuck. I don't know.

Closing my gritty, exhausted eyes, I push my fingertips gently against the lids, as if that will somehow make up for days of sleep deprivation. The darkness and pressure offer a modicum of relief, but I'm no closer to understanding what's going on.

I open my eyes and wait for my vision to clear. *All right. Let's be logical.*

I take a quick peek to make sure the strange girl is still present—yep, still there—and then start breaking down what I know for sure.

Assuming that I haven't experienced a psychotic break—at the moment, I don't think I can count that as certain, but I'm going with it—then Viviane, a resident, is gone, replaced by someone of similar age and size.

But people don't disappear. Especially not cryogenically frozen ones.

Karl. It has to be.

Logic would suggest that if I didn't do anything, then the responsibility must fall with the only other living being on the ship—i.e., the being who is thawed and has a functioning physical body.

That triggers another idea. I stand up, grasping the edge of the tank for balance, and then peer into the tank, searching for details, clues to her identity—and to confirm my own suspicions.

Her skin is pale, fragile-looking, even in this state. Unlike the real Viviane, this imposter's face is thin, no chubby cheeks from childhood. The brow and cheekbones are prominent, as if the flesh has been pulled tight. Her mouth is small and gray, the lips flaking and dried. And beneath the thick and glossy hair, the edge of an ugly scar at her temple.

She looks not only almost dead but *unwell.*

Her stick-thin arms back this up; they're not much more than skin-covered bone. Skin that bears the faint marks of repeated hypo-spray attachments near the shoulder and in her neck.

Son of a bitch. I straighten up. *This is one of Karl's clients.*

I can't guarantee it, and I have no idea why, but Karl must have swapped her out with Viviane. He put her up here and Viviane . . . wherever.

Why? To mess with me? To be a dick?

Fury ignites in me, a boiling hot vat of rage in my chest.

What the fuck, Karl? As if they haven't suffered enough, being frozen in false hope, now he's shuffling them around like decorative vases for funsies?

Or maybe her parents paid more for her to have Viviane's room.

Anger carries me out of Viviane's room, down the corridor, and to the stairs. I pound down past levels SB-4, SB-5, and SB-6, not bothering to hide the clanging of my steps. I doubt he'll hear me coming anyway, with as much noise as he's making.

It sounds more like someone on a rampage—glass shattering, the shrill sound of metal grating against metal, repetitive banging that I can feel through the floor, followed by sudden intermittent crashes that make me jump. I would expect the whine and whir of tools, but maybe he's still demoing . . . something.

I hesitate on the final residential level. A sign points down, indicating the engine room is farther below and Authorized Persons Only beyond this point. There's even a metal chain, painted bright yellow, strung between the railings, blocking the start of the next set of stairs.

Not that that would stop me, but I've been following the sounds of hammering, clattering, and screeching and I can't tell if he's working on this level or farther down.

As answer, a metallic shriek comes from behind the door.

I yank open the door and bat past the construction plastic to enter the corridor.

The smell hits first.

I slap my palm over my nose and mouth to keep from gagging.

It's not hot metal and burning dust, which I might expect in a repair area. Or even the stuffy absence of circulating air.

No, it smells like something died down here. Like, actually died. Rot. Rotting. That thick mildewy aroma that comes from moisture and decay.

Oh, shit. Maybe one of the tanks failed. That would explain Karl's urgency in repairs.

For a moment I almost turn back, to avoid interrupting.

But then I stop. It doesn't matter. Failing tank or not, that's no excuse to do whatever he did to Viviane. Her tank was fine, clearly, judging by the new occupant within it.

I charge down the corridor, past closed doors. This floor is nearly identical to all the other residential levels I've been on.

Except it seems dimmer here. The overhead lights are on but only every other one. And the dark ones appear to be missing entirely, wiring hanging out of a hole in the ceiling. Part of Karl's work, maybe?

Then, on the floor ahead of me, I pick out a lumpy, amorphous shape pressed against the wall between two rooms.

I slow to a stop, my mind combining the shape and the shadows and extrapolating an oversize rat. Not an infrequent sight on EnExx17.

But when it doesn't move, I edge closer. Now I can see the twists and turns in the fabric that tell me it's not a rat but discarded clothing in a twisted and grimy pile. A shirt, maybe, torn and shredded, soaked once and now dried stiff with a dark red substance.

Blood. Right? It has to be blood.

Or some kind of engine fluid you're not familiar with. Come on, let's keep it together and be rational here. What's more likely?

I leave the shirt behind and keep going. The putrid scent is growing stronger. I yank my shirt up over my nose and mouth to help filter it out. Can that be from one bad tank?

Right before I round the corner to the other half of the corridor, I find a half-open door. The resident's room beyond is in shadow, but the smell is oppressive here, like a physical force pushing me to retreat.

The tank is tilted on its side on the floor, the occupant spilled out.

A mixed puddle of bodily fluids, indeterminate organ bits, and flesh—solids, semisolids, and liquids—spreads outward from the tank's lip. At the center of it, the resident, facedown.

He or she is mostly a skeleton but covered in wet patches of flesh in places. Like the bottom of the feet, portions of the back, and the scalp with a long braid still attached, though the scalp has slid down to rest on the shoulders.

I stumble back out of the room before stomach acid scorches up the back of my throat and out. Crouching and choking, I spit it out onto the floor and brace myself against the wall as dry heaves come on. And I can still smell *it*, even over the scent of vomit and with my nose running.

When my stomach calls a tentative truce, I let go of the wall, bending over to press my hands on my knees, panting to catch my breath.

There's one question louder than all the others in my head: *How long?*

How long has the resident been in this state for it to get this bad?

Oh, and *Where the* fuck *is Karl?*

From the opposite end of the corridor, around the corner, faint shuffling noises and murmurs drift toward me.

Seriously? There's something more important than addressing the issue in—I check the door; down here among the non-famous, the rooms are numbered—room seventeen?

Wiping my mouth, I straighten up. With the inside of my elbow pressed against my nose and mouth, I move on. "Karl!" I shout, but my voice is muffled.

When I round the corner to the other half of the floor, I find more of the same. Open doors. Even dimmer lighting. Only one light on for every three fixtures.

"Karl!" I call again through my covered mouth. "Where are you?"

My boot connects with something hard on the floor, and it skitters ahead of me from the force of my accidental kick. I squint, following it from the edge of the light into the next pool of shadow. White, curved, like a bent stick with all the bark removed.

I frown, starting to bend down for a closer look.

But then motion catches my eye. Down the hall, on my left, in an open doorway. It takes me a second to understand what I'm seeing, it's so out of place. Near the baseboard, a hand, fingers extended, is waving at me, but from the floor. The palm is up, shifting back and forth on the inoffensive beige tile, as if trying to summon me closer.

What the hell?

Did Karl fall and hurt himself?

I hurry toward the hand, but something still feels . . . off. I'm not sure what it is. *Maybe because no one really moves like that unless they're trying to be a dick and creep you—*

I stop short of the threshold. Closer now, I can see that the hand is smaller, more delicate than mine. Definitely not Karl's. The perfectly shaped nails are a pale blue. Not polish, but the actual color of the flesh beneath.

Also, the hand is not actually waving but more like sliding toward me, being pushed by a force within the room. And from within the room come meaty snuffling sounds, like a dog rooting through trash.

My heartbeat accelerates until I can feel it in my fingertips. *No, no, no. This is* wrong! *Something is wrong. Go, now!*

But, as always, I'm constitutionally incapable of fucking letting it go. As everyone in my life—Niina, my parents, my college boyfriend Mika—has told me at one point or another.

But isn't it always better to know what you're dealing with? To have a functional grip on the reality surrounding you?

Without moving any closer, I tilt my upper body forward far enough to see around the doorframe.

The first thing that catches my attention is the tank—flipped on its side at an angle, with drag marks marring the floor. It's empty except for the small puddle of water within and spilling out onto the floor.

Then my gaze skips over the center of the room to the tank's resident, lying on her back, one arm stretched over her head into the corridor. Her "waving" hand is nearly at my feet. Her eyes, distant and unfocused, stare up at me, except when she blinks. Her silvery hair is tangled underneath her head. But, oh, God.

At her torso, in her belly, *something* is moving, digging.

A small noise escapes me before I can stop it.

My mind can't parse it at first, make it make sense. At first I see it all as part of her body, as if she has a growth of some sort emerging from her abdomen, shaking and trembling.

That would be bad enough.

But then that "growth" raises its head and looks at me with white, cataract-filled eyes. What I took as a growth is a head, a separate entity. Balding, scraggly hair, decaying nose more slits than cartilage.

It's a person. Or it was. It is an awful, decaying mess of what might be a former human, with limbs that don't bend in the right places. It's what I saw at the foot of my bed, the thing I thought was a nightmare. And it is—except it's *real*.

The only difference now is that its mouth is ringed in dark red blood. Roughly matching the size and shape of the hole in the resident's belly, through which grayish intestinal tubes now trail.

I can't move. My body is in revolt, incapable of reacting to the stimuli my brain is taking in. It's like that moment when you trip and fall unexpectedly, say on a runway to a shuttle, and your mind has just enough time to wonder if this is really happening.

The remnants of its nose, skin flaps near the nasal cavities, twitch, as if picking up a scent.

Oh, shit.

Maybe it can't see me with those messed-up eyes, but it can smell me.

It rises to its feet. No, that's not right. The feet, human-looking but for a few stumps where toes should be, actually dangle above the ground, not making contact with the floor.

Instead, two char-black limbs emerge from the back of the legs, and they end in clawlike feet that scratch against the floor as it shifts position. The arms are much the same; a second set of matching black ones with the same deadly-looking claws poke through the underside of the human arms, leaving those to dangle mostly uselessly.

It's like . . . it's wearing a person costume. But the human head, the mouth, that's still the one chewing, eating, strings of bloody saliva dangling from its lower lip, as it sniffs the air.

A ponderous human belly, ridiculously overproportioned, seems to impede its balance, as it sways slightly. *He*. As *he* sways. The belly is not quite large enough to hide the shriveled penis and scrotum below.

Run. RUN!

Finally, my brain and body sync up, and I turn and bolt on trembling legs.

A shrieky roar of rage echoes in the corridor. I have enough presence of mind to register that the sound is familiar. But most of me is focused on the rapid *click-clack*ing now approaching me from behind. The strange human–whatever hybrid is running. It's fucking running and it's fast. Gaining on me, despite my head start and its ungainly shape.

You're not going to make it.

As I round the corner to the other half of the corridor, I have a split second to make a decision. In that brief moment, I can see how it's all going to play out. It's going to catch up to me before I reach the door to the stairs. And no prizes for guessing what happens after that.

Death smells you. Aleyk's cryptic message comes back to me, along with the creeptastic visual of that thing's flaring nostrils.

In the end, it's instinct, a hope and a prayer, more than any solid plan.

I dive into room seventeen. My feet immediately slip and slide in the puddle of decaying innards, and I start to fall. I catch myself by landing hands-first in that same goo. The smell that rises up immediately makes my throat curl up into itself and threatens to hold me in place with the need to vomit.

But apparently the desire to survive is stronger than even disgust. I throw myself behind the overturned tank right as the rapid *click-click*ing of taloned feet reaches the doorway.

Through a seam in the tank infrastructure, where the lid meets the tank when it's closed, I have a slim line of sight, enough to see it run past, human legs dangling and shaking with the movement.

But it doesn't go far.

I hear it stop, the thick and wheezy sound of its breathing, and then the slow tapping of its claws on the floor as it returns.

When it appears in the doorway, I duck down even farther, crouching in my newly acquired filth.

That snuffling noise comes again, and I imagine it has its nose up again, trying to smell me through the stench of rotting resident.

I have no idea how smart this creature is, how human, despite its appearance. A human would immediately search any open rooms or try the doors to see if they were unlocked and therefore might be hiding someone within.

But something that relies on scent? I don't know.

I'm hoping the deteriorating body in front of me works to cover me.

Endless seconds pass, with it sniffing and me holding perfectly still, except for the drumming of my heart and the smallest inhales and exhales I can manage without passing out.

"Go," a soft voice, creaky with age and exertion, says finally. "Food. Need."

I remain motionless. Is that . . . the human costume speaking? Is he speaking to me? Or the monster wearing him?

Eventually, it retreats, moving away from the door and farther down the hallway, the harsh clacking of its nails getting quieter as it moves away.

I keep still; I'm not stupid. This could be a trap. Also, I'm not sure I can run. I feel weak, limp with relief and wound up with terror. I'm equally safe and trapped, like a rabbit that's found sanctuary in a shady corner, hidden by brush.

Or a tiny fish, right before she gets eaten.

Fuck.

I push to my feet, carefully, slowly. From the corridor, those same distant, wet chewing sounds resume. I want to gag, but if I start I know I won't stop. And there's no way to vomit quietly.

Ignore it. Move now.

I take a tentative step out from behind the tank, but even with the utmost care, my boot connecting with the floor makes a sound. A faint scrape and click.

I freeze, listening, but I can barely hear anything over the blood rushing in my ears. I have no idea how well this thing hears. I was shouting for Karl before and it didn't come running, but it might have been distracted by the . . . food. That's what he called it. The body, the woman.

My eyes water. *Not now. Go.*

I start to take another slow step but then stop myself. If I creep along at this pace, it might get bored or even be done eating before I reach the stairs. I cannot take that chance.

With a grimace, I reach down and tug one boot off, then another, leaving me in socked feet, worn cotton absorbing the various smears of things I don't care to think about on the floor.

But my steps now are whisper quiet.

I tiptoe to the doorway, boots in hand. I can't see around the curve, but this portion of the corridor is empty.

Commit. Waffling is going to get you killed. A lesson from Niina. You can't be wishy-washy if you need to get something done. Apparently this is true whether convincing everyone that you had nothing to do with certain pivotal news-making events or running from something that looks like a creature of the night that villagers would have chased after with pitch-forks and torches four centuries ago.

Taking a deep breath, I step out. Part of me is braced for an attack, a sudden launching at my back. But nothing happens.

So I move. Not quite running, because I'm afraid my feet will slap against the smooth floor, even with the barrier of my socks. But the problem now is that I can't hear behind me very well, not over the sounds of my own motion, faster breathing, fabric rubbing. I can't tell if it's still down the hall eating.

But it's not running after me—at least not yet. The *clickety-clack* of the nails would not be something I could miss.

With every door I pass, I feel the pressure growing, the tension between hope that I've made it and fear that it's getting closer and I can't look over my shoulder.

But I'm also that much closer to stairwell access and a way out of this nightmare. Stairwell access, which is covered in construction plastic. Noisy, noisy plastic.

I slow for a second, staring at the translucent material draped all around the door. *Motherfucker.*

There is no way to get through that undetected. And going back for the elevator . . . I picture myself frantically pushing the button while watching that hand moving again.

No.

Okay, okay, so I'll do the only thing I can. Run.

Heart pounding, knees shaking, I throw myself full speed toward the door for the last ten feet of the corridor, bursting through the plastic sheeting and the stairwell door beyond it.

I start to bolt up the stairs—my only goal known safety—but a flash of yellow catches my attention.

The chain barricading the stairs to the levels below.

I pause, and without letting myself take time to analyze it to death, I follow my impulse. Dropping my boots, I unhook the chain from the far side of the railing and wind it around the door handle, once, twice, and then connect its links on the other side.

Now the chain is barricading the door. Temporarily at least. I scoop up my boots and take off up the stairs.

19

The whole way, I'm expecting to hear the resounding thuds of that abomination trying to break through the door. Or the click-scrape of it chasing me.

Instead, the silence around me feels thick and ominous. Like I'm missing something obvious. Some other route it's pursuing.

Immediately the image of that dangling vent cover above the desk in Zale's study pops to mind. The bare toe prints in the dust. The noises that I hear in the walls . . .

My still healing ribs are throbbing and my muscles burn like I'm on fire, but I push a little harder. Legs and arms pumping, I climb as fast as I can until I reach the main exhibition level, then bolt down the endless-feeling corridor and into the Sec-Office.

I slam the door behind me, flick the now seemingly insubstantial lock from the inside, and drop to my knees, panting and dizzy.

I made it.

Did I? Or did I trap myself in a corner with no other way out? *Stupid, Halley.*

I'll eventually have to leave for food, for water, to get the fuck off this ship. But if that thing is waiting for me on the other side of the door . . .

I lever myself up and over to the control board, shoving the chair out of the way.

The screens still flick through their various views of the floors I'm responsible for, including the main exhibition level.

I stare at it, waiting. One minute, then two. My breathing slows, returns to a slightly accelerated version of normal. The sweat from my panicked escape turns cold and sticky. The smell from my clothes grows thicker and more disgusting until I can't seem to smell anything at all.

But the corridor outside the SecOffice remains as empty and still as ever. The vent covers out there and in here are still firmly in place.

Did I lose it? I frown, scanning the screens for the other floors in my section.

Nothing there either. I don't understand. Why *isn't* it chasing me? What do I not know?

Or maybe you're actually losing it. As in, your mind.

I squeeze my eyes shut tight against the familiar surge of panic and bitterness. I know what I saw.

And what exactly was that? A monster from your nightmares? Something that can't possibly exist? A person but not. Like that old saying about the wolf in sheep's clothing. Only this time, it's, what, a wolf in human clothing?

A hysterical giggle escapes me before I clamp my hand over my mouth.

Those limbs and claws were definitely not of the canine variety. They were like nothing I'd ever seen before. Black, shiny, with their *click-click-click* sounds.

I shudder.

Maybe something like an oversize beetle or roach, but person-size. Something . . . *alien.*

I don't even want to think the word; it's the realm of fairy tales, superstition, and conspiracy theories from centuries ago. We know better than that now; we've never found any sign of intelligent—

"Yo, Halley!" a voice calls through the speaker.

I jump at the intrusion.

Karl.

I go still, and then pivot toward the control board. Karl is on screen. From where I'm standing, I can see a sliver of his face. Beard all fuzzy and sticking out in various directions. Dark smudges along the side of his face.

Shit. He knows, doesn't he? He *has* to know that bizarro Frankensteinian creation is running around the ship. How could he miss it? If not the creature itself, the . . . mess it leaves behind.

But what is Karl's role? Is he ignoring the situation? Or helping out, like a Renfield to someone's Dracula?

And does he know that *I* now know?

"Halllley," he says in a singsong voice. "I know you're there. I can see your arm, you drongo."

I stay where I am.

Karl's the one who told me I was imagining it when I saw that creature on the screens that first day. If he knew, then he was lying to me. For what purpose, I have no idea, but if I confront him about it, start asking questions that I shouldn't, this is going to escalate. Fast.

"What?" I push impatience into my voice. "I'm busy." I step sideways, closer to the screen, so he can see more of me, but hopefully not the mess still clinging to my left hand and down that side of my clothing.

"Yeah, I can see that." He raises his brows at me, leaving a silence for me to fill.

What, what did you see? I squash the impulse to babble, to come up with a lie. That's a total beginner move. I wait, giving him raised eyebrows right back.

Eventually he sighs in exasperation, fiddling with something off screen. "You were late with the button."

I almost laugh. *Now* he cares about the button? Rushing down here to press the button feels like a century ago.

"Yeah. I was." Don't give any more information than necessary. No explanations, no apologies, not until you see where it's going.

He eyes me suspiciously. "I told you to stay out of the theater."

That surprises me enough that I speak before I can stop myself. "I wasn't!" I mean, I was earlier, but that's not why I was late. Does he really not know what I've been up to, poking around upstairs first and then on the lower levels?

My genuine reaction seems to assuage him, and he visibly relaxes. "I'm serious. You can't be late with that shit. Get it together, okay?"

Or else you'll fire me? Use me as food? The carvings on the floor in my quarters upstairs, the superstitious protection marks left by my predecessor, flash into my mind. Suddenly they make a whole new kind of sense. Someone before me, they saw something. I'd bet my life on it.

I nod, neck tight. "Got it." Through clenched teeth, I make myself continue. "Sorry. Won't happen again."

Karl cocks his head to one side, eyes narrowed. "What's wrong with you? You seem . . . off."

Uh-oh. "In case you haven't noticed, my entire life is blowing up all over the news streams," I snap. "Also, I'm being blackmailed *by you,* losing my mind because I don't get any sleep, and the only people I have to talk to are my blackmailer and a partially functioning hologram. What's *not* wrong?" The best lies contain as much truth as possible. And going on the offense is always preferable to being caught flat-footed and trying to defend.

Karl doesn't respond for a moment, his jaw visibly tense.

Oh, fuck. Should I not have pushed? Maybe I shouldn't have mentioned Aleyk. I don't even know if Karl knows he's there. Or what Aleyk really is.

But then Karl gives a huff of faux exasperation. "Blackmail? Please. I'm simply making sure we maintain a mutually beneficial situation for as long as it's feasible for both of us." He gives me that wolfish grin.

And his teasing tone grates. *Where is Viviane, you asshole?*

I want to demand. *What did you do to her? Are these people in the tanks alive still? What is running around downstairs eating people?*

Alien, alien, alien, a soft voice in my head chants.

"Yeah, yeah, whatever," I say tightly.

"Forty-three minutes," he says, raising his bare wrist so I can see it on screen. He taps at it with his finger, and it takes me a second to understand the antiquated gesture.

Time. As in, almost time to push the button again.

"I got it, ok—" I begin.

Karl's face vanishes from the screen before the words are even completely out of my mouth.

The silence of SecOffice feels loud and thick around me, after Karl's blustery condescension.

Now what?

I fumble in my pocket for my holocomm. The second I have enough signal, I'm hiring a transport, somewhere, anywhere.

But that woman . . .

I close my eyes, focusing on the few seconds I glimpsed of her before I was distracted by everything else.

Amli Browning. I'm fairly sure that is . . . was her. Silver hair, longer than in her picture. Bright blue eyes open, staring up at me.

Blinking.

My eyes snap open. I saw her *blink.* What the fuck? Everything I've read about cryogenics indicates that people cannot be woken from it successfully. The cells are too damaged from the freezing process. That's why it fell out of favor. No one could it get to work.

It's possible, I guess, that I, in a moment of terror and shock, imagined it. Conjured it out of thin air because that's what I expected, kind of like how it sometimes looks like the bodies in the tanks are breathing when I don't stare at them straight on.

But what if it wasn't my imagination? What if Zale Winfeld had some kind of secret recipe for cryonics that offered a different outcome and he didn't bother to share? What would that mean for all the people on this ship? What would that mean for Viviane, wherever she is? Could they all still be saved?

None of *that* seems impossible to me now, given what I know about Aleyk and Svalbard.

Aleyk. My heart gives an extra pulse in empathy. He's trapped here. Forever. Until *Elysian Fields*'s central system finally collapses or the ship itself is destroyed.

I can't leave him behind. I won't.

That is not who I am, not who I want to be.

Besides, it's not as if my circumstances outside *Elysian Fields* have improved. I'm going to get caught, and I might still end up dead, albeit in a far more mundane—and pleasant, if such a term can be applied to any method of dying—way.

I let go of my holocomm, leaving it in my pocket.

This is ridiculous. A completely illogical and entirely emotion-based decision.

Just because you feel something doesn't make it real. One of my mother's favorite life lessons, usually when I was upset about something.

She's right. But that doesn't mean I should ignore it, either. Most of her work involves manipulating emotions. She, of all people, should know better than to discount feelings.

And right now, this *feels* right. A piece that I've been avoiding finally clicking into its place, resulting in a wave of relief, oddly. Of certainty, which I haven't had in a long time.

I take a deep breath, instantly regret it, given the lingering stench on me, now in the room, and then cough it out.

So, okay, I'm going to stay here and find out what's going on, how I can help the residents, people who have no one looking out for them. No one keeping them safe from whatever that was—a failed experiment started at Zale's behest, perhaps?

I flinch, hoping that Amli wasn't aware or that if she was, she couldn't feel anything. I can't imagine the horror of waking up to find yourself on the ground in a strange place, with teeth tugging and ripping at your belly and being too weak or unable to scream for help.

I shake my head to dismiss the mental image.

Great. You're going to help them. And how *are you going to do that?*

That is an excellent question. I pace the available space of the SecOffice, thinking. Obviously I'm a little out of my depth here. And it's not like I can reach out for help. Even *I* wouldn't believe me.

But researching, getting as much information as possible, has never hurt anything. I can dig more deeply into the thousands of files on the system in here, maybe. Or even venture back upstairs to Zale's office, though I doubt I'll find anything so obvious as a folder named "Cryogenics Trade Secrets" or "Faulty Lab Creations."

Still, asking questions, peeling back layers, fitting the pieces into place—I'm good at that, I can do that. It's the way I approached everything at the PM's office when tasked with something I'd never done before and everyone else was too busy to show me.

Say yes, assume confidence, and then figure it out.

I step back to the control board, checking the feeds; still no sign in the corridors of . . . anything.

Okay, so a plan. First things first. If the SecOffice is the most secure place to be, with a door that locks and screens that show me what's coming, maybe I need to relocate my essentials and stock up in here. My quarters upstairs are definitely no longer mine. That *thing*—"hybrid" does seem to be the most accurate, the horrific abomination of man and . . . something else—was in my room. At the foot of my bed.

And that scrape on the top of my foot? I'm pretty sure I narrowly escaped waking up without a toe or three. Or maybe the cut happened because I jolted and pulled away. Either way, sharp teeth near my extremities while I'm sleeping is a no-go.

I shudder, imagining that wake-up call, blood spurting every-where and agony radiating up my leg. If I got to wake up at all.

Then, if the relocation part goes okay (aka I'm not attacked or killed), it's on to step two. Which means venturing farther away from the SecOffice.

My hands tingle painfully with an onrush of anxiety as I contemplate opening the door again, moving freely through the corridor and into an open, darkened space where I won't be able to easily see danger approaching.

I shake my hands, left then right, clenching them and releasing them, trying to restore blood flow.

But there's nothing to be done. If time is of the essence, I can't spend it meandering through piles of old data again, especially when I don't even know what I'm looking for. I need some direction. And only one person on this ship has been here from the beginning, or damn near it. And he clearly has some answers, even if he can't easily communicate them.

Death smells you. Aleyk's expression, so desperate, so earnest.

Yeah, I get it now, Aleyk. I grimace. He must have been so frustrated with me waltzing out of there, assuming that I knew everything. Assuming that *he* was the one with the malfunction.

Now, at least, I know better.

20

Dead body goo has to be a health hazard, beyond the aesthetic and olfactory concerns.

Don't need to be a medical professional or an auto-doc to know that.

So my first stop upstairs is the wash-fac. Actually, my first stop is one of the empty rooms down the hall, the one with the discarded IV 'bot. It's a matter of a few seconds' work—maybe a little longer, due to constantly keeping a lookout toward the corridor and jumping at every click, creak, and pop—to unscrew the long metal pole from the 'bot base. Its friendly eyes roll and wobble at me as I pull it free. The pole is pathetic as a weapon, but better than nothing.

And it serves to hold the door closed in the wash-fac, when I brace it between the edge of the handle hardware and the floor. It may not last against a thorough drumming from the outside, but I'll hear the clanging of the pole hitting the floor so I won't be caught unaware while naked and dripping wet.

I feel like I'm holding my breath the whole time in the tiny shower cubicle, caught between scrubbing intensely and trying to listen past the sound of the uneven patter of the water falling out of the corroded shower head to the distorted and broken tile floor.

After I'm cleaned up, I use the same technique with the pole on my room door, while I stuff a change of clothes and a blanket haphazardly into my bag, fabric poking out the top. A quick stop at the galley to add all the food and water I can carry—with the former IV pole in my other hand as a staff—and I'm out of there.

Every second I'm away from the SecOffice feels like one second closer to another inevitable encounter with that multi-limbed monster, the tension winding tighter and tighter around me until I'm practically running down the stairs, out-of-shape muscles protesting at the additional bout of exertion.

But I make it back to the SecOffice, door shut and locked behind me, without incident, something that only makes my dread increase instead of slacken. More and more, I'm convinced that I'm missing important facts or details. If this hybrid is a mindless being simply in search of its next meal, why not come after me? Granted, the . . . "meal" in front of it probably qualified as an easier bet. I grimace. Poor Amli.

But why not before now? It obviously knew I was here. It was in my room, staring down at me while I slept. Jagged teeth positioned over my vulnerable body.

Jesu. The skin on my back prickles, sending chills over my whole body.

So, I can't stay, no matter how comforting the SecOffice feels now with its solid door, stale air, scent of overheated plastic, and worn leather chair that gives off a permanently dejected air as bits of foam stuffing break off around the exposed edges.

I put everything down, pushing it to the far corner of the small space so as not to impede the door if I need to get inside quickly. Then I wait the remaining few minutes for the alarm on my holocomm to go off for my next set of rounds.

When it does, I press the button, starting the endless cycle over again to keep Karl off my back. It's possible that ignoring the button might cause the board to send the authorities. But I'm betting Karl will intervene before that happens. Better to keep him believing I'm being a good little meat puppet for now.

I grab the IV pole and check the monitor for the corridor outside. The relative brightness of the screen sends stabbing pain through my eyes and the top of my head. At some point, I'm going to need to stop for sleep; my head hurts, my eyes feel too big in my skull, and everything has taken on that strange surreality that comes with being awake for too long. Like when the floor is shaking and tilting and you can't tell if it's a grav generator beginning to fail or you.

Flicking the lock back, I tighten my sweaty grip on the pole and then open the door to the corridor. Again, nothing.

What the fuck? I don't get this.

I scurry down the corridor, feeling both foolish and exposed.

The theater doors wait, but this time it feels like approaching an oracle. Or one of those shadowy storefronts on the lower levels of EnExx17, draped in tattered fabrics from the exchange and emblazoned with the promise of knowing your future. In exchange for hard credits, of course.

I grab one of the ornate, grapevine handles and pull.

Inside, the theater is dim and still.

"Aleyk?" I call in a soft voice.

No response.

Come on, not now.

I pause at the back of the theater long enough to recognize my new trick for securing the doors isn't going to work here. The doors open outward and the only hardware on this side is a set of flat metal panels set into the wood.

A hundred-plus seats in dozens of rows, thickly coated in shadow. The floor space between the rows might as well be a tunnel on the dark side of the moon. I can't see anything.

I might be in here alone. Or not.

How funny. Only hours ago, I would have traipsed in blithely, shouting for Aleyk without thinking twice about it.

Now, all I can see is the danger lurking everywhere.

In the end, I go with my instinct. If it hasn't hidden in here before to attack me, why would it start now?

I lean the pole carefully up against the seam between the doors, where it will fall and clatter if they open.

Then I turn and stalk down the aisle, eating up the thick carpeted surface in larger than normal strides and sticking as close to the open center as I can. I still half expect a blackened claw to reach out and snag me as I pass.

But it doesn't.

"Aleyk," I whisper loudly as I approach the stage. "I need your help."

Silence.

"Aleyk. Please!" I clench my fists as I reach the stage. Holding still feels risky, so I find myself shifting my weight from foot to foot, like a runner at a starting line. "I don't understand what's happening. I saw . . . something. And I don't know—"

To my utter humiliation, my voice breaks, and a sudden stinging hits my already burning eyes.

No. I shake my head fiercely. *I will not cry. I'm overly tired. That's it.*

It's not at all about me being left alone, again, to deal with the repercussions of an experience that should have been *impossible.*

You know better than to trust. Better than to count on—

The spotlight above flickers faintly, on and off in rapid succession, before steadying.

A relieved exhale whooshes out of me before I can stop it.

Aleyk emerges a moment later, stepping around the curtain.

"I'm so glad to see you. I don't know who else . . . Well, there is no one else," I babble nervously. "Something happened. Something bad. I was in Viviane's room. I don't know if you know her. I mean, I know you don't know her, but—" I stop myself.

Get it together, Halley. You've presented to the prime minister and colony governors before with less stress.

Then again, none of them were Aleyk. And I wasn't facing being eaten as a consequence of failure.

I draw in a deep breath. "I'm going to start over." But then I clock a better look at his expression. "What's wrong?" I ask.

His face is impassive. Blank. No, empty. That one errant curl dangles over his forehead but he makes no move to push it back. He simply stands there. Staring out at the empty theater.

My heart sinks.

"Aleyk."

His gaze eventually drifts down toward me, but it's as if he's staring through me to the first row of seats behind me.

Oh, no, no, no. "Aleyk. I need you to focus," I say in the same voice I used to get the new interns to listen to me, an authority figure not much older than they were. Only this time I'm shoving down growing panic and despair at the same time. "I need you to tell me what you know."

His blue eyes, still bright in color but utterly flat and lifeless, stare back at me.

Did he give up or did the ancient system finally crash? I'm not even getting the cut-up syllables in response.

"Aleyk. Please. I found Amli. But I couldn't . . . I couldn't save her. If that's what you were trying to tell me." I draw in a breath steadying myself for the next part. "I saw it. I think it's what you call Death. It was *eating* her. He consumes, right? That's what you said to me."

A shudder runs through him, a ripple from head to toe that turns his resolution blurry, as if he's seconds from vanishing altogether.

I reach up, grasping the only part of him I can reach, locking my fingers carefully around his ankle.

His focus seems to sharpen on me, and I resist the urge to pull back.

"Stay with me. I need help. I don't know how to stop this. And I think . . . I think it's coming for me." I glance back over my shoulder, involuntarily. I can't see the pole in the darkness, but I haven't heard the clatter and clang of it falling. Not yet.

He shudders again, only this time it's localized to his upper body. His face shifts, distorts, his mouth bulging.

Instead of being afraid or disgusted, as I was the first time, I welcome the change. Whatever this is, whatever this represents, I know what it means. Aleyk is fighting to free himself.

I keep my grip on his leg firm. "I'm here. I'm right here," I say, over and over again.

It takes longer this time, but eventually the skin splits, a jagged line from his lips up through his forehead, and a slimy hand emerges from his former mouth, followed by the length of an arm, draped in dripping wet sleeve.

The outer version of him bends at the waist, and through the broken-open head, I see a shoulder and Aleyk's damp curls emerging.

"Yes! Keep going!" I have no idea whether my presence or encouragement makes a difference, but I'm willing to try.

But then . . . then he starts to slip back down. The arm retracts back inside, his shoulder vanishing, then the elbow. The hand will be next.

Instinctively, I let go of his leg and scramble up onto the stage to grasp his hand before it vanishes within the gaping, uneven chasm.

His fingers tighten around mine, individual points of pressure.

"I'm here. I'm here," I whisper.

I don't dare pull. I have no idea if it would help or make things worse. This is a metaphoric battle, I'm fairly sure, between Aleyk and whatever controls have been set in place on him. I don't want to break him or screw this up by interfering more than I already have.

Slowly the process begins to reverse itself. His arm reemerges. Then his shoulder, then his head.

My heart thrums at hummingbird speed. Trying not to think too much about this bizarre spectacle I'm witnessing, I back up slowly, carefully avoiding the gridwork of technology on the stage, giving him space as he . . . births himself out of himself.

Jesu. I shake my head.

Eventually, after excruciating minutes, Aleyk collapses onto the floor in front of me, wet and exhausted. The split-open shell of himself staggers backward and away, stumbling and swaying, before vanishing entirely.

The emergency lights stutter, and I catch my breath, waiting for them to go out, but after a moment, they stabilize and grow brighter.

I kneel down next to Aleyk, where he lies facedown on the stage. "Are you okay?" A stupid question to ask of a hologram, and yet I can't stop myself.

He lifts his head an inch or two from the ground, blinks up at me, eyes squinting as if in deference to the brightness. "Did he see you?"

I pull back slightly. "What? What do you mean?"

With a groan, he pushes himself over onto his back. His image wavers and shudders, adjusting in real time, until he appears solid again. "When you caught him feeding?"

I'm taken aback for a moment by his questions, complete with actual words instead of pieced-together phrases and syllables.

"You're talking again," I say dumbly.

Aleyk gestures to where the shell of himself vanished. "The controls. I managed to break through. This time." He sounds grim, determined. "Now, did he see you?"

Oh. "I . . ." I hesitate. I don't know how to answer that. "The eyes . . . they don't look functional. Filmy, white, and I—"

"Did he follow you?" Aleyk sounds more alert, tension thrumming through him. He heaves himself into a sitting position, with an audible sound of effort. But he already looks better than moments ago. His shirt is dried, transformed to the work-dirtied white I'm used to seeing, rather than the sopping wet fabric. His hair is restored to its glorious rumpled state instead of plastered to his skull. I didn't even glimpse it happening; one second it was wet, the next dry.

"Yes," I admit, feeling shame, as though I've done something wrong, though I have no idea *why*. "Until I ducked into a room where a resident was . . . decaying. Outside the tank." I shake my head, still in disbelief, both at what I'd seen *and* what I'd done.

"Not up to full strength, then," he says, more to himself than me.

I gape at him. "What the hell is happening?" I demand. "What is that thing? Some kind of experiment gone wrong?"

"Of a sort." His mouth tightens. "I never should have gotten you involved."

"Which time?" I snap.

He grimaces and closes his eyes for a second. "You were a child. That was wrong of me. But you were the only one listening, actually paying attention, and I was desperate to—" He jerks his head, cutting himself off. Bright blue eyes snap open, fixing on me. "You need to leave. Barricade yourself in the security office until you can summon a shuttle. It might not be too late, if you hurry. I never wanted this for you. For *anyone*."

"I don't understand. Too late for *what*?" Anger *snikts* to life in me, the striking of one friction plate against another. "You do not get to tell me to run and not explain any of this! There are people . . ." My throat works involuntarily over a lump of emotion. "I think some of these people are still alive, even after they're unfrozen. I saw Amli blink, and I don't—"

"I know." Aleyk looks away, running his hand through his hair wearily. "I know."

Horror slip-slides around in me. He knew. He knew that people were trapped in here, along with him and that creature, and he said nothing? For how many years?

A sickening feeling swoops over me. All this time, I've been seeing him as a victim, or at the very least as an innocent bystander. Could I have gotten it that wrong?

"*What* do you know?" I get to my feet, folding my arms across my chest, towering over him on the floor of the narrow stage. "Because I've been trying to work it out, and I've concluded that nothing makes any sense. Least of all, that *monstrosity* that you seem to be awful fucking chummy with."

His head shoots up, and he glares at me. "I am not"—his brow furrows momentarily—"*chummy* with him."

"Then why do you—"

"I haven't been on speaking terms with my father in years. Even before all of this." Aleyk lifts his hand in a vague gesture, presumably to indicate *Elysian Fields* as a whole.

That matches my information, from the research I've done over the years. But it's also a hell of a non sequitur. Before I can point that out, Aleyk continues.

"That doesn't mean I don't understand him, though." He pauses. "Whatever is left of him, at any rate."

I stare at him in a mix of confusion and irritation, even as a yawning chasm opens up in my middle. "I don't understand." My voice comes out too small, too weak. I hate it.

But Aleyk is undeterred. "Of course you do. On some level anyway," he says. "You're too smart to have missed the inevitable conclusion." He smiles up at me, wistful and sad, which twists something distant in my chest region.

My mouth trembles. "I don't . . . I can't . . ." I'm backing away, as if that will stop this chain of events from crashing into me.

"If you need me to say it, I will," Aleyk says gently.

No! Stop! But my protests remain silent, stuck in my head.

Aleyk locks eyes with me. "That 'monstrosity,' as you so accurately and charmingly referred to him, is what remains of Zale Winfeld."

21

An unhinged-sounding laugh bursts out of me, and I clamp a hand over my mouth. I have to resist the urge to count backward by threes from one hundred, another test to see if I'm still awake, still lucid.

"That's not possible," I say. In my head, I compare the deteriorating face, with the patchy scalp, nose flaps, and missing ears, to the iconic images of the man himself, plastered all over the Hall of News, gift shop items, and history texts.

The original Zale was on the shorter side, a little bulky through the middle, but someone who moved with the confidence and ease of a man who'd never heard—or never accepted—no as an answer. That's part of the mythos surrounding him. Zale Winfeld—a masterful mind, a tech genius, a bit of douche, in the old vernacular, but also a towering presence, both mentally and physically.

"That has . . . there are claws . . . these weird extra arms and legs," I splutter.

Aleyk lifts his shoulder in a shrug, as if to ask *What do you want me to say?*

"Even if it . . . even if he was part of some experiment." I shake my head, hoping to jostle this conversation into making sense. "There's no way. He'd have died of old age years ago." Not to mention, who would undergo surgery to do *that* to themselves? "He was what fifty-, sixtysomething when he started *Elysian Fields*?"

"Sixty-three," Aleyk says quietly. "Absolutely terrified of death and in possession of far too much capital and too little humility."

"It's not possible," I say again, stubborn to the end. "Even the most successful life-extending procedures only add maybe a decade or two. Even if he replaced every joint, every organ, it wouldn't work! He'd be over two hundred years old."

Aleyk nods. "Sounds right." He stands, and then starts forward, inching me toward the edge of the stage.

"That doesn't make sense!" I say, backing away. The shrill note in my voice makes me cringe.

He smiles at me, again in that wistful way. "You'd prefer not to see it, which, frankly, is far more sensible. I can't blame you for that. Unfortunately, sense is not the only factor at play here. And right now, the best thing you can do is get off this ship."

My heels reach the edge of the stage, and I'm in danger of teetering off onto the floor below.

He closes the distance between us. "Send a message, request transport as soon as you can. Get off *Elysian Fields* and don't come back. It's the only way."

I almost step down. My head feels too full, my grip on what I know to be real and true lost in a swirling haze of uncertainty and jangled nerves.

"But you reached out to me. You talked to me," I point out.

"It was a mistake, as I said," he says icily. "Go, Katerina."

Anger sparks in me and catches flame on plentiful kindling of resentment, terror, and *so many fucking secrets*.

If I've learned anything, it should be to walk away from an obviously messy situation and keep my mouth shut, but that's how I ended up here. I am done with it. Done with running, done with letting other people decide what value system I'm going to follow.

"No," I say flatly.

"No?" He arches his brows in disbelief.

"It's a complete sentence. No. You wanted my help, you got it. So let's go." I step closer, challenging him to back away this time.

He doesn't, though, and the sensation of his generated body near mine is like standing too close to a field of static electricity. The tiny hairs on my folded arms are on end.

Then he leans forward, his cheek almost brushing mine. "You are in danger," he says in a low voice. "It's only a matter of time until he comes for you, like all the others."

All the others. My heart gives an uneven *thump-bump* and I'm not sure if it's Aleyk's nearness or the sudden memory of those finger bones outside my quarters. The braid of hair in my room. What if that wasn't a good luck charm but leftovers?

Nausea roils my gut.

"He enjoys the hunt, the chase. Once he's at full strength and locked onto your scent, he will not give up." Aleyk draws back, a bitter smile curling the edges of his mouth. "I know my father. What's left of him anyway. The only reason you still have a chance is because Karl doesn't seem to know that you've seen Zale. He hasn't shut down outgoing communications yet."

"Karl. Karl is involved in all of this," I murmur. It's not so much a question as a statement. Of course he is. Some of the tanks were cracked open like those faux lobster shells that are supposed to add authenticity to manufactured seafood. Others were just . . . open. Karl would know how to do that, how to run the awakening sequence.

I look up, taking in the deep lines of concern in Aleyk's brow, and meet his gaze. "Then you should probably stop trying to talk me out of it and start explaining."

A muscle jumps near his jaw—the details in his hologram are unbelievable—but then he seems to come to a decision. "It won't change anything, and you won't believe me," he says in a flinty tone, with a challenge in his eyes.

I don't think he's giving me enough credit. I'm here, talking with him, aren't I?

He sighs. "But if it will get you to leave . . ."

I tip my head in acknowledgment, but I'm not making any promises.

"You'd better sit." He jerks his chin toward the seats below.

Sighing at what feels very much like a stalling tactic, I settle myself on the edge of the stage. Then I hold my hands up in a *Satisfied?* gesture.

He nods, pacing the stage. It takes him a moment to say anything. "I still don't have the whole story. I didn't know it was happening when I was alive," he says finally, using the past tense without flinching.

But I flinch on his behalf.

"This is what I've managed to piece together from being here with Zale, accessing old private files, and talking with Ianthe."

I look up in surprise. "She talks? Like, really talks?"

"She does. We all do." He closes his eyes briefly. "Did. On the other side of Karl's restrictions."

"*Karl* did that to you?" I ask.

"He didn't start it, but he is the one behind the most recent lockdown. I've been prohibited from certain words, phrases, for a long time, but not like that."

"He didn't want you talking to me," I say slowly, realization dawning. "Shit. That's my fault. I mentioned you and I—"

"It's all right."

"No, it's not. He could have, I don't know, deleted you!" The horror of that idea is almost too much. What would Aleyk have felt? Would he have been aware of being deleted, like dying? And it would have been my fault.

Aleyk snorts.

"What?" I demand.

"No. He couldn't have. I mean, he certainly could have tried." His eyebrows arch in amused condescension for Karl. "But he wouldn't dare."

Seeing him like this steals my breath. Aleyk is so *alive*, even though he is just as much a hologram as before.

Aleyk catches the change in my expression. "What?"

"Nothing. It's that . . . Nothing." *This*, this is the person who is asking me for help. He's *real*. He may not have a physical body—or at least not one he's inhabiting at the moment—but that doesn't make him any less a person. Any less someone I like.

I clear my throat. "Why not?" I ask, more to distract Aleyk and myself. "Why wouldn't Karl do that?"

Aleyk's face darkens, his brows drawing together. But when he speaks, his voice is crisp, matter-of-fact. "Karl has to keep me around. For my father."

"Your father," I repeat.

"It's all about keeping him happy, and Zale likes to visit." A bitter smile curls his mouth up at the corners. "Likes to see what I've become. As if he had nothing to do with that." He pauses with a frown. "Though it's been a while since he was here last. He's . . . very much not himself anymore."

I wait for him to continue. Despite the obvious acrimony in the relationship, the pain in Aleyk's voice is real.

He clears his throat, a physical affectation, unnecessary if you don't have a throat or vocal cords, but it doesn't seem put on. Just him, dealing with roiling emotion in whatever form that takes for him in this state.

"I was fourteen the first time Zale had his personal security strap me down." His expression is distant, as if he's retreated within himself to be able to say this. "They grabbed me as soon as I walked in the door at home. Dragged me, no matter how hard I fought, to his study. Where he was waiting with his medical science team to do a blood transfusion, equipment all set and ready to go."

"Why?" The word escapes in an exhale.

"He was scared of death, as I've said," Aleyk says with a casualness belied by the tension in his voice. "But it was more than that. He was obsessed with living forever, with maintaining his youth and quality of life. Blood transfusions were the least of what he tried, to keep from aging. *'I have so much more to contribute. Dying would be a crime against the future of humanity.'* That's what he used to say, as if he were someone special, someone for whom death should hold no sway." He shakes his head. "Nothing else, no one else, mattered, except for Zale Winfeld and what he could do for the world."

"That's when he started *Elysian Fields*?" I ask.

Aleyk laughs humorlessly. "No. First he went through a phase where he pursued every medical possibility, including the incredibly fringe shit. Then it was all about the technology. Technology was going to save him."

Svalbard. I don't want to interrupt to ask, but if I had to bet, I'd guess that's where the singularity angle came from.

"The problem was, none of it offered guarantees. And nothing was as good as living, breathing, and walking around for an eternity."

Svalbard would force him into physical limitations, and *Elysian Fields* would mean betting on future advancements, which ended up not happening.

"But if you know the legend of Zale Winfeld, you know his perspective on bad deals," he says dryly.

If it's a bad deal because of the rules, don't change the deal, change the rules.

"I left when I was sixteen. Lived with my mother, despite the lawsuits Zale threw at her to get me to come back. I hated him," he says, a bland statement of fact.

Years of living with someone whose only interest was in what you could do for them, in what your body could be harvested for. Who could blame him?

My heart aches for him. I wish I could reach out and squeeze his hand. No one deserves to be treated like that.

"So I don't know how the next part transpired. I wasn't there. But Ianthe, who was already working for the company then, said he started diving into very dark arenas, occult bull-shit. Hired archeological experts, biblical scholars, and started collecting relics. Very much his *Hitler searching for the Holy Grail* phase." He pauses, looking down at me, brow furrowed. "Do they still teach—"

"Yes." I nod. "I took a class specializing in twentieth- and twenty-first-century geopolitics and war in college." I don't mention that it focused on faulty strategy rather than the human cost. After the Mosby Education Riots in the late 2100s, teachers, the few human teachers as opposed to the AI ones, had to be careful about what they said.

"To most people, it would seem strange, I suppose, that someone as devoted to innovation as Zale would retreat to the past for solutions, but he had tried everything else, and he was growing increasingly desperate." Aleyk stops. "His own father, my grandfather, killed himself when he was seventy, diagnosed with an untreatable form of dementia. If Zale couldn't fix himself in time, fast enough, he feared there would be no point to living forever."

"But a genetic predisposition doesn't mean—"

"I know. So did he. He wasn't going to take any chances." Aleyk gives me a grim smile. "Other than the ones he chose to take for himself, that is. Apparently he became obsessed with this niche sect of mysticism, Penielia, a very narrow offshoot of an ancient Judeo-Christian religion. More cult than anything else. They believed that biblical references to angels and de-mons referred to actual physical entities. Immortal beings who possessed humans, providing the chosen person with strength and speed well beyond any normal capacity."

"And Zale believed that was real," I say, without bothering to hide my skepticism.

"More than believed. It became his driving purpose. The Pe-nielia have a myth, a legend, about an offering place, a hidden altar of sorts, where worthy souls could give themselves over to the beings. Said to be marked with an otherworldly glow."

Immediately, my mind snaps back to the strange little holo in Zale's office. The cave with the glowing orbs in the wall. The eerie light they projected.

"He was determined to find this place, the ultimate solution to his problem. He bought teams of researchers, emptied out museums. Traveled all over the Middle East and Africa."

"And he found something," I say flatly.

Aleyk nods. "On one of those trips, he came back . . . changed. No longer angry and afraid. Ianthe and I assumed some sort of religious experience, a conversion maybe. Bryck was too busy not looking a gift horse in the mouth," Aleyk adds. "A happier Zale meant an easier life for everyone. He even reached out to me, asked me to come work with the philanthropic arm of the corporation."

Which was how Aleyk had ended up working on the humanitarian water crisis, right before he died. *Was taken.* "That's when he started *Elysian Fields*."

Aleyk taps his nose and nods at me. "Got it in one."

"But I don't understand what any of that, angels and demons or whatever, has to do with that . . . hybrid, with *him*," I say. *Or how he's still alive.* It still felt weird as fuck to refer to Zale in the present tense.

Aleyk sighs and sits down across from me, his arms draped over his knees, as if he doesn't have the strength to support himself through this next bit.

"He found the altar and offered himself up," Aleyk says.

I laugh. "Yeah, okay. But that doesn't mean it actually did anything . . ." I trail off, taking in his all-too-serious expression.

"It took years of digging for me to piece it all together. Fortunately, I had plenty of time on my hands," Aleyk says dryly.

I close my eyes. "You're not seriously going to tell me that you discovered proof that angels and demons are real." It might be time to reevaluate Aleyk's mental capacity.

"No. I suspect that's simply the folklore that rose up when ancient people didn't know what they were seeing. Here." Aleyk flicks his hand behind us, and an image appears.

I twist around for a better look. It's a flat video, not a holo, of a bearded man in a thick tie that appears to be knitted from multiple colors of yarn. This, whatever it is, is old. Late twentieth or early twenty-first century.

"It's certainly an intriguing possibility," the man says, his voice crackling and broken, "the idea that Earth might have been visited by interstellar beings long before we would have understood what they were. Likely, the people of the time would have assumed them to be angels, messengers from God, or perhaps demons. The Penielia sect is a perfect example. Our recent dig sites have found Penielian remains that make no sense based on our understanding of human physiology. Wear and tear on the bodies that cannot be explained other than by playing host to a parasitic entity."

"Aliens?" I ask. But it doesn't come out quite as incredulous as I'd like. I've seen Zale, the hybrid of him and the other creature, and that word was the first that popped to mind. I've never seen anything like it . . . him. The strange glossy black arms and legs poking out of Zale, the grasping claws. And yet Zale—impaled or worn or whatever term is preferred—is not dead.

But aliens are supposed to be impossible. Right?

"Nonhumans," Aleyk corrects. "Here for thousands and thousands of years, living among us. Parasites of a variety who possess a human host, passing on their increased longevity, intelligence, and other abilities in exchange, until they move on to a different one."

"There's never been any sign of other intelligent life . . ." I begin weakly.

"Because we weren't looking back on Earth, thousands of years in the past," Aleyk points out.

"So . . . Zale went and got himself possessed. By an alien," I say slowly, making sure I understand.

"As far as my father is concerned, he was chosen. By God," Aleyk says, his mouth a thin line. "He believes. Or believed. I don't know that there's enough of him left to form any cogent thought as to his condition."

"And that's what's wrong with him? He's possessed?" I ask.

Aleyk shakes his head. "No, what's wrong with Zale is that he's been possessed for too long. His body is deteriorating, despite the parasite's best efforts, and that's why he's . . . changing. The parasite is being forced to take more control. I watched it happen." Aleyk pauses, his gaze shifting to a point over his shoulder, near the front row. "Right there." He jerks his chin in gesture. "He was busy telling me how disappointed he was that I lacked the vision to see the brilliance of his plan."

I wince.

"I saw the first black knobs appear on his arms, right as they burst through the skin and clothes." Aleyk closes his eyes. "He didn't even flinch. He laughed." He opens his eyes, bright blue fury blazing within.

"All right. Assuming I believe this—"

"I don't need you to believe me," he says simply. "I need you to leave. But if you have a more rational explanation, I would love to hear it."

I don't. How can I? Angels, demons, ancient cults, aliens—on that cliff's edge, there's no rational ledge to stand on to even begin an argument. "Why doesn't it take another host and walk right out of here? Or fly or whatever?"

"Because Zale offers it what no one else can—free food and hunting, with no danger of being caught. With more and more people leaving Earth to live on contained stations and domed colonies, it's much harder to get away with fulfilling its needs. *That* is the deal he made."

I stare at Aleyk, the ramifications of what he's saying slowly sinking in. "Zale created *Elysian Fields* not to save people but as a feeding ground. A preserve."

Aleyk nods. "And hunting humans who haven't been cryogenically frozen is its favorite treat. An enrichment activity, if you will. Still want to stay around?"

22

"Behloth goes through hibernation cycles, as near as I can tell, saving its energy," Aleyk continues, while my mind whirls to make sense of this new information. "But once it's eaten enough to be up to full strength, you won't be able to stop it."

"Behloth is . . ." I prompt.

Aleyk grimaces. "That is the name my father uses when he speaks with the parasite. I've heard him. Not as much anymore, obviously. Based on my research, it's a name from the Penielian culture. A demon, in this case, rather than an angel."

Behloth. I repeat the name silently to myself, trying on the unfamiliar syllables.

"You can't hide, you can't run, you can't wait it out. It will—" Aleyk stops, pain crossing his face, making me wonder what he's imagining . . . or oh, God, remembering. His jaw tightens, and then he continues. "It will toy with you, Katerina, until it's bored and hungry enough."

"The other . . . the other caretakers who—"

He nods curtly. "Every single one of them. The longest any of them have ever lasted is three months, and he was a former officer with military training who had fallen on hard times. Some of them, depending on where Behloth was in its cycle, only lasted a few hours." He grins at me, bitterness sharpening the edges of the expression. "We're not a dead ship, Katerina. We're the living dead. Trapped in between, forever. Ianthe,

Bryck, me, yes, but also all of the people Karl hires, and our passengers. The caretakers have hours or days to live and no idea what's about to happen to them. The passengers can be woken, so they're still technically alive, but they don't live, not very long. They're still dying of whatever brought them here to begin with, and the side effects of their preservation don't help. They survive just long enough to be wounded prey for a weaker Behloth."

Aleyk leans closer to me, as if needing to make sure his next words land with enough weight to leave an imprint. "There is no freedom, no escape. Not from *Elysian Fields*."

Dizziness presses down on me, making me feel as if I'm tilting sideways. How is any of this possible? My thoughts scrabble around in my head, searching for purchase, to gain some semblance of order or understanding.

Then a memory pops up unexpectedly.

The bartender on EnExx17, looking at the returned holo-comm in disgust and disdain. *That guy? He's 'interviewed' people from here before. Never seen any of them come back.* That's what she said.

"Oh, God." I feel like I'm falling. I reach out and flatten my palm on the edge of the stage, wrapping my fingers around the beveled corner to hold on.

"Please. Go," Aleyk urges. "Before it's too late." He pauses, seeming to search his memory for details. "Karl has been paying you? To a hard credit chip account?"

Surprised, I nod.

"Good." His gaze unfocuses slightly, as if his attention is elsewhere, then it snaps back to me. "There. Consider that a bonus from the Winfeld Trust." His mouth holds an ironic twist. "You have more than enough for transport anywhere and to start over."

Frowning, I lean to one side and dig the credit chip from my pocket—I now keep it on my person at all times; never let it be said I don't learn from exceptionally painful mistakes—and the balance is thirty times the highest it's ever been. I suck in a sharp breath.

It's more than enough for transport. More than enough to buy a new identity, a good one. A new life, if I wanted. Or a chance to wait out the drama in my old one.

"Aleyk—" I begin.

"I should never have broken protocol, spoken to you that first time. You wouldn't be here now if it weren't for me."

That's not entirely true, but my fascination with him certainly was a factor in my decision.

"What about you?" I blurt. "If I leave, what about you? What about the passengers?" I can't just *leave* them.

He smiles, but it's tinged with sadness. "What about us? Nothing will change. Everything will continue as it has, as it will forever. Until the engines finally give out, the central operating system crashes, or a perfectly placed micrometeoroid penetrates the hull in the right thin spot." He moves his hands apart from each other, in a gesture roughly indicating explosive decompression.

"But that could be—"

"I figure at least another fifty years, maybe a century, depending on our luck," he says.

My head swirls with the numbers—how many will be lost, lied to, *eaten* before that will happen. "I can't do that."

"You can do nothing here except die," he says sharply. He stops himself, his fists clenched, and then draws in a slow breath and releases it. "Let me do this one thing," he adds in a softer voice. "Please. Let me preserve at least one life to make up for my willful ignorance. I knew something wasn't right, that Zale was scheming in some way, and I should have pushed harder. But I didn't."

My throat feels tight with unshed tears. "You wanted to believe. There's nothing wrong with that."

He gives me a weary smile. "Go back to the world, Katerina. Save the people who can be saved."

Tears overflow my eyes, and embarrassment heats my face at hearing my own ambitions laid so bare. It sounds pathetic, needy, when phrased that way, as if I'm not valuable enough on my own, as a person, and I'm aware of that fact and desperately trying to make up for it. Which . . . maybe I am.

Aleyk hesitates, then reaches out. His fingertips brush against my check, a vague, soft pressure against the skin, and my breath catches in my throat. The moisture, however, does not track away, because his fingertips, his hand, Aleyk himself, none of it's real.

More tears spill over. I'm too tired; my emotional regulation is all over the place.

His forehead creases in concern. "I meant no harm, love," Aleyk says, cupping the other side of my face with the other hand, so I am framed in his gentle grasp. Those blue, blue eyes lock with mine before his gaze slowly drifts toward my mouth. "I wish . . . I wish I could—"

But I don't get to hear what he wishes.

A loud metallic *clang* reverberates through the still air, followed by a quieter rolling sound. Aleyk jerks away from me, from sitting to standing without the movement in between. It takes me a moment to process what's happening.

The metal IV pole propped at the door, as my impromptu alarm system. It hit the floor.

I scramble away from the edge of the stage, yanking my limbs away from the floor like a child fearing the monster under the bed.

Only in this case, of course, the monster is real.

Aleyk, staring out at the darkened audience seats, makes a quick gesture, flicking his fingers, and the overhead lights explode on in full brightness.

I wince, instinctively throwing my hand up to protect my closed and watering eyes.

"Is he here?" My voice comes out shrill and too loud, as if my inability to see has also affected my hearing.

Aleyk doesn't respond, which only makes my panicked, galloping heart skip a few beats.

After a few seconds, I'm able to open my eyes to a squint, and I lower my hand.

The theater is bright and dazzling, chandeliers overhead, coated in cobwebs and dust but still sparkling. Row after row of velvet seats flow outward from the stage, like ocean waves.

All of them are empty. There's no movement, either, no strangely deformed head bobbing in and out of sight, creeping down a row.

At the back of the theater, the metal pole lies crosswise across the aisle, caught on one side by the bolted-down metal leg of a chair. Did it fall? It wasn't the most reliable or stable early alert system, obviously.

Aleyk, at the center of the stage, is nearly transparent. The light from above interferes with his projection to the point that he's ghostlike. His face is blank, expressionless.

"Aleyk?" I whisper, getting to my feet in case I need to run.

He stirs himself to life again, shifting his weight from foot to foot. "No," he says finally. "As far as I can tell, he's still below."

Still eating. That's what he doesn't say.

"You have access to the security cams," I say slowly, realization dawning. "And the lights."

"I have limited control over a small number of systems," he corrects. "None of which can help you. Karl and all of those who came before him have made sure of that."

Overhead, the chandeliers dim to a more comfortable level with another gesture from Aleyk.

"My father's not here yet, but he will come, I assure you." He pauses.

I brace myself for another demand that I go. And he's not wrong about that, but—

"And you won't leave if I'm still here, I suspect," he continues.

My eyes widen. "Wait, Aleyk, don't—"

"Goodbye, Katerina. Don't let anyone make you think less of yourself." His image blinks out, Aleyk vanishing for real. Like the ghost he appeared to be a moment ago.

And I am alone—more alone, somehow, than I've ever been.

I edge out into the corridor, the metal pole cold and hard against my palm but also frighteningly insubstantial against Zale.

I waited on the stage. Called Aleyk's name. Threatened to stay until he returned. But the minutes ticked by in bites that Zale was consuming, each one bringing him closer to me. Fear was building up past the point of toleration, and Aleyk knew it.

"Fuck you, Aleyk," I hiss, though I'm not sure what I wanted him to do instead.

I wanted him to be there. Or rather, here, with me. Which wouldn't have been possible, no matter what.

Tightening my grip on the IV pole, I step out, letting the theater door swing closed behind me. The corridor is empty, silent. It might be any other day/night on rounds.

Moving as quietly as I can, which means not moving very fast, I turn left and head for the SecOffice.

My plan, such as it is, is simple. I'll barricade myself in with my supplies, make a call for transport—bribe them to hurry, if need be—and then wait it out until the ship arrives. I have no idea how I'm going to get past the creature—Zale-Behloth. Zaloth? Though I'm not sure how much of Zale is actually left—if it's pacing outside the door. And even if I can do that, I still need to get Karl to extend the bridge.

Escaping at this point feels damn near impossible. But worse than that, it feels *wrong*. Like once again I'm abandoning people to protect my own interests.

But I don't know what else I'm supposed to do. I know nothing about stopping this . . . Behloth. I'm certain I would not be the first to have tried, and I am way less qualified than the ex-military guy before me. It is a nonhuman entity, an *alien*, apparently alive for thousands and thousands of years, that *eats people* for sustenance. Going up against it would be like, I don't know, cloned chicken meat suddenly gaining sentience and fomenting a rebellion against the food-industrial complex.

And, as has been pretty well established, getting help is out because who the fuck would believe me, even with video proof? Maybe one day I'll be in a position to do something, pass a law, demand an investigation, but it won't be anytime soon.

I pause as I pass Amli's room. The woman within the tank, not-Amli, draws my attention, the familiarity of her once again plucking at my memory.

Even though I should keep going, her presence draws me closer. The jewel implanted on her cheek should have been a dead giveaway, no pun intended, that she wasn't Amli. She's too modern.

Karl must be subbing his clients into rooms when needed. Maybe in case the board actually does show up? It makes sense. He might be able to get away with some empty rooms on the lower levels, but if they arrive for even a cursory inspection and find missing tanks on the main exhibition level, he's toast.

I move closer. It's very eerie how much the girl in the tank resembles the old me. The hair, the height. And I don't know why that keeps tripping me—

I freeze. Wait. I *do* know her.

Back on EnExx17, when I was waiting for the transport. That departure board, the one featuring all those missing people. The girl that caught my attention and nearly sent me into a panic spiral because, for a second, I thought it was *my* picture up there. She looked like me, sort of.

But she looks exactly like the body in this tank.

This girl—and she is a girl, just nineteen or twenty—is one of the missing.

Sarai, I think. She vanished from EnExx17. Her brother was looking for her. She left for a job interview and never came back.

Oh, Jesu.

So she came on board for an interview and for whatever reason ended up in a tank.

That feeling of falling from a great height returns.

Is Sarai the only one? What if she's not? Karl may have some clients, but not enough. What if all these people I've been walking past every day are more people like me? Just trying to survive or help their families or even hide from something that's hurting them?

And I'm supposed to walk away?

In the tank, Sarai rests peacefully, her hands folded across her chest. But now that I'm looking for it, I pick up on the blood from a torn fingernail, pooled and frozen on her index finger. The faint purple mark on her cheek might be the start of a bruise.

I didn't, couldn't see it before.

I squeeze my eyes shut. How much damage we do, running from things, refusing to see what's right in front of us because we need things to be different, because we want to wait for someone else to come along and fix it. In the end, the only person you can count on to do something is . . . yourself.

Anything else is a deferral of responsibility at best and wish fulfillment at worst.

Leverage. Power is nothing but leverage appropriately applied, rypka.

Not sure that adds up from a physics sense, but a lesson my mother swears by.

One person wants me alive badly enough to come here and collect me, despite the unusual circumstances he may encounter. One person mistrusts UNOC enough not to get them involved, which is important. Not everyone in the collective government is corrupt, but I suspect there are more who are open to "persuasion" than I would like to think.

One person has the right to know the truth, even if I despise everything he stands for.

Plus, the whole "private security" thing. If you have an army you can call, and you need an army, you do what you need to do.

After leaning the IV pole on the wall, I pull my holocomm from my pocket and establish a connection to my relay accounts. The connection indicator flickers a weak but visible green along the side of my holocomm. We must finally be close enough to Amster-York now to piggyback on their signal.

Green light go, as the old saying goes.

Then I start my one and only outgoing message, directing it to Ayis's former campaign headquarters. *I can't believe I'm doing this.* My own image stares back at me in disbelief from the holocomm display.

"This message is for Rober Ayis." I clear my throat against the bile rising up at the mention of his name. One day this message will be in history texts and I will be either praised for breaking ranks to support true democracy or vilified for helping a democratically elected tyrant take office. I'm betting on the latter.

"My name is Katerina Weiller. Former assistant to the chief of staff for Prime Minister Bierhals. I have the information you're looking for. As you can imagine, I'm not in a position to trust anyone. If you want what I have, then I'll need you to come to me. I'm—"

The connection indicator abruptly flashes red and my image disappears, replaced by my account's index page. I've lost service.

Shit, shit, shit!

Automatically, I reset the holocomm, but nothing happens. Still red. But there's no way we've moved out of range that quickly.

Okay, okay, breathe. Everything is fine. It's probably a glitch. Give it a second and—

A mechanical *ka-thunk* sounds outside in the hallway, and I spin around to face the open door behind me. The *ka-thunk* is followed by another, and another, like dominoes falling. And with it comes darkness and shadows.

The generator is failing. Or . . . someone is turning off the lights.

I grab my makeshift weapon and bolt for the door, but a *ka-thunk* outside turns everything dark in this room and the corridor beyond. I pull myself up hard, stopping before reaching the threshold.

The only light is from the tiny status indicators on the tank behind me and from my still open holocomm.

Otherwise, I am surrounded by a blanket of blackness so thick it's practically palpable. I can no longer see the doorway ahead of me. My frantic and raspy breathing dominates the silence around me, but not quite enough to drown out the familiar rustle and scrape in the walls. Distant for now, but growing closer.

I know that sound.

And this time I know what it means. Behloth is coming.

23

I instinctively lurch toward the hallway, finding the doorway by tilting my holocomm away from me to shed its light ahead of me. It helps, but it also makes me all too aware that I'm broadcasting my position. Yet I can't turn it off; I can't handle the idea of Behloth creeping up on me in the dark while I'm blindly facing the wrong direction.

As if facing it would somehow change the outcome. My mind helpfully supplies the image of Amli on the floor again, her whole body bobbing with the force of Behloth buried face-first and gnawing on her abdomen. Only this time, in my head, it's my face in place of hers, blankly staring up at the ceiling, tears sliding silently from the corners of my eyes. How long would it take to die that way?

What do I do? What do I do, whatdoido, whatdoido?

My panic sends the question on a loop in my brain, over and over again, until it becomes nonsense syllables.

Okay, okay, shut up. I need to think.

"Halllley." Karl's voice echoes up and down the corridor, coming through the vid screens, seemingly all at once.

Hearing his voice jolts me into taking a step or two toward the theater, toward Aleyk. Toward help. Could he help, though? His physical presence is limited to the stage, and I'm not sure he's strong enough to actually intervene if needed. I'd be stuck there, waiting for Behloth to reach me. I'd just have company while I waited.

As if in answer to my unspoken question, the emergency lights buzz to life behind me, one after the other, leading me in the direction of the SecOffice.

Aleyk.

I pivot and run for the SecOffice.

"Don't make this more difficult than it already is, Halley. Or should I say Katerina? Which do you prefer?" Karl's sigh, rolling down the hallway through the series of screens, sounds like wind coming off the water. "Doesn't matter. All I'm saying is you've already fucked us. He's not ready for you yet, but I clearly can't leave you to your own devices. Who knows what you would come up with in another day or three?"

I skirt the fountain near the main entrance. *Almost there.*

"Now you've put me in an awkward situation. He's very touchy when I get involved, but I can't risk you hurting him in one of your death throes or something. We have a deal, and I've given up far too much already to stop now." He gives a breathless laugh, and in the background I hear the metallic clomping noises that I recognize immediately from my own escapades around the ship.

Footsteps on the metal stairs.

Oh, shit. I stop midstep. *He's coming.* Karl's *coming.*

A lock might keep Zale out for a time, but it would barely slow down Karl, who most certainly has keys and access codes and whatever else is needed to reach every inch of this ship.

In the distance, perhaps fifteen feet away, the door to the SecOffice beckons, like false hope, a mirage in the desert. If I lock myself in, I've just cornered myself for them.

In the walls, Behloth scrapes and shuffles closer.

Overhead the emergency lights, once showing the way, fade to almost nothing, as if Aleyk has made the same realization.

But now what?

"Sometimes I think it's cruel to see a great man in such sad shape," Karl continues conversationally. "And I'm ready, more than ready. But his stamina is amazing, and they've been bonded so long, I'm pretty sure Behloth would hold a grudge if I tried to push, you know?" He forces a laugh, trying to cover the sounds of exertion. "I mean the last thing you want is to be possessed by a pissed-off demon, no matter how hard you've worked to be here. There's immortality and then there's an eternity, if you get what I'm saying."

Wait, Karl *wants* to take over as Behloth's . . . host? That's why he's here, why he's stayed around for so long? I don't know how long, actually. He wasn't in charge when the ship was open as an exhibit, but—

I shake my head. He's trying to distract me, and it's working.

"I mean, there's power hungry and then just hungry. A man has to have his standards," Karl continues.

I ignore him as he chatters on. Where? Where can I go? If I can't hide, I need to fight. But how? I don't have any weapons, no way to call for help, no access to anything useful. I've got empty corridors, dead ends, and not much else.

I'm like a mouse in a fucking maze, exactly as intended. Except I don't even have a piece of cheese to run for, a prize hidden at the center. No bolt-hole to call home.

Do something, Katerina!

Desperation makes it hard to concentrate. Sweat trickles down my spine. Any second now, Behloth is going to come slithering out of some room or vent and I'm still going to be standing here.

Hidden. Home. Hidden. Home. Prize.

The words echo in my head, giving me visions of a darkened room, angular furniture, carpeting thick with furry dust.

Upstairs. Zale's family quarters. So? Why is that coming to mind? Hiding up there won't do me any good, and I don't remember anything that would serve as an adequate weapon.

No convenient blades or old guns on display, not that I have any experience with wielding either.

But something . . . a submerged thought is nagging at me, bumping into the edges of my mind as it swirls around.

Frustrated, I blow out a breath and try to calm the chaos in my head and tune out Karl long enough to focus. If I'm going to have a chance at surviving this, I can't let panic take over.

Working backward through my memories of that exploration, I still find nothing—tanks, Aleyk's sad empty room, the mirror in Ianthe's room, the desperate wall of praise in Bryck's.

And then, finally, it clicks. I straighten up, an electric-like shock cascading down my spine.

When I broke in upstairs, the metal letters on the wall—signage—indicated that the quarters were in one direction. But in the other?

The bridge. The fucking bridge!

That level is not only the private family quarters but also the *Elysian Fields*'s former center of operations. Karl said he'd rigged everything to be controlled from the engine room. But that doesn't mean I couldn't attempt to de-rig it.

Rumor has it, I'm fairly good at destroying what's meant to remain untouched, unexamined. If nothing else, odds are good that I can cause enough of a problem to distract Karl, at least. Change the ship's course, aim for the nearest solid object. Or break things until he has to stop coming for me and put out whatever fire I've started.

Tightening my damp grip on the slick metal IV pole, I slip out into the corridor and head for the stairs as quietly as possible.

I'm not sure there's any point, though, in trying to hide my intent. As soon as I'm on the move, it's only a few seconds before the increased rustle and scrape behind the walls tells me that Behloth is on to me. Tracking me by scent, if Aleyk is right.

How had I missed that for so long, writing the sounds off as the regular creaking, popping, and settling of an old ship?

They're so deliberate. So . . . predatory. I shudder.

Probably because it never occurred to you that something out of a nightmare was hunting you, outside of a nightmare.

"Ah, Katerina, I thought you weren't going to make this so difficult for me." Karl's voice drifts after me as I speed toward the door next to the SecOffice.

Fuck off, Karl.

I charge up the stairs, feet banging on every step. Below me, but not far enough, I can hear Karl's echoing ascent. He's maybe two, three floors away? Not running, making slow, steady progress in a strangely uneven, clomping gait.

But I don't stop to consider it further. My destination is so close, I have to keep my focus on what to do next.

Comms, first. If I can work it out. I don't know if I'll even recognize the comms system, this ship is so old. And even if it wasn't, I haven't spent a lot of time on bridges. I'm hoping for a lot of clearly labeled buttons.

If that's not a possibility, then navigation. Throw us in the middle of a highly trafficked shipping lane and I bet that gets some result. Possibly an undesirable one, if we end up on a collision course with a heavy freighter. It'll cut through us like a knife through a rotting orange. And I still want to try to get everyone out of here. Let scientists or authorities or whoever, someone who knows more than I do, sort out whether any of the preserved bodies are still viable.

Now that I've had time to consider it, I suspect that very few of the "residents" are original. Even the first Viviane. When I really think about it, my own memories of her are vague. The bow, for which I got the color wrong, is mainly what I remember. Karl has been very smart about how he's gone about that—preserving the elements that people are most likely to call to mind. Even the board members, if they bother to check, which I'm beginning to suspect they deliberately don't, might be fooled. After all, no one wants to look too closely at death—their own future.

The entrance to the private level remains as I left it, hanging open, caution tape now dangling around it in torn curls. It's dark inside, of course, as before.

At the threshold, I hesitate. Karl is clanking and clattering closer than ever. In a moment or two I'll be able to peer over the railing and see him below me. But I can't hear Behloth moving in the walls anymore.

It makes me wonder if he knows a faster route, through the innards of the ship, through the vents and gaps that exist within the walls, to get here faster. It makes me wonder if he . . . *it* is standing on the other side of this door, waiting for me.

"Katerina, you're only making this harder on both of us," Karl calls from below. "There's nowhere else to go. I can hear you up there."

Holding my breath, shoulders tensed, I slip inside. Standing in the sliver of light from the stairwell, I swing the metal pole into the darkness in sweeping gesture, but it doesn't connect with anything.

Still . . . I can sense a tension in the space that wasn't present before. Not anything so definitive as sounds of movement or breathing. More like a sharpness, an alertness that *feels* like awareness. As if the space itself were sentient, holding its breath to see what will happen next.

The door to the bridge should be around the curved edge of the corridor, and there's no sense hesitating on the threshold. If Behloth is in here, that's bad, but Karl coming up after me is no better.

Gritting my teeth, bracing for an attack, I move into the shadows in the direction of the bridge.

It's not more than fifteen feet before I run into the entrance, stopping short of a heavy, utilitarian door before my knee collides with it. An imposing vault-like swivel handle holds a place in the center of the door, an old-fashioned keypad set into the wall on the right. The whole thing is probably intended to seal off the bridge in the event of a hull breach or intruders.

My heart plummets toward my feet before I even get a chance to try the handle, and it takes me a moment to recognize why: the keypad is dangling from loose wires, and deep gashes and nicks surround the thick metal handle, some even digging into the handle itself, the matching creamy white paint nicked and dinged at various points.

I'm not the first one to have this idea, nor the first one to try to get in. And whoever they were, the ones who came first, they definitely appear to have had better tools than I do. If I had to guess, those inches-long gashes, driving deep into the metal surface, were from a fire ax. Which is part of the standard ship fire safety kit, along with fire extinguishers, placed at mandated intervals. (Bierhals had supported the bill for it, back in his MP days.) I hadn't seen any on this ship, not that I had noticed until now.

So it seems that in addition to the missing emergency escape shuttles, *someone* has taken away the best weapons one might use for defending oneself.

What else had I missed?

I try the handle, but it shifts to the left less than an inch before halting with a loud metallic clank.

I wince, imagining the sound traveling down to Karl. And then I realize he's gone silent.

Panic ignites in me with an audible *whoosh*. I spin away from the bridge door, half expecting to find him looming behind me, but the corridor is still empty.

For now.

I can't stay here. My back is literally to the wall. There's nowhere to go. Not even space to try to dodge or fight.

I rush back toward the door to the stairs. If I can slip past Karl before he gets up here . . .

As I close in on the door, my hand reaching out for the

space, I have just enough time to recognize that the light from the stairwell seems dimmer than before.

Bad. Wrong. The part of my mind working overtime is reduced to mere words and phrases. I instinctively snatch my hand back, and I half stumble, half throw myself to the side, right as an arm reaches inside the opening, grasping for me.

Staggering sideways, I get a better look at the arm as I attempt to regain my balance against the opposite wall.

It's not a normal arm or hand. No. From the wrist down, it's gleaming black, the digits and bones represented in patched-together metal and plastic. A 3-D-printed hand. Only the digits aren't fingers but claws, sharpened on the inner edges. The first two are claws, but the others have stranger shapes that I can't even recognize. A curved blade, a straight tube with an end that appears to retract and move even as I watch.

Even worse, from the wrist up until the start of a ragged sleeve, red divots and bumpy purple scars cover what remains of the skin, down to what must be almost bone. Most disturbingly, one of the marks, right above where the crudely engineered hand attaches to the arm, looks like human teeth have scooped the flesh away from the limb, like biting ice cream off the top of a cone. All disturbing ridges and valleys.

What the fuck? Did . . . did Behloth bite his hand off?

Or did Karl feed it to him?

The shadow outside the door shifts, and Karl ducks inside, pushing the door open with that monstrosity of an arm.

His face is familiar, but nothing, *nothing*, else is.

He towers over me by nearly a foot, putting him closer to seven feet tall. Taller than he should reasonably be. His other hand looks normal, undamaged. But both his legs are gone below the knee, replaced with contraptions similar to that on his arm. Except the feet look more like spiders. Each is a solid, rounded shape in the center, where it attaches to the slender peg of his former calf, with six or eight independent phalanges ringing the edges.

No wonder he stayed in the engine room. No one, not one single person, would be desperate enough to stay, once they saw Karl in person.

He clomps forward toward me, the spider-leg toes pushing off the ground and moving him faster than he should be able to move.

I want to scream. I can feel it bubbling up in my chest, but it won't come out, caught behind the horror of what I'm seeing.

Scrambling forward, I trip over my own feet as I try to watch him and get away at the same time.

I fall before I can catch myself. My hands and knees hit the carpeting hard, knocking the air out of my lungs, sending dusty plumes up into the air, and scraping layers of skin off my palms in the added indignity of rug burn.

Breathless, I flop to my side, trying to get my feet back under me in time to run.

Karl grins down at me, holding up his altered hand and clicking the clawlike fingers together. "What, you didn't think there would be a sacrifice? To be Behloth's next chosen doesn't come for free."

24

"I feel like there's a requisite arm-and-a-leg joke here, but I think we're past that, aren't we?" Karl continues, looming over me.

I crab-walk backward, keeping my eyes on him. "What happened to you?" I ask between fits of coughing.

"Sometimes frozen *isn't* as good as fresh. And sometimes he gets a little temperamental. Most geniuses are, you know." Karl sounds dreamy, a man in love.

"You let him . . . you let him eat parts of you?" I ask in disbelief.

He scowls down at me and I scramble to my feet, backing down the corridor, toward the family quarters. It's the only route available to me. Once I'm in, there's no other exit that I'm aware of, but it's better than standing here, waiting for Karl to snap at me with those hands.

"You don't need to make it sound so crass," Karl says, following me. "I made a willing sacrifice. A necessary sacrifice. And it wasn't as gruesome as you make it sound." He gives an offended sniff. "It was surgical. Precise."

"Is that why you have a bite mark on your wrist?"

Anger tightens his expression, visible even in the dim light. "You don't understand. People who think small never do."

The back of my leg collides with edge of something sharp. One of the side tables by the sofa. I shift slightly and keep backing up. Maybe if I can reach one of the bedrooms, I can barricade myself in. *For how long? What then?*

I shove those questions down to keep my focus on Karl and the immediate problem. "You're right. I don't get it. Please explain how turning yourself into *food* is part of some grand master plan."

But instead of reacting with more fury, he simply nods smugly, as if I've said what he expected. "Every brilliant man is misunderstood in his own time. Da Vinci, Galileo, Tesla, Jobs, Musk, Winfeld—"

"And you?" I scoff. I can't help myself, in spite of the danger of pissing him off too much. Also, given what I've learned, I sincerely doubt Zale should be classed among them, either. The man was—*is*—a selfish bastard, afraid to die. Pretty sure that doesn't make him misunderstood or brilliant.

"No one wanted to listen to me." Karl says, closing the distance between us as I round the corner of a sofa.

I risk a glance toward the nearest doorway. Bryck's room is *right there*. But I can't risk it. Karl will grab me before I have the chance to shut the door. I have to keep going, to put some distance between us.

"Did you know I ran my own company, Peerless Innovations, for almost ten years?" Karl demands. "Translucent Transports was *my* idea. It was the wave of the future."

That almost stops me in surprise. I remember hearing about that. "But that . . . that killed a bunch of people, didn't it?"

"Because they wouldn't listen." He glares at me, as if this is evidence that I am not listening, either. "Sometimes you have to step outside the box to truly see that certain limitations are unnecessary."

From what I remember at the time, aerospace experts deemed his brainchild a failure from the start, triggering all sorts of regulations around transportation safety. "And that's how you ended up here? Because they fired you." From his own company. Ouch.

He shrugs stiffly. "It happens when you're dealing with small-minded moneymen who are more interested in covering their own asses than advancing the fate of humanity."

It was a fucking balloon. A see-through balloon that would lift tourists up from a planet's surface to see into space.

"But that doesn't matter, because it sent me on this quest and I found what I'm looking for."

Two missing legs and a missing arm?

"Zale had the right idea. If you're too far ahead of your own time to be appreciated in your life span, then you find a way to extend it."

I gape at him. That is not at all what Zale had done. It wasn't as if he had spent the past hundred or so years innovating or creating or doing anything but purely surviving. But the shining fervor on Karl's face told me that attempting to explain that would not go over well.

Zale Winfeld, cult leader, even still today. How do people not see it?

But I know the answer to that already. Because you see what you want to see, what you need to see. The people who signed up for *Elysian Fields* back in the day saw a guarantee against death. Those paying Karl now, based on Zale's reputation and past, saw one last chance for a miracle.

Just as I saw what I needed to in Bierhals, I realize with a sinking feeling. I needed him to be a decent person who made the right choices, someone who cared about other people more than his own success or ego. And I needed to be right. So much so that I completely missed—or ignored—any signs to the contrary in him, in Niina.

Then I didn't have the courage to confront my own mistake.

A charismatic leader is a mirror of our own desires. And I, apparently, am not immune to it, any more than anyone else. I needed someone to be what I was looking for in the world, and Niina was happy to play that role for me, for everyone, as long as it got her what she wanted.

Behind me, the fireplace triggers with a sudden *whoosh*. Reflexively, I glance over my shoulder. And immediately freeze.

Behloth is crouched on the floor just past the threshold of Ianthe's room. As I'd feared, he managed to bypass the normal routes within the ship to arrive here before me.

Zale's bare, bony feet barely touch the ground, his body stretched like an ill-fitting suit over the darker limbs—and presumable structure—beneath. His human hands shift restlessly, like vestigial flippers, while the alien arms and hands, sprouting claws in a triangle from a small circular palm, brace against the floor. The anatomy appears not at all dissimilar to what Karl created for himself.

Karl attempting to further ingratiate himself to Behloth, perhaps? Sickness washes over me at the idea, nausea flooding my mouth with saliva.

Zale's head, though, is still human. Mostly. Thick black spots and seams show through in random constellations across his forehead and cheekbones where the skin has gone thin or been torn away, like those rough and ridged scars on the holo depictions of dinosaurs. The eyes are silvery white with cataracts, reflecting the flickering light of the fireplace back at me.

But when he cocks his head to look at me, it goes a little too far to the left, as if the joints there aren't what they should be. It stands, elevating itself to its full height, more than a foot and a half over my head. Zale gives a soft moan at the movement, sending a whisper of fetid and rotting meat breath in my direction. Then he grins at me, revealing a mouth full of jagged and sharpened black teeth, mixed with a few yellowing human incisors and molars. Somehow the combination is worse than one or the other alone.

Instinctively, I clamp my hand over my mouth and back away. Almost directly into Karl.

I spin around in time to avoid the snap of his claws over my upper arm. But I'm caught, pinned between Karl and Behloth.

Short of leaping over living room furniture to run for the door, which I doubt would happen in the quick, effortless manner it would need to for success, I have no way out.

My heart shakes and judders in my chest. *You're going to die. Right here. Bits of you in his teeth. That'll be all that's left. This, this is what running away gets you. You didn't want that confrontation, so now you have this one instead.*

"This doesn't have to be difficult, Katerina," Karl says, hands out in a soothing gesture as he steps toward me.

I move back into the center of the living area, until the coffee table knocks gently into the back of my calf. "Don't call me that," I snap, more for the sense of doing *something* to fight.

Karl reaches into the pocket of his stained and torn jumpsuit, pulling out a capped syringe. An old-fashioned one, with an actual needle beneath the plastic molded cap. "You won't feel a thing. Well . . ." He pauses to reconsider. "You will, but you won't care. At least not until the very end. And it'll also slow you down enough when you run that you won't be a threat." He laughs.

He glances over his shoulder toward Behloth, as if expecting him to chuckle along with the joke.

But Zale is looking past him, his focus entirely on me. As if Karl doesn't even exist.

"Young . . . healthy . . ." Zale's voice sounds like handfuls of gravel being rubbed together. Grating, broken. *"Female."*

Oh shit. My heart free-falls toward my belly, and cold spears through me, goose bumps rising along every inch of my skin. Is he . . . is Behloth thinking about changing up hosts?

Being eaten by the monster is bad, horrific beyond imagining, but becoming the monster, the thing that eats? Trapped and fully aware but unable to control your body, make your own choices? Hurting people to survive, watching them suffer?

His mouth works in a swallowing motion, then his lips part. He gives a faint groan as something dark snakes out between his cracked lips—a tubelike protrusion caked in a thick white slime. Searching, it whips itself from side to side, extending from Zale's mouth like a tentacle seeking something to grasp.

I have a sudden mental image of lying on the floor, helpless, while that *thing* scrapes its way inside me, down my throat, up into my brain. And, oh, God, what if it can reproduce? What if it *uses me* to do that?

I need to get out of here.

"No," Karl says tightly, turning to face him. "No. We talked about this. You promised, Zale."

I don't think there's much of Zale left in there, so there's little point in making an argument like a whiny kid. Maybe Karl should have thought twice about feeding pieces of himself to the thing he wanted to become. But I don't care as long as they're both distracted.

I take another cautious step back, then another, around the edge of the coffee table, toward the sofa and the closest route to the door. Almost there.

"I'm next. You said—" Karl stops himself, spinning to face me. "No, you don't."

He charges toward me, syringe in hand.

Lights blaze suddenly, from dimness lit only by the fireplace to the full force of every source of illumination in the apartment.

Zale cries out, shrinking back from the light with an animal-like cry of pain.

"Aleyk!" Karl roars like a younger sibling thwarted by an older one.

Aleyk.

Tears flood my eyes, only partially from the sudden explosion in light. He's trying to help, trying to save me. It makes my chest ache with a powerful emotion that I don't have time to contemplate.

I scramble onto the couch, two steps up and over the low back, and out into the hallway leading toward the stairs. The open door is right there, ten feet away, freedom summoning me through a sterile slice of harsh white stairwell light on the dusty, nubbly carpeting.

Putting on as much speed as I can, I lean forward, hand out, as if someone will be there to pull me out, to save me.

Aleyk. A mental image of him reaching down to pull me up from the stage crosses over, superimposes itself on my reality.

But then sharp edges catch at my ankle, and something in the mechanism of the joint gives way with a loud and nauseating pop.

Fuck!

The floor flies up to smash into my face, the rough carpet tearing skin off my elbows, palms, chin—anywhere it can reach.

Waves of agony scream up my leg. Karl or Behloth, one of them, must have grabbed me. Curling to my side, I roll over. But before I can rally and try to crawl away, Karl looms over me.

He brings that syringe down, right into my neck. I don't even have time to turn away. The needle pierces my skin, and a flood of warmth spreads out from the puncture point.

"There," Karl says breathlessly, straightening up. "That's better."

Behloth shuffles up to stand next to him, staring down at me. "Young. Healthy. Female," Zale says again, making no immediate move to fall upon me and start chewing.

His face a dark cloud, Karl kicks me in the ribs with his modified foot. Hard.

The metal connects, and it feels like my still healing ribs bend with the force. I would scream but all the air is gone. My lungs are two wet plastic bags, the sides firmly sealed together.

He leans down over me with a sneer. "You should run now."

I can't. I can't even move. I try to breathe, but the air won't go in. It's like being in a box with the lid slammed tight against my face.

Eventually, a small sip of oxygen makes it through, and

then another. With the return of breathing, though, comes the agony of moving my damaged ribs. My vision blurs further, moisture collecting in the corners of my eyes.

"Run," Karl bellows at me, while Behloth, the intelligence peeking out from Zale's murky eyes, shifts between looking at him and then at me.

Get up. Get up! But between the pain radiating outward from my chest, the electric shock of whatever has happened to my ankle—I'm afraid to look, afraid I'll see it dangling from my leg by a slender scrap of flesh—and the rising cloudiness from whatever Karl injected me with, I am lost. A spot of nothing on the floor. An emptiness that has not quite finished vacating.

Beneath the haziness, though, I wonder if Karl wants me to run because that will trigger a prey drive in Behloth, distracting him from the idea of a new host. Some . . . some creatures work like that, right? They don't chase you unless you run?

This thing, though, is not from Earth. It doesn't have to follow Earth rules, if there are rules . . . I don't know. I don't know anymore. This drug is making me feel so . . . apart, like disconnected. But I feel so much and not anything at all at the same time. My body is a cumbersome cloak of physicality that I would love to shake off. To be free.

Like Aleyk said. Like Aleyk asked.

An alert pierces the air, a loud and insistent siren, rising and falling. Karl's head jerks up toward the ceiling, toward the sound of the noise, as if that might provide more information.

Aleyk again?

Oh, Aleyk. My eyes overflow with tears, from emotion rather than pain this time. I wish it could have been different, that he could have been real. Alive now instead of hundreds of years ago. That I could have saved him.

But Karl seems less annoyed this time, more mystified. His brow furrows. "A collision alert? That shouldn't be possible.

There's nothing in our path, unless one of those fucking trawlers crossed the lanes—"

The alert cuts off as suddenly as it started. But then a new sound takes over, a grinding from somewhere below us.

Karl drops the empty syringe, his face pale in the slant of light. "That's . . . that's the doors. On the main exhibition level. They must have a warrant override. We're being boarded."

Rober. Rober Ayis. My message must have gotten through. It worked. My plan worked. A tiny spark of elation trembles in me before going out under the weight of sedation.

Behloth straightens up to its full height. Zale's head tips back, sniffing the air through the holes in his face that serve as nostrils. Tension quakes through all four of his limbs, sending Zale's weak human hands shaking.

Karl's eyes widen. "No," he says, holding his hand out. "They're not invading your territory. They're here for her, not—"

But Behloth ignores him, bounding over me, out the door, and down the stairs.

Karl, cursing, follows him.

I should get up now. This is my chance. But the urgency has faded to a faint screaming in the back of my mind.

A faint screaming that is replaced by a short, sudden shriek in real life.

Shit. I need to warn Ayis's people. They came for me, and they might die for that.

Rolling over to my side, I manage to get my hands on the floor and push myself half upright. I drag my good leg up, and then, bracing myself against the wall, try to stand.

My right ankle feels wrong, disconnected somehow. Blood. So much blood. But it's still attached, sort of. The pain is muted, thankfully, under the drugs.

I have to reach down and lay my foot flat against the floor. I can't lift my toes or raise my heel anymore.

Using the wall, I pull myself along to the doorway and then onto the landing, where I can grip the metal railing to keep myself upright. I take each step as a hop, a movement that jars everything broken, bloodied, and bruised in my body, like being stabbed. Repeatedly.

This is taking too long, too long!

I keep expecting shouts, bursts of gunfire. But there's nothing, not since the final thud of the main entrance doors. What is happening?

I can't imagine Ayis's people showing up unarmed, even if they were expecting me to cooperate. Especially with a warrant override.

A warrant.

I frown.

My foggy brain struggles to grasp thoughts . . . How did Ayis's team get here so quickly? That shouldn't have been possible.

I reach the curve in the stairwell, which turns me toward the second level and my room. One more floor to go.

My ribs are on fire, and it feels like inhaling shredded glass every time I try to breathe. That can't be good.

I hobble down the next half flight, turn, and . . . stop.

At the next landing, a body lies crumpled in a lake of blood. Karl. His hands are still clawing at the wall with an automated *click-clicking*, even as his eyes turn glassy. The middle of his torso is cored out, torn free, in several swipes. I think . . . I think I can see white beads of spine.

My hand tightens on the rail, and to my shock, his gaze shifts upward to me. Tears streak down his dirtied and bloodied face, creating trails of clean. "Wa . . . wa . . ." His mouth opens and closes frantically, a bubble of blood forming on his lips and then popping.

What happened? Why did he do this? I don't know what he's asking, and probably wouldn't have any answers even if I did.

"I'm sorry." Because I am. No one should die like that. Except maybe one who's forced others to, for the sake of his own ambition.

Clutching the rail, I edge around Karl, my boots smearing his blood. It's unavoidable and adding to the mess I'm leaving in my wake.

But it's not only me. The blood trail, mixed with gobbets of dropped flesh, continues down the stairs ahead of me.

I swallow hard. Does that mean . . . Was Behloth eating, gathering strength, as he went?

When I reach the threshold to the third floor, the main exhibition level, the door is partially open. A clot of chewed-up fabric with a zipper is caught in the gap between the bottom of the door and the floor.

Nausea wells up, combining with the deep throbs of pain, and I retch. Which only makes the pain worse. Whatever Karl gave me is wearing off.

I need to hurry.

After I manage to stop gagging and catch my breath, I limp out onto the floor. Everything is quiet, still. The emergency lighting is back on. But there are no teams with oversize weapons or crackling comms.

Aleyk? I want to call for him. To ask him to turn everything back on. But that might only make things worse.

Searching the shadows for Behloth as best as I can, I move cautiously past the door to the SecOffice. Keeping my hand braced on the wall, I limp past the public restrooms, heading for the central fountain, where the main entrance is.

Warrant. Warrant. Warrant. That thought keeps echoing in my head, along with the disconcerting speed with which Ayis's team arrived after receiving a partial message. Something is wrong.

I shake my head. Or it's just a combination of well-earned paranoia and my inability to accept a little bit of good fortune in this complete shit show. *Let it go, Halley. Keep moving.*

Except, as the rounded edge of the dry fountain appears out of the shadows, a bright light flicks on from the other side of it.

I stop and hold up my hand to block it, squinting as it moves to engulf my entire body.

A figure moves into the light, creating a familiar silhouette. Petite, striding with purpose toward me.

"Jesus, kid, what the hell happened to you?" Niina asks brusquely.

25

Oh, no. No, no, no. A searing wave of panic spreads over me. "What are you doing here?" I manage, my voice emerging more like a scared squeak.

But even as I ask the question, I realize I should have known. *The warrant override.* Ayis's people wouldn't be able to get a warrant because they weren't in power. It could only be the Ministry of Justice, likely acting on Bierhals's orders.

Fuck. I take a step back, away from Niina, then stop myself. I don't know where Zale and Behloth are.

Niina steps closer, her body now blocking the light so I can see her more clearly. She's dressed down in a snug black jacket over equally nondescript pants, but for the wide-legged style and thick cuffed hems with gold buttons holding them in place. *Always leave an impression.* One of her earliest lessons. Apparently, even on illicit missions to co-opt former employees. "You think we were going to let you go without keeping an eye out? Or an ear, in this case?"

I reel back a step, the dizzy, surreal feeling of the last few moments increasing. Niina and Bierhals *knew* I was here. The whole time. And they were listening. Probably had a team at the ready, waiting to move in if I spoke up. Or even hinted that I might.

"You know this would have been a lot easier if you had stuck around and let us work things out. We would have protected you," Niina continues, before turning to nod at someone behind her.

Jahn steps out from the shadows to stand next to her, his face solemn. Of course he's here.

He greets me with jerk of his chin. A shiver of recognition runs through me. He's not wearing the mask, and the tattoo on his wrist is covered now. But the primitive part of my brain, the amygdala or brain stem or whatever, *knows* it was him that night. *Danger, danger! Be careful!*

At a gesture from Jahn, a dozen men and women in black UNOC IEA uniforms, all their insignia removed, spread out and start heading deeper into the ship, carrying battered metal crates with them. It's hard to miss the weapons slung over their backs and in holsters at their sides. They're marked with red slashes, indicating they're hull-safe, but still.

"What are they doing?" I ask, alarmed. "Don't let them go into the ship. It's too dangerous." Even now I'm on edge, listening for the slithering, *click-clack*ing approach of Behloth. "In fact, we should leave, right now. Just . . . let's go." In direct comparison, Niina is definitely the lesser-of-two-evils choice, though not by as a wide a margin as I would like.

Niina cocks her head at me, regarding me strangely. "We had to have a reason for the warrant. This old ship is the perfect cover for Daze distribution." She pauses. "Dangerous?" She gives a half laugh. "There's no one here, except for a caretaker. Somewhere." Niina frowns, looking around, as if expecting Karl to pop out from behind a corner somewhere.

Karl. Rising up with his clickety-clackety prosthetic limbs, insides still leaking out onto the floor . . .

I shudder. I need to get out of here.

"That's why you chose this ship, isn't it?" Niina nods with grudging respect. "Smart."

Neither the compliment nor her easily admitted falsification of the conditions for the warrant faze me, not now. "I'll leave with you," I say, limping forward. "But we need to do it fast."

She narrows her eyes at me and steps in front of me to block my progress. I'm not playing my part correctly in her scripted drama. "That's good," she says slowly. "You're willing to listen. You have a choice. We have proof now of your collaboration with Ayis in the Nova Lennox riots."

I stare at her, startled into distraction. "That's not—" I begin and then snap my mouth shut. She must mean my message to Ayis's people, but it's partial and dated after the riots themselves. Is she threatening to manipulate the facts? At this point, unless she's threatening to eat my liver, she's picked the wrong place and time to try to scare me.

I shake my head. "There is a monster on this ship. It's . . . it eats people. And it's coming."

She laughs uneasily, her gaze meeting mine. But her laughter stops short when she sees I'm not smiling. "Clearly your time here has given you the opportunity to reconsider your options." Niina reaches out, as if she might take my arm. But then she pulls back, her nose wrinkling in distaste at my unwashed clothes, the blood on them.

I want to push past her, head straight for the extendable bridge and whatever ship she and the others came on. Fuck her. But Jahn still looms behind her, hands on his weapon, and I'm not certain he'll let me pass.

"We'll blanket your absence as a mental health issue, stress of the election. You'll testify that everything before the election was a blur, blah, blah, blah. There will be a stir in the media for a few days, and you'll have to get your parents on board with the messaging. But then everything will go back to normal. That's what you want, isn't it? What we all want?"

Desperation pulses beneath her smile. I can feel it like an ache in my molars. The tide is turning. They need me to come back—or at least to be verifiably not dead or missing.

"You've been out there, on the stations, in the muck, with the Daze dealers and the briners. You can see now, can't you?" She edges closer, into my personal space. "How important it is for us to represent those who need us. The people don't know what they want. We have to guide them, save them from themselves." She steels herself and gently rests her hand on my forearm. "I know you, Katerina. You want to make a difference. You want to change lives. I do, too."

She already has, just not in the way she's trying to convince me of.

From the darkened corridor, a muted sound, like the soft scratch of something sharp against the floor, drifts toward me. I snap to attention, my flesh erupting in goose bumps. But I can't see anything. It might be the agents moving crates . . .

Niina smiles at me. "The circumstances of our entrance to this sphere may have been . . . less than ideal. But think how much good you can do now, with the power of the prime minister's office behind you. One day, maybe even the prime minister herself." She gives me an elaborate wink.

Implying, what, that one day she'll be in the running, and I'll be in her role?

In that moment, it strikes me with the force of a gut punch how much I once would have wanted the future she's depicting. This woman I admired, in whom I believed, leading me to follow in her footsteps—serving people, listening to the long-ignored, trying make government work for the benefit of its citizens instead of the other way around.

And she's right. With Ayis in charge, the suffering and chaos would be so much worse. The very citizens who voted for him would likely be most hurt by his proposed policies of station- and colony-centric self-sufficiency.

But she's no different than any of the others—willing to help, to serve, but only for the perks that come along with the role. Power, prestige, ego. The moment serving others comes into conflict with her own needs, it's clear which one will win out.

Even still, it would be so easy to say yes. I could make different choices than Niina. At a minimum, I would be able to push for an investigation into *Elysian Fields,* to untangle the mess Karl has made, get the residents out of here, and find *someone* to deal with Zale and Behloth.

Not that I would be able to tell the truth about what was going on here. No one would believe me.

Suddenly I'm right back where I was. This is the problem with relying on others to do the right thing, to step up and intervene when you can't. Or think you can't.

The only certain way is to take the risk and step up yourself.

I edge around her, heading straight for Jahn and the exit behind him. "Call your people back now," I say to him.

He blinks, surprised, moving to block me automatically. But then he looks past me to Niina, seeking direction. *Shit.*

Niina stalks toward me, yanking me back around to face her, her expression contorted with an ugly rage. "You think you're better than me?" she demands. "All high and mighty, sitting in judgment? You only took this job to prove your parents wrong."

I bite back a scream of frustration. "I don't care right now, okay? We're running out of time. If you want to argue about who did what and why, we can do that. On the *other* ship. Please!"

"How much good do you think you were really doing at that tiny NPO with no budget and no resources, living off Mommy and Daddy's money?"

My face flushes. "We were trying—"

"Fuck trying," she spits. "What does *trying* do for anyone? You can't make a difference unless you have the power to enact change. Anyone will tell you that. Even *you* know that. That's why you left that pathetic shit show for us."

The jab at H_2OPE stung. "Then why not run again in three years? Take the loss and try again."

She gapes at me. "Do you know how much damage he would have done in—"

"They chose him, Niina. Or they would have. And that's it.

That's all you know. Except that you were willing to sink to his level to win. How does that make you any better? You . . . and Bierhals?" My voice cracks on the prime minister's name. It was an inadvertent question, one I didn't realize I was still harboring.

Niina sighs. "Katerina. Yes, he knows. Of course he knows."

Even though I assumed as much, it still hurts to hear that he's not the person I believed him to be.

"He, unlike you, understands the need to sacrifice a little to gain a lot. Integrity doesn't keep people fed—"

The loud clatter of a crate hitting the floor echoes up the corridor, followed by a piercing scream cut short.

Oh, fuck.

Jahn turns, weapon raised in that direction. It leaves Niina and me in the relative dimness of the main pavilion.

"What was that?" Niina demands, after a glance over her shoulder.

"I told you, the monster. He's hunting," I say flatly.

Her mouth opens and closes, her brows drawn tight in a frown before she manages to say, "The caretaker?"

"No," I say evenly. "The 'caretaker' is eviscerated on the stairs behind that door." I jerk my thumb back the opposite direction in the corridor, toward the stairway. "It's Zale Winfeld, or what's left of him after being possessed for the better part of a couple of centuries." I pause. "By an alien."

A spluttering noise, something between laughter and a snort of disbelief, emerges from Niina. "Are you fucking kidding me right now? Zale Winfeld." She shakes her head. "Jesus Christ, Katerina. You've lost your mind."

I meet her gaze without flinching. "You can try to paint me as ignorant or unstable, but you, of all people, know I'm not."

Jahn turns, takes one look at my face, and then jogs past us in the direction I indicated, heading for the stairs.

From down the hall, where the other agents had vanished,

muffled shouts of panic. They're discovering the body, or the absence of one. Hard to say.

Jahn returns, only faintly out of breath. "Dead guy on the stairs. Like she said."

Niina returns her attention to me. "What the fuck is going on, Katerina?"

"Like I said, Zale's possessed. And the alien inside him— well, it's coming out of him, at this point—is evidently very territorial." It's funny; it's so much easier to sound calm and collected in the face of what sounds like sheer insanity when you've had a little practice at it. "It will—"

Distant gunfire—the thick *thud, thud, thud* of hull-safe rounds—cuts me off, followed by screams and then an inhuman roar that makes me flinch and throw my hands up over my ears.

Behloth's pissed now. I don't think that's a noise Zale's vocal cords could make.

Rushed footsteps, bobbing lights, and then pale panicky faces arrive back at the fountain. Three, no, four out of the original dozen. "It's coming," one of the men shouts in a shaking voice. "It was climbing down from the—"

His voice cuts out in a gurgle, a black claw sticking out through the front of his throat. He wobbles back and forth for a moment, like he's trying to get his balance. But then he finally drops, sliding off the clawed portion of Behloth's hand.

In the space behind the man, centered in the darkened corridor but highlighted by Jahn's light, is Behloth. It snaps its hand several times, shaking off the remainder of the blood and flesh. The agent hadn't been moving at all; rather, Behloth had simply been trying to free its hand.

Then it straightens to its full height. Zale's body dangles limp and pale about the center of its body, like a skin about to be shed. Bullet holes, blackened but not bleeding, cover his torso and lower half. Zale's head remains in place, but it's misshapen and distorted, like a discarded and stretched-out mask. Beneath it, through gaps, wet, slick skin is emerging, the bright glow of yellow shining through Zale's dulled and cataract-filled eyes. Behloth is definitely advancing to some further stage of transformation.

It surveys the humans gathered in front of it, and then locks straight onto me.

Shit.

It starts forward, and I duck instinctively behind the stone fountain. "Run," I shout. "Get back to the ship!"

But Jahn and Niina ignore me.

"Fire, fire, fire!" Jahn orders, and the loud *thwack* of bullets crashing into Behloth and the surrounding space commences at once.

Behloth squeals—a hurt, almost insulted sound, as if someone had stepped on its toes rather than attempting to blast holes through its entirety.

A second later the firing slows and then stops, while the screaming begins again.

An arm, now detached from its body, flies toward me and lands near my ducked-down position, rolling and tumbling end over end, its fingers spasmodically trying to squeeze the trigger.

Niina, still standing out in the open, tracks the severed limb with her gaze, to where it finally skids to a halt. Her eyes are wide to the whites with horror.

"Niina!" I flap my hand frantically at her, directing her to come toward me while I scoot backward on the floor under the edge of the fountain. If we can get away while Behloth is distracted . . .

But it's too late. Niina freezes and then slowly turns to look up at something I can't see from my angle. I can guess, though.

A moment later, she's gone, jerked upward, leaving only empty space where she once stood. And one of her delicate, pointy-toed flats.

26

I brace myself for the rain of body parts. For the crack of bones, followed by the gurgle of lungs filling with blood and the wet smack of intestines hitting the ground.

But there's nothing.

Just high-pitched ringing in my ears in the sudden silence.

I poke my head out above the edge of the fountain.

Beams of light splay out in crazy angles from the discarded weapons, casting strange and malformed shadows in the smoke-filled air.

But no Behloth lazily tearing Niina apart or burying his face deep in her belly in an obscene mockery of an intimate act.

I swallow hard over the dry lump of terror in my throat and make myself look up, half expecting to see him dangling from the ceiling, dragging Niina along behind him.

But there's no Behloth there, either.

And—I frown—no Niina.

Keeping my balance with a hand on the stone lip of the fountain, I rise to my knees. Cooling blood on the floor soaks through my pants immediately.

It's difficult to see far in these conditions, but it's clear that the arm near me is hardly the only body part in the vicinity; there's part of a leg in the fountain proper. A chunk of torso, spine trailing out of the bottom of it, rests along the fountain

ledge, like it decided to stretch out for a quick nap in the artificial sun.

All of the parts appear to belong to the UNOC enforcement
agents, given the remnants of black clothing and the boots.

Where is Niina? Why would Behloth have taken her—

My mind flashes back to that horrible moment upstairs, Behloth looming over me. The strange, mucus-slicked tube that
had emerged from Zale's mouth, like a tongue . . . but not.

I shudder.

Young. Healthy. Female. Behloth's gravelly voice echoes in
my head.

Niina is nine years older than I am, but what is a decade to
a being who might be immortal and has definitely been living
in the body of a more-than-centenarian?

Oh, shit. Behloth is probably at full strength now and looking for a new host while it's powerful enough to take one.

I carefully push myself up to my feet. White-hot pain blazes
up from my sliced ankle. Blood, sticky and wet, has filled my
boot on that side, making each step squish unpleasantly.

I start to edge around the fountain. Movement from the
shadows—someone or some*thing* emerging from the remnants
of the old food court—makes me flinch back. But it's Jahn,
hobbling toward me and hauling one of the injured agents with
him. The woman appears only half-conscious, bleeding pro-
fusely from a gash on her arm. Her blood *pitter-patters* on the
floor, sounding like the steps of a small, dazed creature running in circles.

Jahn himself doesn't look well—too pale, and holding onto
his side with his free hand. He will be of no help. Not that
there is necessarily any help that will make a difference.

This is it. There is no one else to take this on. No one else to
step up and solve the problem.

My heart is a stone, layering itself in protective granite
against the fear and the terror, then it sinks to my belly. Not in
despondency but in a measure of calm resolve.

I ran before. It solved nothing. I can't leave *this* to someone else.

"Get everyone out of here," I say, my voice raspy. I must have been screaming at some point. Again.

Jahn blinks at me, slowly, dazed, a pained expression contorting his face. "Niina," Jahn says. "She—"

"It took her," I say. "Probably for food, or as a host." Or—it strikes me now—as a lure. Maybe it still wants me and figured this was the best way to get me away from the chaos. "Close the doors, retract the ramp. We cannot let it off this ship. If I can find Niina and she's unharmed, I'll try to get her back to you." In the flatness of my tone, I hear how unlikely I consider that possibility to be.

Jahn eyes me, then nods, a glimmer of respect showing through.

He shouldn't. I don't have a plan. Not really. Other than making sure Behloth is contained, no longer hurting people. And if Karl was being truthful about the condition of this ship and the level of maintenance required simply to keep it functioning, I have only one idea.

"Desperate" would be a generous term for it. "Suicidal" would be more accurate. *Is* more accurate. I curl my hands into fists, palms damp with sweat.

Jahn and the agent stumble around the fountain and back toward the primary entrance. And then a belated thought occurs to me.

"Wait!" I call.

Jahn tenses and swivels around.

"Just . . . wait. One second."

I dash—as much as one can with a foot that no longer lifts properly—into the closest resident's room, Amli's. Amli is gone, but this girl, Sarai—her Karl-provided substitute, the one whose family is searching for her—is not. It's a matter of a few seconds' work to disconnect the tank from the central power and unlock the wheels from their bolted positions on the floor.

The independent battery, a backup in the event of a ship-wide power failure, immediately kicks on with a high-pitched whine. Zale really did think of everything. The only noticeable difference in the tank is in the dimming of the indicator lights along the outside frame.

I push Sarai's tank into the hall and then toward Jahn. It moves easily enough, smoothly enough, that I can direct it with one hand against the cool surface. Nothing but the best for Zale. "Take her with you. She doesn't belong here." I can't save everyone, but I can save her. One person.

Jahn stares at the tank and then at me, in disbelief. "You want me to bring a frozen corpse—"

"She's not. Or she might be. I don't know. Take her with you." I push the tank to Jahn's side. "Try to find someone who knows about cryogenics. They might be able to save her." I don't have time to explain more. Behloth will surely be heading back this way before long, and I need them gone before that happens.

After a moment, Jahn gives me a grudging nod. He leans on the tank like a support, elbow braced against the top. He guides the tank toward the doors while using it to keep himself upright, his other arm still locked tight around the injured agent, who is drooping more and more by the second.

I watch their unsteady progress, making sure they aren't attacked on the way. That would mean Behloth is up to something else and I might have to recalculate.

But they clatter onto the extendable bridge without incident, and then are out of sight. It'll take them only a few more seconds to close up shop on their side. Then Jahn will, I'm sure, use the warrant override to close the doors on *Elysian Fields* and retract the bridge.

Leaving only me and my "plan." Right.

It's an odd thing to confront certain death by your own hand. I can't think too much about the details, or the fear currently bubbling in my veins might take over and I'll bolt after Jahn on shaking legs.

I take a deep breath and head as fast as I can to the engine room.

But I don't get very far.

"Katerina."

Aleyk. It's Aleyk, calling to me from the stage—his prison—as I pass the theater.

"Katerina!" His voice booms this time, echoing down the corridors, even with the theater doors closed. I wince.

I should keep going, but this might be my final opportunity to see him, to say goodbye. I don't know if I'll be able to get back up from the engine room before . . .

A mental image emerges, fire roaring all around, engulfing me, a dark shadow at its center, as my skin crackles and bubbles, my bones charring as my mouth falls open in a silent scream.

I shudder, then shake my head to clear the thought away. *Before. Just . . . before.*

I pull open the door. Aleyk doesn't even wait for me to fully step inside. "What are you doing?" he demands, as I head down the aisle toward him. "That ship is trying to leave. They've closed the external doors, and I can only hold the bridge in place for so long."

Now that he mentions it, I can hear a faint metallic whine behind me, buzzing like a cloud of oversize mosquitos thwarted from their target. The bridge mechanicals are fighting conflicting orders from the UNOC vessel and from Aleyk within *Elysian Fields*.

"Aleyk." I pause, trying to find the words and the nerve to speak them around the lump in my throat. "I'm not going with them. I can't."

He crouches down at the edge of the stage, his expression wild with fury and panic. That one floppy errant curl still dangling over his forehead. Of course it is. He will look the same for-ever, or until the *Elysian Fields* is destroyed. Why does that make tears sting my eyes?

"What are you talking about?" he demands.

I lift my chin defiantly. "I can't walk away and wait for someone else to handle this. That's not right. I've done that in the past and look what—"

"This isn't your mess to clean up," he says. "What are you going to do?"

"I'm going to the engine room. It can't be that hard to make something . . ." My throat works. "Karl always said the ship was on the edge of blowing up, so that's what I'm going to do. Figure it out." Preferably before Behloth finishes eating or changing hosts, if that's in fact what's happening.

Aleyk gapes at me in disbelief. "Are you joking? No. Abso-lutely not."

"What do you mean, no?" I cross down to the base of the stage, moving past the jumbled remains of the velvet barri-cade to stand below him. "There aren't any other options! I can't . . . I can't let this go on and I—"

"You're going to get on that ship. I'll close it up behind you. As soon as they've reached safe distance, tell them to fire on us." He pauses, his gaze turning inward, perhaps gathering whatever information he can from the *Elysian Fields*'s instru-ments. "They have multiple weapons systems that should be sufficient."

It's a UNOC IEA ship, Viper class mostly likely. A half dozen or so of them used to accompany us and the PM every-where. So, yeah, sufficient is an understatement.

"The engine room is a good idea, a point of weakness." Aleyk returns his attention to me. "It shouldn't take much." His tone is thoughtful now, as if he's playing out scenarios and running probabilities of success.

I stare at him, horrified. "No!"

"Why not?"

"Because . . ." All of my reasoning vanishes in that instant. "Because it's not right," I say finally, too aware of the feebleness of that explanation.

"Because you'll need them to listen to you? Because you'll need to take a risk in speaking up and then standing your ground instead of throwing yourself into the weaker option, one that conveniently involves self-sacrifice?"

"Yes, because I can control that option," I burst out. "Because then I don't need them to listen to anything!"

He arches an eyebrow. "And what if that gambit fails? What if you only destroy yourself in the process? Take out an engine, or maybe part of the guidance system? Or what if Behloth catches up with you first?" he asks, his expression stony. "How long will it be before someone else comes on board? Perhaps the board members that Karl was forever going on about. They are real, even if they haven't been paying as much attention as he implied. At some point, someone will come to check on Karl and his lack of responsiveness. And any destruction you might manage to cause will certainly draw them in. And then what?"

Then more people will die, and Behloth might even take the opportunity to switch things up with a different host, one powerful and wealthy, and leave the relative confinement of *Elysian Fields*.

My heart sinks slowly, a pebble in an ocean stirred by a hurricane. He's right. My way is riskier. Assuming I can convince Jahn or whoever is left to follow my directions.

"I won't leave you here to die alone," I say, my throat growing tight.

He sighs, tipping his head to the side to look at me with a sad smile. "Katerina. We died a long time ago. It . . . takes a while to sink in. That's all. True death would be a freedom of its own."

Tears well up and spill down my cheeks.

"Come here." He opens his arms to me, and I step into range, allowing him to hold me.

I wish, in that moment, I wish so hard that I could feel the tightness of his grasp, that I could smell the salt of his skin under the rough cotton of his shirt.

But it's just pressure, generic pressure, gently and evenly distributed around my neck and shoulders, roughly where his arms would be. If he were really here.

Stupidly, that thought only makes me cry harder. For a man who died a hundred years before I was born.

"It's frightening, I know," he says. And it would be a whisper in my ear, if he were able to make it so. But instead it's his quiet voice over the targeted speakers in the range of my ear. "To step out and leave the familiar, even when the familiar has become dangerous. But you need to go. We are not yours to save. You have other responsibilities, other people waiting for you."

But my feet remain firmly planted, as if my boots have melded with the floor. I don't want to. Don't want to take the risk.

To Aleyk's point, though, it's a risk either way.

"You can do this," he says, pulling back. His gaze searches my face, and I close my eyes, lashes wet against my already damp cheeks.

He presses a kiss against my forehead, a light brush of sensation, and it makes my throat ache.

"Awww," someone behind me says in a mocking voice, and Aleyk and I jolt apart. For a moment, I'm convinced that Karl has managed to drag himself, exposed spine and all, down the stairs and into the theater.

I turn automatically, my hand up to block the lights so I can see into the dimness of the theater. Someone is coming toward us, down the aisle.

It takes only a few seconds for the shadowy form to clarify into a recognizable personage.

That trim jacket, those pants with the three gold buttons on the cuffs. Her sharp, dark bob, cut right at her chin. The gun, a small sidearm likely retrieved from one of the dead agents, in her hand.

I suck in a breath of surprise, moving instinctively closer to the stage and Aleyk.

"This?" Niina waves her gun in a loose gesture at the space between Aleyk and me. "This is adorable. Whatever this is."

27

"Niina. You're—" *Okay.* The word catches and dies in my throat as soon as she steps closer, into the cast of the spotlight.

She's limping, one shoe gone. The other foot is bloodied and bare. But not actively bleeding. Her jacket and the white shell top she's wearing underneath it are slashed on both shoulders, to her collarbone, and both layers appear soaked in red.

But the bare skin of her collarbone and shoulders, exposed by the slashes and tattered clothes, is unmarred. No damage.

Or, perhaps, no *unhealed* damage.

Oh no.

"You know, I thought you were crazy for doing this," Niina says, continuing down the aisle toward us. "Running away to this ship. Running away in general. I mean, we were in on the ground level. Bierhals would never be able to leave us behind. The ladder was ours to climb, to wherever we wanted. You just needed to keep your mouth shut and let me handle it. But then you fucked off and made Mather all panicky. I was so pissed at you!" She laughs, a giddy sound. "Now, though . . . Now I think you were cleverer than I gave you credit for." She pauses, her eyes flicking toward Aleyk kneeling on the edge of the stage behind me. "And look at you, you got yourself a life, finally. Or some version of one anyway." Her nose wrinkles in distaste.

"Niina. What happened—"

"Oh, don't play coy. I won't lie. That tube thing? Fucking disgusting. Freaked me out." She touches her mouth reflexively and shudders. "But after that? It's weird. I feel stronger, already. It's in there. I mean, I can feel it like a secret, all tucked away in my mind. But I'm still me. I just know all kinds of things."

"Niina," I try again. "Stay back. Please."

"Like Zale." She shifts her focus to Aleyk, and the pressure that would be his hand returns to my shoulder. "He was proud of you for fighting back. Even though he could never say that. It ate him alive, that contradiction. He wanted you to be proud of him, but if you had been, he would have lost all respect for you." She shakes her head with a *tsk*ing noise. "Complex man. Geniuses usually are." She winks at us.

"You seem to think you know my family well," Aleyk says, but he sounds distant, distracted. The way he does when he's focusing on something else in the ship.

"A hundred years of Zale droning on and on, some of that has to transfer," she says. "I don't know you at all, but I can hear *it*, whispering in my head. All snuggled in tight." She grins. "So many good ideas. And when it's all settled in and recovered—"

"It eats people, Niina." I cut in. "That's how it gets stronger. *You* will have to eat people . . ."

Her lip curls faintly in disgust. "We'll see about that."

"No," I say, feeling almost sorry for her. "There's no bargaining or negotiating. It doesn't work like—"

"Enough," she snaps. "Here's what's going to happen. You, Aleyk, are going to open the doors so I can catch my ride. And *Halley* here is going to come with me. She's my safety net. You fuck with my escape, and I'm going to fuck with her." Niina holds up the gun, as if to illustrate her point. "You let us leave, and she gets to stage her remarkable comeback, after a devastating mental break. She won't remember anything from before, which is too bad." She affects a deep pout. "But she'll go on to great things. Until she decides to retire to a less stressful and more private life. Very shortly."

In other words, long enough for the speculation to die down. And then maybe I'll get to walk away, or maybe I'll simply vanish again. This time by her doing instead of my own.

"You believed in me." I hate that my voice shakes even as betrayal burns through me. "I was worried about disappointing you. You told me that I could make a difference, that I was a valued member of the team." *That I meant something.*

"And you were. You did," she says evenly. "But you couldn't be flexible; you didn't want it badly enough. It's not only about helping people," she says impatiently. "It's about doing whatever is necessary to keep yourself in that position where you have the power to make a difference. It's not my fault if you didn't get that. You had the right instincts, and holy shit, your parents. Their contacts, their access? That alone made you a good get for the campaign."

I flinch.

"But once you proved yourself unreliable, we couldn't keep you around."

"You mean *you*." I start to step toward her, but Aleyk tightens his grip on my shoulder, holding me in place. I glance back at him, startled. He gives me a pointed look, communicating without words, as he had before he could speak freely.

He wants me to stay put.

Niina edges closer. "That's right, baby girl. At what point did I ever give you the impression I was the self-sacrificing type? If you can help me along my way, I'm going to take you with me. If not . . ." She fires the gun, above her head.

Something shatters above us, bits and pieces raining down.

Movement flashes on stage, and when I turn to look over my shoulder, Ianthe and Bryck are now on either side of Aleyk. But something is wrong. Ianthe is mostly see-through in her upper half, more ghost than hologram now. Bryck is flickering in and out of sight.

Niina must have damaged the hologram setup.

"What is this?" Niina asks with laugh. "You're bringing in reinforcements? I hate to tell you this, but that's not going to—"

A pained look crosses her face, and she puts her free hand to her forehead, pressing hard enough that her fingers go white. "Shut up, shut up," she snarls. "I don't need you right now."

"Niina?" I ask warily.

She immediately lowers her hand. "I'm fine. Let's go." She gestures for me to step forward. But she's paler than she was a moment ago. I'm not entirely sure that she's ready for whatever the final stage of this possession will look like, or feel like.

The pressure of Aleyk's hand remains tight on my shoulder.

"Oh, come on. Seriously? I don't have time for this." Niina lurches forward, closing the distance between us.

Crossing that discreet, faded caution tape without so much as a look down at it.

She grabs for my arm, preparing to pull me away, but as she does, Aleyk releases me, giving me a shove past her.

Then he and his two siblings reach over the edge, grasping at Niina, holding her by arms and shoulders. It takes her a second to process what's happening. Based on the shock on her face, I'm betting she didn't know they could do this.

Then Aleyk looks up at me, his face showing the strain, as Niina shrieks and struggles to free herself or aim the gun. "Run!"

So I do.

28

It's more of a fast hobble than a run up the carpeted aisle, but it's the best I can manage. I don't know how long they'll be able to hold her. That gentle pressure I'm accustomed to from Aleyk won't be enough.

The second I push through the theater doors, I can hear the locks attempting to ratchet into place, even before the doors are closed.

Aleyk again.

I almost stop. I want to look back through the sliver of an opening to see him one last time. But he's giving me this chance, the only chance to get out of here alive and stop Niina, and Behloth within her.

I have to take it. I have to make his sacrifice worth it. He felt guilty for not stopping Zale, though I don't know if he could have done anything, then. But now he's going to stop Behloth, at least from getting off the ship. The rest will be up to me.

The short stretch of darkened corridor between the theater and the main entrance has never seemed longer. I'm waiting for Niina's screech and the battering sounds at the theater door, any second. Will Behloth have enough strength to give her to break them down? No idea. Better to be long gone if so.

I pick my way through the mangled agents near the fountain, trying not to trip over a hand or foot or random rib cage in my path. The dizzying tangle of weapon lights helps a little, though they nearly blind me almost as often.

I dart around the fountain, and the silence behind me is more frightening than the clamor I was expecting.

At the threshold to the main entrance, both sets of airlock doors, exterior and interior, hang half-open. The smell of over-heating metal and that mechanical whine are stronger here. The open doors reveal the extended bridge and the *closed* air-lock door on the Viper.

I stumble to a stop. Fuck. Fuck! Of course they would seal themselves off. They're trying to leave.

I hurry across the extended bridge to bang on the outer doors. "Listen. You need to listen to me!" I back up, searching for the sec-cam above the door. "Niina's not coming back. Behloth has her." Not quite in a way they would recognize, but I'm not get-ting into those details now. "You need to destroy this ship. Aim for the engine room."

I wait, panting, my breath rushing too fast. The bleeding on my ankle, which had slowed, is hot and wet again, and I'm starting to feel a little dizzy.

There's no response from inside. Nothing. Not even a warn-ing to evacuate to the area.

"Are you fucking kidding me?" I demand, beating against the door again. "I'm trying to save—"

The door opens abruptly, and Jahn, his midsection heavily wrapped, reaches out, yanking me into the airlock almost be-fore there's space enough for me to squeeze through.

He releases me and I stumble forward, onto my knees. My whole leg screams in protest. The airlock door immediately re-verses course, slamming shut and sealing with a hiss behind me.

Sarai's tank is just beyond the threshold onto the ship proper. Across from me in the airlock, though, the wounded female agent is on the floor, a rough blanket pulled over her face. Her blood is still pooling out onto the ridged metal floor. *Shit.*

"Close the doors. Pull the bridge," I say to Jahn, through gritted teeth. "The override should work now."

Jahn speaks over his shoulder to someone deeper in the ship. A moment later, when I'm able to pull myself to my feet, using the safety harness straps along the wall, I watch on the airlock sec-cam screen as the bridge slowly retracts and the doors to the *Elysian Fields* close.

"As soon as we reach safe distance, you have to blow it." My voice is hoarse. "You have missiles or some shit. Hit it with everything you have."

"Mission objective was to retrieve you, alive," Jahn says flatly.

I turn to face him. "Yes, I'm sure my well-being is of the utmost concern to you."

He doesn't even flinch. "Following orders."

"Right off a fucking cliff," I mutter. I don't belong in this world. I don't believe in it anymore. I can't believe I ever did. "You saw that thing. You saw what it can do." I gesture toward the dead agent in the airlock. "If we don't do something, it's going to find a way off that ship and you know what will happen." And while Jahn might be picturing the half man, half monster he witnessed, I know the version that looks like my utterly human mentor will be far more dangerous.

Still, he remains silent.

From the corner of my eye, I see the gray wall of the *Elysian Fields* slip away, turning to a black field of stars. We're moving away. Panic rises in me, making my hands tremble. This is it. It'll all be for nothing if I can't get this done. They'll have teams out here in no time investigating the "incident" and Behloth will gobble them up and hitch a ride back, wearing its Niina face.

I straighten up, smear my hands across my bloodied and tearstained face, and put on my best Niina take-no-shit expression. I did, after all, learn from her. "Fine. You want orders? *I'll* give them to you. I accepted Niina's job offer." Retroactively, but close enough. "That makes me assistant chief of staff to the prime minister again. As she is *indisposed* at the moment, I am ordering you to fucking hit the ship, for our safety and others'. I'll take the responsibility for the decision, testify to whoever needs to hear it, and I will gladly go to prison if it means that fucking abomination doesn't come anywhere near anyone else ever again." I pause. I may not want to be a part of this world, but I do know how it operates. "Unless you'd like to explain why you did nothing, in violation of direct orders, when it starts mowing down anyone who comes to follow up. That won't bode well for your future or your legacy."

Fear. That's the key. Fear of being made irrelevant. Being abandoned, left powerless and insignificant, after working so hard to attain a position that never felt quite secure.

Jahn doesn't move, and panic swells in me, like a high-pitched scream with nowhere to go.

Then he turns and gives a sharp jerk of his chin to whoever is waiting behind him.

I move closer to the screen on the wall inside the airlock. I should go find a seat, strap in, and watch from a viewport somewhere, but I feel like I can't move, can't risk missing anything.

Streamers of light burst forth from somewhere underneath me and streak toward the *Elysian Fields*. We're far enough away that I can almost see it in its entirety.

I grip the edges of the screen, my face inches from the image, looking for a sign, any sign, from Aleyk.

But there's nothing. No flashing signal light. Nothing to call me back or say goodbye.

Just that one last memory of him telling me to run. Just him trying to save me from myself, one last time. *True death would be a freedom of its own.*

The *Elysian Fields* is quiet, serene, and still. Until the streamers reach it and vanish inside, like a magician behind a curtain.

A bright line splits the ship almost in half, and as I watch, the edges along the line seem to bow inward first and then explode outward in a flash.

I raise my hand instinctively to block the light, and when I lower it again, the *Elysian Fields* is gone. Aleyk's gone. Ianthe. Bryck. All the residents, both original and Karl-provided, are gone. One person's greed preserved them, but another's destroyed them.

I despise the parallel.

A scattering of debris and two or three large chunks of distorted and tangled metal—I catch a glimpse of what might be a tank within a shattered room—are all that remain. They spin outward, away from the center of the explosion, off screen in a matter of moments.

Dizzy again, I release my grip on the screen and step back before slowly sinking back to the floor, feeling every bruise and break in my skin as a fresh sting, salt in every wound.

I should be relieved, and I am.

But that doesn't stop me from folding in on myself, sheltering my face in my arms, and for a few moments letting myself *feel* for all that is lost. My shoulders shake with silent sobs.

Eventually I dry my face on my sleeve and then, using safety straps again, haul myself up, putting my weight on my good leg. "You have a medkit on this ship?" I ask, limping out of the airlock. I need stitches. At the very least. Possibly a whole new tendon or ankle bone or whatever is broken.

Jahn stares at me, then nods his head, gesturing for me to follow him.

"We need to talk about what we're going to say," he says after a moment, as we cross through the central passage, where strike force members would be gathered, if there were any left.

"Is that your version of 'We need to get our story straight'?" I ask through gritted teeth. With that last rush of adrenaline fading, everything hurts. I shuffle next to Jahn, dragging my bad foot across the floor.

"They're not going to believe us. They're not going to believe *you,*" he says. He gestures to a small alcove to the right of us. It's an auto-doc, built into the ship, bandage wrappings discarded all around it.

"I know." With a sigh, I sink down into the auto-doc exam chair and pull my injured leg up onto the footrest area, trying to keep my ankle from bending in ways it shouldn't. The auto-doc sensors immediately chirp in alarm. Good to know I'm not overreacting.

"And?" Jahn presses.

"And I don't care," I say. The truth is the truth, even when it's fucking inconvenient and completely unsupported by general logic and rational thought. Too bad it cost me so much to learn that.

"Now pass me the anesthetic spray."

29

"It is a small storefront, but I think you'll find it will work for your needs." The station rental manager brushes the chip in the back of her hand against the security pad, which signals access with a faded green light and a faint beep. "It used to be a boot repair and exchange!"

With a delicate grunt, she lifts the battered metal gate blocking off the darkened space and beckons for me to follow her. "Lights. Lights, please!" she calls, as she enters. Her voice sounds strained, despite her determined smile. Probably because there isn't much demand for the abandoned shops on this level. Generally speaking, the need to step over zoned-out Daze addicts on your way to a location isn't a great selling point.

Or maybe it's because she recognizes me. That would be enough for some people.

Sometimes it felt like the *Elysian Fields* aftermath was never going to end. Despite all my bravado with Jahn that day on the ship, I had no idea what I was in for. Inquests. Inquiries. Investigations. Indictments. All the bad *I* words. And lawsuits, so many lawsuits—from the Winfeld Trust, from the families who believed their wealthy relatives were still on board (they weren't, except maybe as a pile of gnawed bones somewhere on a lower level). Even a couple of the families who had "contracted" with Karl tried their luck.

I was, and still am, a figure of ridicule. Who believes a story about an alien possessing a titan of industry from a couple centuries ago? Especially when all the proof has been blown to bits. It is, in the purest sense of the word, unbelievable.

Or, as the UNOC prosecutor called it, "a little too convenient."

Which, of course, meant the experiences I relayed about Niina, Jamez Ildris, and Bierhals suffered the same scrutiny. Bierhals finished out his term but under a cloud of shame. Rober Ayis looks set to win the next election, based purely on outrage from the last one. In other words, nothing I did mattered.

Inside the storefront, the overhead lightbars flicker to life resentfully, like teenagers pulled from a deep sleep. "We'll get the lights fixed if this ends up being the right fit, I promise," the rental manager, Lilyy, says with a nervous laugh.

"That's fine," I say, trying to reassure her. I'm not looking for perfection, just the right place. And SL-23 is where I can do the most good. I hope.

"If you'll follow me into the back . . ." She turns away, and the rest of her words are lost to me under the dull roar of the air-circulation system and the buzz of the lights.

I start toward her, only to freeze at the threshold, foot midstep—automatically waiting for permission to proceed.

I've been out of Whitehall Camp for a few weeks, but old habits die hard. The UNOC minimum security penitentiary station where I served my eight-month negotiated sentence is considered the luxury hotel of the UNOC prison system. It was nothing compared to the asteroid mining labor camps, certainly, and I'm grateful for the deal my parents' lawyer managed to wrangle in exchange for my testimony.

But prison is, to some extent, still prison. At Whitehall, your ability to roam the station freely—to meet with visitors, buy products in the commissary, work in the station garden—was limited by your points, which could only be acquired by good behavior. And wandering into a section you don't have access to would result in a suspension of your points and your privileges.

And the delivery of a mild electrical shock via the tracking chip in your neck.

With an instinctive shudder, I reach up to trace my finger over the thin line below my ear, where the chip was removed.

Based on my experience, it only takes being shocked a couple times before you find yourself hesitating at every threshold. Even once you're free.

"Is everything okay?" Lilyy asks, bustling back toward me.

I make myself cross into the storefront to meet her. "Yes, sorry."

She nods uncertainly, making sure to keep distance between us. "Because of the central location on this level, you'll have easy access to the freight elevator from the terminal. And the storage area will give you plenty of room to organize your supplies for . . ." She lets the end of her sentence hang, waiting for me to complete it.

"Project Sunlight," I say. A nonprofit supplying oranges, dried beans, vouchers for time under the sunlamps. Anything and everything I can convince people to donate. The good news is that right now a lot of journo-streamers, conspiracy theorists, and even politicians want to use donations to Project Sunlight as entry into interviews or evidence of their support for whatever they see as my "true cause." Fine with me, as long as they give, and give generously. I've told the truth, and nothing is going to change that.

The nonprofit is a small thing. Practically nothing in the grand scheme of what the briners really need. Like massive regulatory changes, for one. But it helps a little, to focus on something other than my mistakes. It will be years before the events on *Elysian Fields* are not the first thing I think of when I wake up, and even after that, I'll still have the memories.

All those people I couldn't save. The young Benadrian man whose mothers left him to be preserved, hoping one day he could be healed. Karl, who, though greedy and selfish, was suckered in like everyone else with the promise of a future that couldn't exist.

Niina, whom I loathe and yet still find myself missing, depending on the day or even the moment.

Aleyk.

Even Sarai, the one person I managed to rescue—whose disappearance and return in an active cryogenic tank from a century before she was born somewhat backs up elements of my story—remains in a coma.

Every time I look in the mirror, I despise myself for not doing more, not being braver, smarter, fucking faster.

But one night in Whitehall, while I was obsessing over everything from the moment I spoke to Karl in Seven Fathoms to the instant that bright light split the *Elysian Fields* into pieces— trying to find all the ways it had gone wrong, all the ways I could have done things differently—the memory of that little boy asking for paddle cakes sprang up in my mind and wouldn't leave.

The big difference I wanted to make is impossible. I had to accept that, and then accept that my choice was only between doing nothing or doing *something*. And the idea of doing something brought such relief that I couldn't ignore it. It's not enough, not even close, but it is better than barricading myself in my parents' home, where I stayed for a few miserable days after my release, or taking one of the many "employment opportunities" my mother kept pushing. I'm done with their side of politics. If they want to see me, they'll need to see me as their daughter rather than their newest pawn.

"There's even room for a small living space in the storage

area, if you want to have an overnight manager," Lilyy says brightly.

I try not to snort. What she means is *You better have someone on site overnight if you want anything left by the next morning.* Poor Lilyy either doesn't know or doesn't remember that my experience on EnExx17 is more than theoretical. That's fine. I can stay here. I'm not going back to the hostile hostel.

Outside, on the concourse, the sound of retching and coughing drifts toward us. Someone is waking up.

Lilyy squeezes her eyes shut in a grimace, forehead furrowing in despair, before forcing herself to look at me again. "So what do you think?" she asks, teeth clenched in a smile.

"I think it's where I need to be," I say simply.

Her mouth falls open before she recovers herself. "Oh. Oh that's fantastic news. Let me send you the contract right now."

My holocomm buzzes in my pocket, startling me. My UNOC ID and credentials have been restored, so I can be found and contacted—and tracked—at any time. But it still catches me by surprise sometimes, being so connected again after *Elysian Fields* and Whitehall.

I check, but I don't have any new messages.

I frown. That's weird. "I'm sorry, I don't seem to have—"

"I can send it again," she says, fingers flying across her holocomm. And then she watches me expectantly.

The same thing happens again. A buzz, but no new message.

Then it dawns on me. I'm connected to the EnExx17 servers again, where I set up my relays so long ago, and I haven't gotten a new holocomm yet. Not really top of the priority list. So her message might have automatically diverted, based on my old settings.

I haven't been back into my relays since I left the *Elysian Fields,* so I brace myself for the flood of hate messages, fan holos, and whatever else might have come through.

But the relays are worth the money I paid for them; no one

has managed to track me through them or connect me with them.

In fact, aside from the two messages from the EnExx rental agent, there's only one new message. Text only, no holo, and the icon is the blank-faced, vaguely head-shaped image used for an anonymous sender.

I frown. Anonymous is never good.

"I've got it," I tell Lilyy, to her obvious relief. "Give me a few minutes to review the terms."

I reach out to swipe the anonymous message away as junk, but the time stamp makes me freeze in place, my hand still hovering in midair. *21-4-2223, 10:17:32.*

I *know* that date. Specifically, I know that time, down to the second. It's been plastered all over every legal document I've seen, read, been forced to sign over the past two years. This is the exact moment the *Elysian Fields* was blown up, destroyed. Rather, the exact moment *I* destroyed it.

Except that's . . . strange. Back then, no one else knew yet what was going on. No one even knew where I was. Only the few of us on the Viper ship.

And Aleyk.

Aleyk, who had access to almost everything on board the *Elysian Fields.* Aleyk, who would know about my relay accounts because I used them on board.

Beneath the anonymous header is a string of numbers. A protocol address. One that could belong to the *Elysian Fields.*

Stop it. There's wishful thinking and then there's being completely delusional.

But my hand is shaking when I tap the message open. The body is two simple words.

THANK YOU.

That's all. Two words, but I hear them in Aleyk's voice, thick with sorrow and mixed with sheer relief.

A choked noise escapes me before I can stop it, and I clamp a hand over my mouth. The image blurs before me, my eyes stinging with tears. The stress and tension of the past two years, petrified into a solid and seemingly permanent mass in my gut, softens. I did it. That one thing I accomplished—I got him out. Not at all the way I wanted, but he is free. Gone, but free. And he was aware of it at the end.

The sense of weight lifting off me is almost dizzying.

"Are you okay?" Lilyy asks, edging closer with a worried look. "The terms are definitely negotiable."

"Yeah." I lower my holocomm to meet her gaze. The Aleyk-shaped ache in my chest is less. Only slightly, but it's enough. "Everything's all right."

ACKNOWLEDGMENTS

I am so wildly and incredibly grateful that I get to write creepy space stories and share them with you! A whole bunch of amazing humans make that possible in a variety of ways, and I'm so, so thankful for them.

My agents, Suzie Townsend and Sophia Ramos. Thank you for your encouraging words at just the right time and your brilliant feedback!

Everyone at New Leaf Literary & Media, especially Tracy Williams and Keifer Ludwig, who have brought *Dead Silence,* *Ghost Station,* and *Cold Eternity* to the world, and Olivia Coleman, who helped so much during a crazy (wonderful) time earlier this year. On the film side, thank you to Pouya Shahbazian and Katherine Curtis, for all the things we cannot yet discuss!

The Nightfire coven! Kelly Lonesome—I love working with you, and I look forward to our editorial Zoom calls every time (Tater Tot)! Kristin Temple, Giselle Gonzalez, Jordan Hanley, Valeria Castorena (Hi, Valeria!!), Michael Dudding. The Google Meet we all had earlier this year, when I was in my car at school, remains one of my peak publishing experiences. Thank you for all that you do. I am so grateful.

Katie Klimowicz and Emmanuel Shiu, thank you for the gorgeous and eerie cover! It is so creepy, and I LOVE it!!

And the larger Nightfire/Tor team: Jessica Katz, Jacqueline Huber-Rodriguez, Rafal Gibek, Greg Collins, Devi Pillai (Hi, Devi!), Lucille Rettino, Will Hinton, Claire Eddy, Eileen Lawrence, and Sarah Reidy. This book exists because all these people work hard to turn a collection of words on a page into the magic that is a *book*. Thank you!

Chloe Gong, Ally Wilkes, Darcy Coates, Philip Fracassi, Yume Kitasei, Kali Wallace, David Wellington, and Gretchen McNeil—thank you for taking time out of your insanely busy lives to read and offer kind words on *Ghost Station*. I am so grateful!

Susan Bischoff, my coach at WBFA. You helped me feel grounded and capable when I was really struggling. Thank you. I continue to benefit from your advice and expertise, and I look forward to our next conversation.

Zura Johnson, you are a joy. And I'm so happy we know each other now. Thank you for bringing Ophelia and company to life with your *Ghost Station* performance. It felt like listening to these people in my head draw breath for the first time. So cool!

Linnea Sinclair, my mentor, my critique partner, and my friend. Thank you, as always, for being willing to drop everything and help me when I'm in panic mode! I love the way your mind works, and I'm so happy to have it and you on my side.

Susan Barnes Oldenburg, for always being my first call on everything, good and bad.

Matt Oldenburg, for always being willing to help the Barnes collective with whatever shenanigans we've gotten ourselves into. Thank you! Also, Ben.

Becky Douthitt, you were literally sitting at my side while I was writing portions of this book in Michigan, but you've metaphorically been at my side for all of them. Thank you for being excited with me, for helping me, for caring about what is going on in my writing life. It means the world.

Allison Klemstein, for dinners and our conversations. Love you!

Amy Bland and Kimberly Damitz, so grateful to have you in my life. Our talks mean so much to me!

Read Between The Lynes, my awesome independent bookstore, thank you to everyone on staff—especially Natasha—for all your support and the fantastic launch for *Ghost Station*!

Mundelein High School staff and students, for encouraging me and being excited with me! Special thanks to Rebecca, Karen, Diane, Kathryn, Hope, Heidi, Melissa, and Meredith. Because of you, I enjoy coming to work every day. (Except during state testing.)

Mom and Dad, Judy and Stephen Barnes, for unwavering support in so many ways over the years and celebrating with me! (Yes, it's another scary one. No, I have no idea why I am the way I am, but Susan likes horror, too! It's not just me.)

Greg Klemstein, my partner in non-crime for the last twenty-five years, for always encouraging me to order dessert, supporting my book obsession (buying, reading, *and* writing), and hauling me out of my writing cave into the daylight every once in a while.

ABOUT THE AUTHOR

Mila Duboyski

S.A. BARNES, author of *Dead Silence*, *Ghost Station*, and *Cold Eternity*, works in a high school library by day, recommending reads, talking with students, and removing the occasional forgotten cheese stick as bookmark. Barnes has published numerous novels across different genres under the pen name Stacey Kade. She lives in Illinois with more dogs and books than is advisable and a very patient husband.

staceykade.com
Threads: @authorstaceykade
Instagram: @authorstaceykade